BULLETS IN THE WATER

BULLETS IN THE WATER

CONOR MCANALLY

Published by

Stoney Creek Publishing Group

StoneyCreekPublishing.com

ISBN: 978-1-965766-32-3
ISBN (ebook): 978-1-965766-33-0
Library of Congress Control Number: 2025910055

Cover design by MacShinny Graphics

Printed in the United States

For
Kay,
Áine, and Nuala

CHAPTER ONE

MIKE CARSON'S head snapped up when the brunette started mewling. Two guys had her pinned against a pinball machine in the corner of the bar, trying to remove her T-shirt. Mike had been bourboning his way through a Rolodex of regrets when the gang of twenty-somethings whacked through the double doors like they owned the place half an hour earlier. Loud and lewd. There had been an edge to the air ever since.

"Just show us the damn tattoo," one of them demanded, hauling at the flimsy fabric.

"Stop it, Karter, please." She was getting desperate. The girls in the group looked away in embarrassed silence as the guys started to chant.

"Show it, show it!"

Mike looked around the bar. Everyone acted as if nothing was happening. He stood and walked over. The brunette was blush red and crying, sensing the battle for her dignity would soon be lost.

"OK now," Mike said, "let's take it easy and settle down."

"Get lost," the Karter kid said, looking up at Mike, "and mind your own goddam business."

"Look, some of us are here for a nice, quiet drink. Why don't you knock it off?"

"Do you know who he is?" asked one girl, a small, feisty redhead.

"Sure, he's the bully, trying to humiliate this young lady, who clearly doesn't want to show off her tattoo right now."

"You'll stay out of this if you know what's good for you," Karter said.

"Yeah? Well...no." Mike stepped forward and snapped the kid's wrists from the brunette, turned him sideways and pushed him away. He straightened to his full six-feet, two inches and squared off against the Karter kid, who nodded to Mike's right with a sly smile. There was a blur of movement in Mike's peripheral vision, and then something hit him in the head. Hard. It seemed a long way to the floor. He was surprised when it arrived so quickly.

"Oh my God, Jess...." One of the girls.

"Screw him, he shouldn't mess with us." Presumably, Jess.

"You could have killed him."

Mike started to get up when a pair of tan cowboy boots filled his vision.

"That's enough, leave it, Karter," Jess' voice said.

"No way." One boot connected with Mike's jaw and the darkness enveloped him.

He came to in custody, arms pinned behind his back, handcuffs biting into the flesh. Two uniformed cops hauled him to his feet, marched him to a police SUV and eased him into the back seat. He looked to his right at the line of young, taunting faces in the window of Gold Spurs Bar and Grill as Karter and the redhead shot him the finger. The brunette was nowhere to be seen. The officers climbed in and the SUV pulled away.

"Am I arrested?"

"Yessir," said the cop in the passenger seat.

"What for?"

"Assault for starters and whatever else comes up."

"Assault? I was hit in the head and kicked in the face."

"We heard. Self-defense, according to the witnesses. Probably best not to say more till we get to reading you your rights at the station."

"I want a lawyer," Mike said.

"I'll bet you do."

They hustled him through a side door when they got to the station. A sleepy civilian receptionist looked up in surprise.

"Chief here yet?" asked the chubby driver.

"On his way," she said.

They moved him into a gray institutional interview room, sat him on a metal chair, removed one handcuff and refastened it to a metal table that was bolted to the floor.

"You have the right to remain silent and refuse to answer questions. Anything you say may be used against you in a court of law. You have the right to consult an attorney before speaking to the police and to have an attorney present during questioning now or in the future." The passenger said. Mike now saw he was a sergeant named Green.

"I would like an attorney present during questioning."

"What attorney?" said the driver whose name tag read Brown. Green and Brown, both white.

Mike was stumped. He didn't have an attorney here. "John McKinney."

"Honest John," both officers laughed. "OK, we'll see if we can find him. He's not always in his own bed this time at night, if you know what I mean." Brown winked. It didn't suit him.

CHAPTER ONE

Honest John McKinney had to stoop low to enter the interview room. Taking off his hat would have spoiled the image. He arrived around 2:30 in the morning. Underneath the Stetson was his usual attire, a gray Western suit with black suede front yokes. His starched white shirt and longhorn bolo tie completed the image. He was somewhere in his sixties and looked like he could be related to Ray Benson from Asleep at the Wheel. Mike had seen Ray's huge cardboard cutout beside a little restaurant in the Austin airport as he headed toward arrivals just forty-eight hours earlier. *Doing great,* he thought, *only took you two days to get arrested.* Honest John looked him over.

"Chief tells me you're Tom Carson's son."

"That's right."

"I went up against your pappy a time or two. I'd say we came out even in the end, though he'd say he had the edge. Never met you, I don't think."

"No, we've never met."

"So how come you asked for me?"

"I saw your face on that billboard outside town and I don't know any other lawyers here. Been gone a while."

Honest John smiled.

"'Honest John McKinney for All Your Legal Needs.' Nice to see the power of advertising making a return on investment. Well, let's say I agree to represent you."

He pulled out the other metal chair and sat sideways at the table because his knees would not fit under. He took some reading glasses from his inside pocket. They looked small on his head as he opened a brown folder.

"Let's see now."

His finger moved down the page from a worrying distance.

"Assault, battery, disturbing the peace, drunk and disorderly, public nuisance, resisting arrest. Someone has been busy."

"This is complete bullshit. They were molesting a young girl, trying to haul her T-shirt off. I went over to help her and got cold-cocked for my trouble and then kicked in the face."

"So, you started the fight."

"I pulled the guy's hands off her and pushed him away."

"That's the assault and battery and disturbing the peace. How about the drunk and disorderly? Could you have passed a sobriety test?"

"I wasn't driving."

"Check that box too, then."

"I'm the one who got assaulted."

"By whom?"

"I didn't see who hit me in the head, but I heard the name Jess. The guy who kicked me in the face was called Karter."

"Oh, see now, that's bad. Probably Karter McMillan. We could press charges, kinda like a counter suit, but I wouldn't recommend going up against the McMillans."

"As in Duke McMillan?"

"You know the McMillans?"

"My brother Andy was best friends with Zane; never heard of a Karter."

"Younger brother, different mother. Anyway, my advice is the same. Best not to go up against the family."

"So, what are my options?"

"These are all just misdemeanors, but you don't want them on your record. Maybe if you were to apologize and be on your merry way back to New York City, they might all just go away. That's where you live, right? According to your driving license."

"I can't go back to New York right now. Unfortunately, I need to be here for a while."

"I see."

Mike wasn't sure if it was the kick in the head or the bourbon that fogged him, but the haze suddenly cleared.

"Wait, a second. They Mirandized me, but I haven't been charged with anything."

Honest John smiled and closed the folder.

"Right. These are charges they could bring if they want to." He got to his feet. "I'll just go talk to them and get some clarification." He paused at the door. "Just what is a *New York Chronicle* investigative journalist doing back in little old Taborville? You here for a story?"

"A story here? Hell no." Although he needed a story—desperately. A big national exclusive might just....

"What then?"

"I'm just here to sell my uncle's house and mind my own business."

"Doesn't sound like you did a good a job of that tonight."

He was released an hour later. Charges were not being brought at this time, but could be filed at a later date. Police Chief Walter E. Gates, according to the nameplate on his office door, issued a warning.

"It would be best if you stayed out of trouble."

"I'm sure my client will be careful," Honest John assured him.

Outside, he offered Mike a ride in his silver Cadillac, but Mike said he needed a walk.

"Where do you want me to send the invoice?"

"1927 North Street."

"You living there?"

"No, but it's where I get mail."

With a tip of his Stetson, Honest John folded himself into luxury and glided away.

Mike began to walk as a cruiser screamed past him, lights on, siren wailing. The officers looked worried.

CHAPTER TWO

MIKE KNEW he should have walked straight from the police station to the welcoming sheets of his bed at the Holiday Inn, but, in spite of his pounding head, made for Uncle Harold's instead.

The old part of town was a strange mix of nineteenth and twentieth century. Single story, stone-fronted ranch houses, dating from the 1970s, squatted low on their concrete slabs between the scattered, antebellum two-story mansions.

It was election season and little yard signs were everywhere, declaring support and allegiance. There'd be knocks on doors soon, flyers shoved into mailboxes, and poorly attended public forums. Taborville wasn't known for the excellence of its political discourse. There was a quaintness about it, Mike thought, a far cry from the vicious and moneyed knife-fights he'd reported in New York.

It was still cool when he got to Uncle Harold's. The house dated back to his great grandfather Jeremiah Carson, town constable of Taborville in 1901. It was a corner plot, just over half an acre. Jeremiah's grandfather had built a dogtrot cabin there. "Cedar logs and sweat," Uncle Harold used to say, "and a large helping of belief." The dogtrot was demolished and, in its place, Jeremiah had a Sears Catalog home assembled. Plans and all materials delivered to the frontier for $872. A single-story structure with six rooms and a front porch.

These days it was ideally situated on the corner of North and Live Oak, diagonally opposite the Cornerstore, a short walk for farm fresh eggs and bacon by the slice. Even in the early light, Mike could see the decay. The house had inherited Uncle Harold's cancer and was now in need of urgent care. Or hospice.

He sat on the front porch steps. A chubby squirrel scampered across the lawn and stopped, rose on hind legs to study the new occupant, but found him uninteresting and gamboled on.

The town slowly blinked awake. Trucks, SUVs, and the occasional sedan rolled by—commuters on their way to jobs in San Antonio. Every driver's head turned in his direction as they moved out of the four-way stop.

Another police siren shattered the early morning birdsong. The cruiser flashed by, barely pausing at the four-way stop, and screamed on up North Street. Mike's hand automatically went for his phone to find out what was going on, then dropped back into unemployment. He sighed and climbed off the steps, stretched, and walked around the outside of the house. The head-jerking scent of skunk hurried him on. A missing inspection hatch gave free access to the underside foundations. God only knew what else was in there. The corrugated roof was almost all rust now, paint peeled from every wall.

When he graduated from the University of Texas with his journalism degree, Mike had called on Uncle Harold to say goodbye. He was on the porch swing, monitoring the Cornerstore across the road, ever vigilant for a story.

"I think they're dealing drugs over there. Lot of kids going in and out."

"The new high school is just around the corner," Mike said. "Maybe they're just getting a Coke before they go home."

"Oh yeah, and Clinton did not have sexual relations with that woman. Give me a break."

They sat in silence for a few minutes, watching the comings and goings. A lifetime of smoking Camel cigarettes had taken its toll. Uncle Harold's breathing was a constant rasp. There was a hesitancy to it, as if he could not afford to cough.

"*Dallas Morning News*. Ain't you the great I am?"

"I'm very lucky, Uncle Harold, and I owe so much to you."

"No. You worked your ass off for that degree. You deserve it. I'm proud of you. Now looky here. You tell me that's not someone who just bought drugs."

Two young guys were walking away from the store, hoodies up despite the heat, hands stuffed low in pockets in case their genitals snuck away. Mike didn't buy it. It was just kids trying to act cool. After a few minutes, Uncle Harold asked him.

"Are you getting any good with your hands?"

"Why?"

"Because I'm going to leave this place to you one day and it needs some fixin'."

Sure does, Mike thought, sitting on the same porch swing. *Can't sell it the way it is.* He pulled his phone and started googling contractors as an ambulance, fire truck, and a third police car screamed past. *What the hell was going on?*

CHAPTER THREE

VISIBLE POWER in Taborville was displayed every morning at Longhorns Grill. The farmers were gone by 7:15 a.m., having traded stories about prices and the weather. The good ol' boy table was strategically placed front and center of the restaurant and had seating for eight. Occasionally, someone might pull up a chair and sit on a corner, but it was a rare indulgence and always generated gossip. Half the table was occupied by bankers and developers, Duke McMillan chief among them. Politics and the law occupied the other half—city council members Xander VanDorn and Isaac Brook sat with county commissioners and Police Chief Wally Gates. Gates was always last to arrive and first to leave.

The combined wealth at the modest wooden table ran to eight figures most days. Today, the table was muted, anxious even, as speculation slithered around the restaurant about the murder north of town.

"Anyone heard from Gates?" asked Duke McMillan, rising from his half-eaten breakfast. "No? Well, I guess he's still at the scene. I've got that chamber opening. Need to prep a few remarks."

"Don't know why," VanDorn scoffed. "You say the exact same shit every time."

"Just like your campaign speeches, I guess."

Duke stood to one side of the speaker's podium and tried to look modest. He remained in the shade. The president and CEO of Taborville Chamber of Commerce was giving her usual ribbon-cutting speech, hitting all the chamber talking points. She was well upholstered, Duke thought – bouncy. After a few pinot grigios at chamber functions, she got a little flirty, and sometimes he wondered if she would or if it was just tease. The husband was never around—so maybe. Not that Duke would. Probably.

Fidelity was not something he expected of himself. His first wife hadn't been a looker, but she was a catch. Her family had a lot of acreage-–enough for her father to have people manage his interests while he ran for the state senate. He enjoyed the corridors of power and the status it gave. The senator loved Duke, who flattered and listened as the single malt whiskies leaked insider information the Duke could profit from.

Duke's tolerance of his wife, whose temperament was volatile at best, reached the breaking point when she got pregnant with Zane. She became impossible to deal with but, fortunately, Duke had accommodating lady friends, women who knew men and their needs, in ways his wife never could or would.

Zane was six when his mother left. Duke had dismissed the gossamer-thin rumors of his extra-marital exploits during those years, blaming the suspicions on her delicate state of mind. But being caught *in flagrante* with the nanny could not be denied. Zane's mommy had run home to daddy. His daughter's diagnosis of bipolar disorder and several of her more deeply embarrassing incidents tempered the senator's desire to crush McMillan.

Duke scanned the audience and smiled. What you knew about who you knew was a key component of his success. It surprised him how many people thought their dirty little secrets would never be discovered.

"And now, before I ask the mayor to cut the ribbon on Dolly's Allsorts Candy Store, it is my distinct pleasure to introduce the man who has made so much of our downtown revitalization project possible, Mr. Duke McMillan."

There was a smattering of polite applause from the small crowd on the sidewalk and on the street.

"Thank you, madam president, for that lovely introduction, but honestly, I am the one who should say thanks. Thanks for all the opportunities this wonderful town has given me. It is my pleasure to invest in these fine old buildings, bring them up to date without losing their heritage, and make them available for exciting new retail outlets like Dolly's. It's my pleasure to join with the city and the chamber to breathe new life into our downtown and make it thrive. Thank you."

Mayor Bill Pryor posed with a giant pair of scissors next to the red ribbon strung across the front door until all the photographers settled.

"Ready?" He sliced through. More applause and everyone moved into the store. Chamber staff had erected portable tables in the center and laid out the obligatory champagne, orange juice, and canapés. The mayor sidled over.

"That went well."

"It did."

"Have you heard anything more abou—"

"Not here, dammit." Duke walked away. The man was always a potential liability, a little anxious lap dog ready to roll into submission, but one who needed far too many belly rubs for Duke's liking.

Dolly accepted congratulations from all the usual ribbon-cutting crowd – bankers, realtors, tourist office staff, other retailers.

"It's up to you now," Duke said. "You've got to make it work."

"I know. Thank you for your help with the rent."

"My pleasure."

He had lowered Dolly's rent in exchange for a stake in the business, just as he had for most of his other tenants. Rents in downtown Taborville were as high as in Austin. Duke said it was because of the cost of renovations. If the owners got three months in arrears, they forfeited the entire enterprise. Stock, goodwill, furniture, and fittings all became his.

"You'll have lots of good publicity from this and great word of mouth."

"You don't think that awful murder—"

"You shouldn't worry. People have very short memories." He patted her on the back and quietly made his way through the small gathering to his car. Zane had texted. An urgent issue needed his attention.

The boy was a constant worry, and Duke was forced to admit he was a little crazy. Fortunately, that hadn't mattered in football. It gave him an edge, an uncaring ruthlessness, that served him well on the field. The Destroyer. Feared and respected by teams everywhere. Tolerated in victory by his coaches despite the injuries he caused and the resulting penalties incurred. A player Duke admired in the stadium, but would rather not have taken home.

The nanny stayed on after the break-up but three years later, Wife Two replaced her. Wife Two was of sound mind and even sounder body, a vision of Southern charm and manners, a near-perfect corporate wife but not much of a mother or a stepmother. Zane hated her even before she gave birth to little Karter, and she hated him right back. She spoiled and indulged Karter in ways that were far beyond healthy.

The Taborville Industrial Park was home to seventeen businesses, two founded by Duke. McMillan & Monarch Engineering was on the road to his right, but he guided his BMW Alpina through the open steel gates of Horny Toad Couriers and drove through the sliding door into the vast warehouse. He took the steps two at a time to the glass-fronted office overlooking the panel vans and box trucks below.

Duke greeted and acknowledged the staff of six and walked to the sound-proofed office at the back where Zane waited.

"Tell me."

"The Houston Port driver got in a wreck. He's in the hospital."

"Before or after the pick-up?"

"After."

"Where's the truck?"

"Police towed it to the impound. They called to let us know."

"And the driver didn't call?"

"He's unconscious. He's hurt pretty bad, they said, in the ICU, and the two people in the car he hit are critical."

"Damn. Who else knows about it?"

"Just me and you. What do we do?"

"Seriously? You can't figure this out? Sometimes I think I should never have signed this business over to you."

"I just thought I should check, see what you thought."

"Get your ass down to Houston right now with the tow truck and bring it back here."

"What if they don't release it?"

"Get Karter to drive another box truck and transfer the cargo. They can't impound the contents."

"Karter? You're kidding. Hasn't he done enough damage today? I'll take one of the drivers. Anyway, I don't know where he is."

"Then go find him. We keep this close."

Zane hovered. "Scroggin's pissed because we missed delivery."

"I'll deal with him." His son didn't move. "What, Zane?"

"Why do you think Mike Carson's back?"

"Just go get the cargo, will you?" He sat down on the black leather couch in Zane's office. Carson was unsettling, but there were ways he could be made to leave. Duke didn't need any more of this crap today, not with what else was going down.

Council Member Xander VanDorn learned everything he needed to know about business at the Battle of Bloody Ridge in Korea. Know your enemy. Direct brute force with precision. Achieve your objective by any means necessary. Never underestimate the importance of luck and happenstance. *Hell, if we'd been seven miles away at Heartbreak Ridge, they'd have put me in the movies.*

The water workshop was well attended. He scanned the audience in the San Antonio City Council chamber—the agitated little movements of those about to speak. This one checking his notes, that one looking at graphs, other ones silently rehearsing their speeches. Pathetic. The whiny conservationists hadn't turned out in great numbers, which was a bonus. He'd walked in solo, armed with a simple, powerful weapon. *I have what you need and I can get it to you cheap.*

One by one, they got to their feet, and tried to convince the city there would be plenty of water for the future if the council would simply enact strict measures to curtail its use, introduce xeriscaping, replace leaking pipe infrastructure, subsidize installation of low-flow, water-efficient toilets. On and on. When the San Antonio mayor had invited Xander to the hearing, VanDorn agreed to share his expertise on the condition he spoke last.

"Xander VanDorn," said the mayor.

"Thank you, Mr. Mayor, council. My name is Xander VanDorn. I'm the former CEO of the Wichita River Authority, and I am a member of the Taborville City Council. You cannot address your current and future problems in San Antonio solely with surface water solutions. We have seen historic droughts lately. Certainly, the measures proposed tonight will help conserve your supplies going forward. But you need to ask yourselves, 'Is that it? Is that the end of growth in this wonderful city?' I think the answer should be an emphatic 'no.'"

Two of the council members leaned forward. Good.

"Deep groundwater wells drilled in Tabor County—which, as you may know, sits on three plentiful aquifers—can guarantee your future growth. I've run the numbers and I assure you the water can be brought here inexpensively. But you must act quickly and decisively. Thank you for your attention."

VanDorn sat, content. *Chew on that.*

CHAPTER FOUR

MIKE WATCHED Maria Elena's cleaning crew move through Uncle Harold's like a chattering army of locusts, devouring every scrap of dirt and dust in all the rooms. After her initial walk through, Maria Elena immediately dispatched her daughter for reinforcements and now four ladies chatted happily in Spanish while they vacuumed, swept, mopped, and scrubbed. Now and then, one left for more supplies.

When the bright-green six-yard dumpster arrived in the driveway, she called her sons to haul out beds, mattresses, carpets, and other heavy stuff. In a couple of hours, it was already half full. She parked Mike on the front porch swing and emerged frequently, holding some fresh piece of biohazard in her rubber-gloved hands. Rat-chewed bedclothes, moth-eaten rugs, soft furnishings stained with God knows what.

"Bye-bye, Señor Mike?"

"Bye-bye, baby, bye-bye." And they laughed every time. The dumpster ate it all. When they finished, she invited Mike back inside the front door. The ladies stood like a greeting line at a fancy cocktail party, all beaming in the knowledge they had crushed it. The rooms sparkled, the bathrooms gleamed, the stovetop looked like it had just been installed. They had gone over every single inch of the house. There was more of an echo now that all the floor coverings were gone. The original long-leaf pine boards had been meticulously scrubbed, steam cleaned, and lemon oiled. The shock on Mike's face at the scale of transformation delighted the women. He turned and applauded, and they did little giggly, self-conscious curtsies and bows.

After they had gone, Mike settled with Maria Elena.

"Thank you so much. There was no way I could sell the place like it was." As he was writing the check, she blessed herself and asked, "You hear about that awful thing, Señor Mike?"

"The shooting?"

"Yes, oh my God. Terrible."

"Uh-huh?"

"The drugs. So bad. Bad people. *Demonios*."

"Drugs in Taborville?"

"Oh yes, Señor Mike, bad everywhere."

Mike handed her the check and counted out a generous tip in cash. He looked at the faded walls.

"Do you know anybody who could help me with some painting?"

"Yes, Señor Mike. Wonderful family."

She checked her phone and wrote the number in Mike's notebook, along with the name Alvarez.

The Houston Police Department Vehicle Compound at 1300 Dart Street was rarely silent, being so close to the mad spaghetti of interlacing interstates 45 and 10. Metal fencing encircled the compound, painted a dull brown and reinforced by both barbed and razor wire to deter intruders.

Zane and Karter McMillan parked their trucks on the street and checked in with the office. Zane presented proof of ownership and waited. The sergeant at the desk made four different calls to determine if they could move the cargo. It took almost an hour to get the green light. The gate opened and they drove inside. The wrecked box truck was up against the fence on the Hickory Street side. Zane could see immediately it was a write-off. The whole front end was destroyed, and the cargo department sat at an odd angle.

Under the watchful eye of an overweight officer who would rather not have been sweating in the heat, he and Karter began to transfer the load.

"I don't know why I had to come," Karter said. "Any of our drivers could have done this."

"Believe me, I didn't want you here. Not today, but Dad said to keep it tight."

"Dad said, Dad said. What are you? Three?"

"Keep it up, Karter, I dare you, keep it up. See where it gets you."

"Ooooh. The Destroyer speaks. Should I be scared?"

Zane dropped his end of the large oil rig drill-bit and stepped forward, eyes twitching, muscles flexing.

"Jeez, man, calm down. Some people can't take a joke," Karter said.

"Are you on something? Tell me you're not sampling product."

Karter laughed. "Do you think I'd be that stupid?"

Zane stared, then raised an eyebrow, unconvinced.

"C'mon," Karter said, "this shit ain't going to move itself."

The engineering items were difficult to lift and maneuver in the tight space close to the fence, but eventually they packed them safely in the second truck. The cardboard boxes were awkward but lighter. Many of them were battered, corners crumpled, some split. There would be damage to some of the contents, depending on how well things had been bubble wrapped. After he signed all the paperwork, Zane took a last look inside the wrecked truck and left the yard satisfied. He didn't notice the small patch of powder in the buckled corner behind the cab.

"Fancy a beer?" Karter asked.

"What? And leave the truck where, exactly?"

"Park it. We could keep an eye on it from inside. There's a cool place a couple of blocks over."

"Gimme the keys. You drive the wrecker back. This stuff doesn't leave our sight." Zane shook his head as he climbed into the cab. He called the hospital before moving off.

"Are you family?" the nurse asked.

"No, I'm his employer."

"All I can tell you is he's in intensive care," she said.

"I should come over. I need to speak with him."

"I'm afraid it is family only."

"Can you give me a break here? This man has worked for us for years."

"Look, there's no point coming over. He's in a temporary coma. Head injury."

"How awful. Thank you for letting me know."

Relieved the driver wouldn't be talking anytime soon, Zane headed straight back to Taborville. Karter had left already and driven God knows where.

CHAPTER FIVE

LEVI FORREST SPOTTED Mike Carson in the back corner of The Copper Kettle, a place that served mediocre food but had an enormous selection at the bar. He was surprised to get Mike's call. He'd rather have eaten with his wife and daughters, but Carson had sounded needy and he felt obligated since he'd had the yard contract on old Harold Carson's place for years. The neighbors might complain about the house, but they couldn't say a word about the yard. Levi made sure of that. He had his Tabor Yard and Lawn crew over there every two weeks mowing and weeding, leaf blowing, and picking up the dead pecan branches. But it was like cleaning the plate around a rotting piece of meat. All it did was draw attention to the real problem.

Mike was a customer of Tabor Transport, too. Levi had picked Mike up from Austin-Bergstrom airport a couple of days back and couldn't figure why Carson hadn't hired a car. But when Levi stowed the single suitcase in the back of his Escalade and Mike climbed in beside him, he got his answer—the guy was loaded and fell asleep soon after they hit the highway.

"Thanks for coming," Mike said when Levi got to the table. "What can I get you?"

"I'll just have a beer. Coors, I think."

Levi watched him waiting at the bar and realized he knew very little about Mike other than the occasional mentions of him in the local paper. Mike's older brother, Andy, on the other hand...what an arm! Andy took Tabor all the way to the state championship and Levi had been right there with him, one of the offensive guards making damn sure they protected their quarterback. They were proud of that, all of them. Andy Carson had never once been sacked. But Andy was gone, and young Mike was back and nobody knew why.

Mike returned with the beer and another double bourbon for himself. After they'd ordered their burgers, he said, "I got arrested."

"I heard. Down at Gold Spurs."

"You heard?"

"Small town. Word travels fast. Especially when it involves a McMillan."

"What's with the McMillans? It wasn't like this when I left."

"The Duke's a big deal these days. He's made a lot of money over the years, but he's investing it right here. Pretty much turning downtown around single handed. "

"You guys close? You were tight with Zane, right?"

"Hardly." Levi took a swallow of beer. "Let me ask you a question. Do you think I enjoy driving folks and tending yards? Do you think that's my dream—the height of my ambition?"

"I guess not."

"I had plans—big plans. It's why I stayed. I could have run off like you, but I didn't. Worked my ass off to build a stake. And you know what happened?" Mike shook his head. "I was persuaded I needed partners, connected people. The Duke. And if I invested my stake with them, I'd be on my way."

"It didn't turn out?"

"Lost it all."

"How?"

"Ever hear of Magnolia Trails?"

"No."

"I'll take you there sometime and—"

The food arrived and Levi stopped talking. When the server cleared the half-finished plates, Mike ordered more drinks.

"What's the story about this Karter McMillan?" Mike asked.

"Youngest son by Duke's second wife. He's on his third wife now, but not for long from what I hear."

"The kid seems like an asshole."

"Crazy little prick, spoiled and nasty with it." Levi took a swig of his fresh beer. "But the Duke looks after him, gets him out of trouble."

"The other night he was trying to rip the T-shirt off this girl—"

"I heard."

"And everyone just sat there. Bar staff, everyone. Nobody did a damn thing."

"Well, they wouldn't dare. Duke owns the place."

"Oh."

"You didn't know?"

"Wouldn't have made a difference, I don't think."

"Should have. Best not to mess with the McMillans."

After his third beer, Levi said he'd have to leave. Mike showed no sign of moving.

"I think I'm going to rent a car," he said. "Could you take me to Alamo tomorrow?"

"Sure thing. Mid-morning work for you?"

"'Round eleven at the Holiday Inn?"

"See you then."

"I appreciate you coming, Levi."

Mike perfected the art of walking drunk after a couple of years in New York. The NYPD was always on the lookout, so Mike walked home super carefully, in short bursts with small breaks and surveys of his surroundings in between. Walking back to the Holiday Inn from The Copper Kettle, he noticed a homeless man sitting on a bench on North Street. Seemed as good as any place to take his next break.

"Hey, man," Mike said, sitting at the other end of the bench.

The guy pulled his Walmart bags closer and shoved a sleeping bag out of sight with his heel.

"Just saying hello, wondering if you'd like a drink?"

The eyes said it all.

"So, what's your name?" Mike asked, passing the pint bottle of Jack Daniels he'd just bought at outrageous restaurant prices.

"Jack." The homeless man put the bottle to his lips and opened his throat.

"Steady on there, Jack. This is for sharing."

"Sorry. Name's not Jack. I was talking about the bottle. Ain't seen Jack in a long time. Me and him used to be friends. Real good friends, till he got so damn 'spensive."

"What's your name?" Mike accepted the bottle, wiped it with his hand, and took a slug.

"Raul."

"Mike."

"Ain't seen you before."

"Only been back a couple of days."

"Yeah? I've been out in the woods, but them asshole kids cut my tent when I was getting supplies."

"Where you get your supplies?"

"Ain't none of your damn business."

"Look, I'm not trying to boost your patch. Seriously. Just wondering is all. I got food and money." He reached in his wallet and handed Raul twenty dollars. "See?"

"The Whataburger is good. Get a lot of sandwiches there that gets too old to serve. I like the double meat but you don't get much of those. Standard Whataburger isn't bad."

"Oh man, I'd have given anything for a Whataburger when I was on the streets in New York."

"You was on the streets?"

"Yeah, long story."

"I got time. Nothing but. You gonna pass that bottle?"

After a short time at *The New York Chronicle*, Mike realized the extraordinary level of talent at every desk. He couldn't compete with these reporters on regular assignments. He was the hick from Texas, the country boy with talent they tolerated but did not accept. The news editor, Ron Knowles, protected him, but there was no respect. Eleven months into the job, Ron asked him to take leave.

"You need to take two weeks. Otherwise, it rolls over, and I get questions from up top. They don't like accumulated leave; screws up their planning or something."

"I don't need a vacation."

"You'll think of something. Now get out of my hair, what's left of it. To think I gave up journalism to do vacation rosters. Go."

No way Mike was going back to Texas. No triumphs to tell. He walked to his apartment, wondering how to fill the time.

"You got change?"

Mike walked on.

"I'm not the freakin' invisible man here. I asked if you had change?"

Mike stopped and turned. Sitting on a sheet of cardboard with his junkyard dog, there was a guy surrounded by bags, wearing two coats and holding a cardboard sign: "Need money for bullets in case I have to off myself."

"Sorry." Mike said. "That was rude."

"Situation normal."

"Here's my change."

There was maybe two dollars and a quarter.

"You hungry?" Mike said.

"Always."

"Let's go get something to eat."

"Can't. This is my spot."

"Alight. I'll bring something back. What kind of food do you like?"

"The kind you put in your mouth and doesn't make you puke."

"Come on, man, help me out here; American, Italian, Chinese, what? Something close so it stays hot."

"They got good Chinese at Mama Moto's."

"I'll be back."

He was Staff Sergeant Corey Thomas, a Korean vet who came home to nothing, a family who moved without telling him, a girlfriend who left him, and a VA that didn't care. He came to New York looking for the girlfriend but ran out of money and hope. Eventually, he accepted his inexorable slide into oblivion.

"The thing that's really hard, you know," he said blinking

back some tears, "I'm the freakin' one percent that goes out to defend our country, a hero when I'm there and a piece of shit when I get back. They don't even look at you on the street. It's like you don't exist. I'm a damn human being. A soldier. I served, which is more than any of you shitheads did."

Mike spent the next two weeks living homeless, sitting on cardboard, begging in the day, sleeping in shelters when he could at night, recording all he saw and felt in his mental note-book. He spent hours talking to the others at the hostels, and sharing the Everclear and flavored Sveda when they were on the streets.

After a few days he felt the pain of being blanked by all the passersby, understood the fear of police who moved them on, sensed the terror of hostels where all you had of value could be stolen, understood the need for a friend, and the paranoia of knowing you could not trust them.

The two weeks turned into 2,000 words in the *Chronicle*, his first major feature. Other papers mentioned it, they talked about it on radio, and it got the attention of the New York City Council. Activists quoted it in speeches asking for reform.

Mike knew this was his path. To go where others would not dare. To deep dive the story at whatever cost. This was the glory road and he loved it.

Mike gave Raul another ten dollars before he walked to the hotel.

"You be safe now."

"Oh, I'm always watching. Checking it all out. They don't see me, but I got eyes on them." He waved goodbye with the half-empty bottle.

CHAPTER SIX

MIKE PAID Levi at the Alamo rental and waved him off. He was going to rent a compact, but the midsize Nissan Sentra was only a dollar a day more, so he opted for the upgrade—a little extra room for his legs. After signing a two-week contract, he walked out to the parking lot with the enthusiastic sales assistant, stopping as she headed for a brilliant red car.

"Excuse me," Mike said, "do you have one in another color?"

"Don't you like it? Scarlet ember. I think it's kind of cute."

"It's a little too flashy for me."

They had another in gray—gun metallic, she called it. The chance of a police stop in a bright red car was exponentially greater, and Mike treated speed limits as more of a suggestion, designed for drivers much less skillful than himself.

Next stop was the drive-thru ATM at Wells Fargo. He'd had a savings account since he was thirteen. Uncle Harold had encouraged him to save a little every week for the inevitable rainy day.

"Happens to us all at some point or another," he said, "and

always when you least expect it. Life serves you up a plate of nothing, and it's nice to have some cash to fill it."

Mike saved a little every month—a lot more when he got older. He'd been frugal in Dallas and New York—until he met and married Liz. Before her, he'd had no interest in anything but the job.

Looking at a bank balance that would sustain him for a year, he was grateful for Uncle Harold's advice, something he never got from his parents. His father obsessed about the friends he ran with and was concerned they could land Mike in the penitentiary. All boys who did not man up to play football were suspicious.

His mother didn't give advice. Didn't say much of anything. Mike often wondered why she had kids since she didn't seem to like them. His parents were as much of a disappointment to each other as he was to them.

On the way to the house, Mike's phone started howling loud and long and scary. Frank Wolfe, his friend from *The Philadelphia Inquirer*.

"Hello."

"Hey, Skippy, where are you?"

"Texas."

"Seriously? It's true then."

"I'm afraid so."

"What in the hell did you do?"

"You know, you must have seen it. Went off half-cocked on a story."

"Word is you didn't fact-check a damn thing."

Mike tried to think of something witty to say, but no words emerged.

“Do not tell me you did not fact-check the story,” Frank said.

“Guilty as charged, your honor.”

“Skippy, Skippy, Skippy...what the hell? Were you drinking?”

“Again, guilty as charged.”

"Man, I’m scared for you. I thought you had this under control. Any chance of getting back with Liz?"

"Nah. Says we’re through. No do-overs."

“How come?”

“She was the source. Impeccable, but unfortunately it was office gossip.”

“Wait. She gave you the story?”

“Not exactly. She told me over dinner, and I went with it.”

“Oh man, what is wrong with you?”

INVESTMENT BANKER
GRILLED FOR TEEN MURDER
DEAD GIRL FOUND IN APARTMENT
By Mike Carson

He should have warned Liz before it hit the streets. She deserved that, at least.

When word of Charles Coolidge being questioned by the NYPD Sex Crimes Division for the murder of a teenage girl reached Hansacker Capital Bank, the rumor flitted around the building like a drunken butterfly and found its way to Elizabeth Carpenter’s office. She’d kept her maiden name for work. Liz had told him the story over dinner, and he had decided to run with it.

Neighbors discovered the body of a 14-year-old female in an apartment

building on Mercer Street, SoHo. NYPD was alerted when EMTs found signs of strangulation.

Liz and Mike each had access to troves of confidential information through their jobs. In the early weeks of marriage, they decided it was dangerous to keep secrets from each other and introduced a Las Vegas policy to the apartment: what was said at home, stayed at home. Mike's last two investigations had been expensive failures. His regular reporting was patchy and often late. He was under pressure to deliver. This was too good a story to ignore.

NYPD will not comment on the investigation, but it is known sex crimes detectives are questioning Charles Coolidge, an investment banker with Hansacker Capital Bank, in connection with the murder.

When he got home that evening, she had a packed bag waiting for him in the hall. Her rage was a physical thing, a force-field he could not penetrate, whirling and gathering speed. Her questions peppered him like paintballs, but his bourbon brain had no answers. All he had was "sorry," and each sorry pushed him farther out the door.

The first rebuttal piece ran in *The New York Times*. Charles Coolidge had been questioned but was not a suspect. WNYC reported Coolidge owned the apartment building on Mercer Street where the victim had been found. The *Post* gave lip service to his innocence but started digging in the darker New York places and found their tabloid gold. The refined Ivy Leaguer liked to play it rough—sweaty, bloody, sadist rough.

Prostitutes of both genders and some in-between revealed saucy details day after day in salacious column inches. Social media went crazy. Clients slipped away. In a week, his reputation was ruined.

Liz filed divorce papers the day Charles Coolidge hanged himself.

"And Ron Knowles couldn't protect you?" Frank asked.

"Nothing he could do. He only had a week left before he went to the *LA Times*. Editor no less."

"I heard. Damn. But, Mike, you know..."

"Yeah, I know. What else could they do?"

"Where are you staying?"

"I'm movin' into Uncle Harold's place."

"Is it even habitable?"

"Barely, but I'm doing some renovations before I sell it."

Frank chuckled.

"Using what? Your legendary DIY skills? Seriously, though...and I am serious, you need to get help, not for the house—well, for that too. You're too good for this shit. Not sure Texas is the right place for you. You know, the boredom."

"Not that boring. We just had a murder."

"Just the one?"

There was a pause and Frank chuckled again.

"Now I'm thinking this is your worst screw-up since Helmand."

"Don't remind me," Mike laughed.

"I mean, who runs at two Taliban machine gunners waving tidy whiteys and screaming 'PRESS' at the top of their voice?"

"It worked, didn't it? We got out."

"That we did, that we did. Look, I don't know what I can

do from here, but if you need anything just hit 'dial,' OK? How are you for cash?"

"Thanks, Frank. No. I'm fine. I had some for a rainy day."

"Let me ask you this question, then. Is it pissing down enough for you to get your shit together?"

"I'll let you know."

"Take care of yourself, Skippy. Don't want to lose you."

Mike noticed the light-bar on the cruiser flash in his rearview just before the *whoop*. He pulled over and waited while the officer called in the number plate. *What was it with these Taborville cops?* He kept both hands on the wheel as the young Black policeman approached an eternity later, violation book in hand. Mike had already lowered the window.

"Good afternoon, sir, do you know why I pulled you over?"

Am I getting real old or are they recruiting straight from high school now?

"Absolutely no idea, officer, none whatsoever. Since this rental is practically brand new, I'm guessing the taillights are not an issue, or am I wrong?"

"There're a hands-free ordinance in town, sir."

"Is there really? How very advanced."

"License and registration, sir, and watch the tone."

They went through the whole rigamarole. Mike's license was clean and the registration matched the rental, as the cop must have known it would. He came back to the window and Mike noticed his name tag.

"Wait, a minute. You're, you're...dammit..." He snapped his fingers. The name was there, flirting with the edge of his memory.

The officer stepped back, unsure, hand moving towards his holstered weapon.

"You're, I've got you, you're Jacob Washington, right? Hell, the last time I saw you was on the top of your brother's shoulders, beating on his head like it was a big bass drum. You were maybe four years old."

"You know Sam?"

"I was in high school with him. He used to take you to games sometimes. I had to baby-sit your ass."

"You're that Carson?"

"Guilty." Mike looked over at the young man in uniform. "I see you've gone into the family business, Jacob."

"I go by Catch these days, Mr. Carson."

"Ah, wide receiver?"

"Yes, sir. Here's your ticket. Just a warning this time. Try to be more careful."

"Sure will. Where's your brother these days?"

"Oh, he's up in Austin, special investigator for the state attorney general."

"Good for him. You tell him I said 'hey.'"

"I will."

The officer walked back to his cruiser and switched off the lights. Mike pulled away slowly, fully aware at least a dozen cars had seen the stop. It wouldn't take long before word got around the town.

CHAPTER SEVEN

COUNCIL MEMBER NADIA NAVARRO studied every item on the city council agenda and all the backup material with great care. When she was small, learning to read, the words danced around the page, flitting here and there like insect-hunting bats. The letters moved to their own gavotte, sometimes left, sometimes right, sometimes back to front. It took all her effort to nail the letters to the word and stop the word from waltzing away from its meaning.

There were some who called her stupid, some who said she did not try, some who simply laughed and made her cry. But every day she took her butterfly net and her hammer, captured the erratic letters, and nailed them to the words. Slowly, she made sense of the sentences, the paragraphs and pages. The psychologists said she was brilliant, had an exceptional mind, but she still failed most of her tests at school.

It had become less hard over the years but never easy, and there were still moments when she looked at a page and the words mocked, danced a crazy cha-cha, and lost her. Thankfully, today was not one of those days.

She was super careful because she never knew when the

next piece of privileged pilfering would pop up. The sneaky little back-scratching attempts at the taxpayers' expense came with astounding regularity. From the moment she took office, the brazenness and the sheer, all- pervasive banality of the corruption baffled her.

Generations of good 'ol boys had been doing this since the birth of the town. Favors for their friends, denial for their enemies, and a vise grip on the power that permitted it. Businessmen funded and endorsed "their" candidates for public office and were rewarded with special treatment, often writing their own regulations. When term limits were introduced to curb some of the worst excesses, they all switched positions like Lanigan's Ball.

I stepped out, and he stepped in again.

He stepped out, and I stepped in again.

A revolving carousel of calculated corruption. Tacky, tawdry, tiresome. The amounts were rarely life changing, but the sheer unfairness and injustice made Nadia bristle every time she came across another little scheme. By the time her first term was over, she had concluded these folks had a different moral compass and she had learned how to fight them. Hard, mean, angry, and public. They had met her polite questioning in the first two years with the pitying head shakes of old white men who had to tolerate her "lack of experience." How could she possibly understand the business of running a city when (a) she was a woman, and (b) she was Hispanic? This was never overtly stated but always implied in the condescending commentary.

"Very interesting..."

"Worth considering..."

"A different view of things, certainly..."

The vote would finish four to one and nothing changed.

She vowed to fight differently after her re-election, to

oppose every attempt to cross the line ferociously, to call them out publicly for their venality. No concessions, no compromises, no quarter. She might get beaten, but at least the citizens would realize the backroom dealing she had been battling for years. This was her last term, and she thought she had nothing to lose.

In an attempt to appear inclusive, two of the five seats on the council were unofficially assigned to minorities. One for Black, one for brown, but the balance of power was always white and ancient. Any time a council member or citizen started with "My family has been here for five generations," she could be sure a steaming pile of dung was about to land, as if simple presence was an entitlement, a golden ticket to privileged treatment. Five months or five generations were all the same to her. You paid your property tax and got the same rights as every other citizen.

Even Oscar Huff, who held the Black seat, would spout it from time to time. Huff-and-Puff loved to talk and preen and strut about, wearing his position like a uniform. Hanging out with the white folks, financed by the white folks, voting with the white folks. Huff got just enough vanity projects through the council to keep him happy. Concessions that cost little but allowed him some extra swagger and prove to his community that he was the man.

The funding for the African American Heritage Center was a fraction of the cash awarded to the historical society or the arts center where rich white ladies indulged their hobbies in buildings lavishly financed by every citizen's taxes. Someone had complained to Nadia in the street: "If you threw a brick into either of those buildings, it would come clear through to the other side without ever hitting a person of color."

Nadia didn't trust any of them, not a single one, and cultivated her paranoia in order to remain vigilant.

She made a note to ask Chief Wally Gates about the latest on the murder investigation when her cell rang. *Dammit, Sofia, what do you want now?*

"Yes, Sofia?"

"Are you in the middle of something?"

"As a matter of fact..."

"You will not believe this. He has a huge dumpster now, came yesterday, very ugly color, and he has removed your signs from his yard."

"Who has?"

"The man next door."

"What's the problem with the dumpster?"

"Part of it is on my property."

"Sofia, I love you. You are my sister but stop now. I am busy, and I have to represent everyone in the city, not just you."

"It's so bad. And what about the signs?"

"Did you ask him if it was OK?"

"No. We always put signs there. Everyone knows that."

"You need to ask him. I'm hanging up now."

"They are your signs, you know, for your election."

"Hanging up."

"You are mean."

"Bye-bye, see you Saturday."

Nadia returned to her reading but couldn't concentrate. She got into her Highlander and drove over to North Street, hoping her sister would not spot her as she cruised past. She pulled into Cornerstore's parking lot and watched. The dumpster was a horrible shade of green but was not encroaching on Sofia's property. She saw a man sitting on the porch swing, gently swaying. He seemed to be talking on the phone. Not bad looking if I was ten years younger, she thought. He got up and paced the porch, still talking on the phone. Nice ass. She laughed at her foolishness and drove home to finish her packet.

CHAPTER EIGHT

MIKE WAS SIPPING beer on the swing under the creaking porch fan when a battered Ford F-250 dually rolled into the driveway. He squinted against the early evening sun but could not make out the driver. The paint on the hood and roof had peeled away, adding a tone of rust to the once-shining silver. The driver's door opened and a woman climbed out. She looked entirely too small for a truck this big. She strode towards him and he remembered that cowgirl gait. Holly Kingston. Stunning as ever. Kick in the gonads gorgeous. Mike had not seen her since prom night.

"Hey, stranger," she said as she came up the four steps to the porch. Blonde, shoulder length hair, checked shirt, and faded blue jeans.

"Jesus Christ, if it isn't Holly Kingston."

"Don't you go takin' the Lord's name in vain, Mike Carson. You know better than that."

"When did you get all religious?"

"I've always been a woman of faith."

"You weren't always a woman, but you sure are now. You look good, Holly, real good."

"Gets harder every year."

"Can I get you a beer? Some tea?"

"I'll take some unsweet if you have it."

"Watch the board there. It's rotten. I'd invite you in, but the air's not working yet."

"Porch is fine."

Mike pulled the AriZona Tea from the fridge and rooted around the cupboard for a suitable glass. When he returned with the tea, she had taken his place on the swing. He handed her the glass and rested his butt on the porch rail.

"You sure you want to sit there? Don't look too secure to me." She looked around the porch. "This whole place looks like it could fall down any minute."

"I'm sure it will be fine." He took a slug of beer. "Joe, over at the liquor store, told me you're working at the bank nowadays. How have you been?"

"I'm not going to lie; I could be better."

"What's going on?"

"You hear about the shooting?"

"The newspaper delivery guy? Polley? Some drug connection."

"He was my husband."

"Husband? Oh, my good God, Holly, I had no idea."

"That drug story is pure crapola."

"I'm so sorry. God, that's awful."

She took a sip of tea. "Thing is, he was clean. Going to meetings and all. He was just doing his job, delivering papers same as every morning. Well, that's not his main job. He works for the county; the papers is a second job 'cos we need the money." Her face was angry now. "The story the police chief put out is total bull."

Mike waited. She hesitated.

"Can you please get off that rail? I can't concentrate expecting you to go flying any second."

Mike sat on the porch steps. She leaned forward.

"I know it's been years, Mike, but I need some help. You know how to find things out." She put the glass down. Her blue-gray eyes were a kaleidoscope of emotion, hurt and grief, anger and determination. "Something's wrong here and I can't get anyone over at the police department to make sense of it. Adam was a good guy, not perfect. None of us are, except our Lord and Savior Jesus Christ, blessed be His name. But we were getting back on our feet. Working two jobs, the both of us. No way he was doing drugs. No way. He had seen the light. He had found his way to Jesus, and I don't know why the Lord had to take him. I just don't know." A tear rolled down her cheek. She gritted her teeth. "I wouldn't even take his name."

"I don't understand."

"Well, I kept my name. Didn't want to be Holly Polley." She started to cry. "How could I have been so stupid?"

The tears forced their way through her like grace in a sin storm. Mike had questions, but this was not the moment. He got down on one knee in front of her and took her right hand in both of his.

"It was so darn selfish of me and so darn dumb." She sucked a quavering breath. "He said he didn't mind me not taking his name, but it must have been embarrassing, don't you think?" She looked down at their hands, then licked her left forefinger and tried to rub away the black mark on the underside of his wrist, like he was her child.

"It doesn't rub off Holly. It's a tattoo."

She looked closer at the small question mark inked on his left wrist.

"I had it done after my Uncle Harold passed, to remind me."

"Of what?"

"His philosophy. To give the readers facts—the who, what, where, when. The how but not the why. 'Cos why is a matter of opinion,' he'd say...'without facts, most folk's opinions aren't worth dog spit.'"

"He was a good man, your Uncle Harold, not God-fearing, but good all the same."

"Uncle Harold feared nothing. Not in this world. Or any other."

"Are you good, Mike? Are you good like Uncle Harold?"

"I'd like to think I am. There are some who'd disagree."

"Like who?"

"Ex-wife, ex-employer, my parents."

"Oh. I'm sorry. I don't think your parents got cause to judge. Not after...."

"Yeah."

"You ever see them?"

"No, not for a long time. We have nothing to say to each other. I get a Christmas card from my mother every year and another one for my birthday. Saccharine Hallmark stuff I'm sure they don't believe. No message."

"You shouldn't lose touch with family."

"There was no touch to lose."

"The Lord sent you, Mike, I know it. I prayed on this, asked for His help to find out what really happened. The Lord answered. Here you are."

"I wouldn't be too sure about that. To be honest, I don't think I'm your best option right now. I'm going through some sh—stuff. It's not a great time for me."

"You're not my best option, believe me—you're my only option. I've got no one who has your skills."

"My skills aren't...."

"Are you saying you won't even try?"

"Alright, alright I'll do what I can, try to find the truth or as close as I can get. Can't guarantee you'll like it."

A car drove past.

"Get up off your knee, fool. Folks will think you're proposing."

Mike jumped to his feet. She snatched her hand away and walked back to her truck. As she hauled herself up into the cab, she paused.

"I'll be expecting to hear from you. Soon."

And then she was gone in a black cloud of diesel smoke and a screech of wheel-spun tires.

CHAPTER NINE

THE POLICE STATION in Taborville sat just outside the historic downtown. The squat brick building was ugly—all function, no form. Mike had noticed little of it when he was arrested. Black-and-whites, some unmarked cars, and a few personal vehicles baked in the parking spaces at one side of the building. A forty-foot incident command-post trailer occupied the corner. Mike wondered if it had ever been used.

He slid the Sentra into one of the visitor spaces at the front. Inside the entrance, dark brown doors flanked a small lobby. A middle-aged lady in civilian clothes sat behind a shield of glass facing the door. A different receptionist on the day shift.

"Good morning. How can I help you?" The voice sounded metallic through the little louvered window.

"I'd like to see the chief, please."

"And you are?"

"Mike Carson."

"And what is this in connection with?"

"I have some questions about the shooting on Bluebonnet Road."

"I see." She was making notes. "Do you have any information for the investigating officers? I can get one of them."

"No. I'm a journalist."

"Oh, in that case I will get our press relations officer. The chief likes him to deal with the press."

"I'd rather talk to the chief." But she was already walking away, past some empty desks, and through the door at the back.

Mike had a look at the small notice board on the left-hand wall. The usual public safety stuff. Nothing of interest. The door on the right opened, and Sergeant Green stepped into the lobby.

"Well. We meet again. How's the face?"

"Healing."

"Shauna tells me you're a journalist."

"That's right."

"For the *Chronicle* in New York, yes?"

"Actually, I'm freelance at the moment."

"Interesting. Your press card, please?"

Security had forced Mike to surrender his *New York Chronicle* press card when they escorted him out of the building.

"Look, you know I'm a journalist. I have some questions about the Bluebonnet shooting," he said.

"You tell me you're a journalist. Our protocol here is to check press cards before discussing any ongoing investigations with reporters. It's just the way we do things. Lots of folks claim to be reporters with this citizen journalism and all. So, we check bona fides."

"I don't have my press card with me."

"How about you come back when you do? The chief made a statement. I brought you a copy."

Mike studied the single page.

Taborville PD officers were dispatched to a motor vehicle crash on Bluebonnet Road today at 7:50 a.m. On arrival, they found the single male occupant in the vehicle was deceased. It has now been determined that the man, identified as Adam Polley and known to the police, had been struck by gunfire. Based on ballistic investigation, the department believes two suspects were involved. The killing may be drug-related and connected with recent gang activity in San Antonio.

"Any progress on the San Antonio angle?" Mike asked.

"Early days of the investigation, can't really say." Green shrugged. "You try to stay out of trouble now."

He turned and Shauna buzzed him back in.

The Taborville Times sat next to the Opera House on Button Street. It was a classic, small town Texas Victorian building, two story, flat roof with three doors on the ground floor, and three matching sash windows on the first. The brick around the doors and windows was painted a dark green to match the frames, and the lettering of *THE TABORVILLE TIMES Est 1889* above the door. The building itself was a little older. Just below the roofline, the year 1884 was picked out in relief and painted white.

The glass in the door frame rattled hard. He closed it carefully behind him. An old counter of burnished hardwood ran the width of the office. Sitting behind it, head down over a keyboard, was an ash blonde. The young woman who looked up at him was a younger Liz, his Liz from courtship, the same shaped face, the same hair, the same smile. A gut punch.

"Hi."

She even sounded similar, but something was off. Something in the eyes. Guarded. Like Liz in later years, when he opened the front door. Eyes fearful of what he might say or do. Eyes that had once been open, inviting, and admiring now steeled because of him. Mike drew a breath.

"Hey, I wondered if I could speak with the editor."

"Quintin. He's back in his office. Who will I say?"

"Mike Carson." A flicker of recognition in her eyes.

He watched her walk to the wood and glass-framed office, which looked original to the building. She was confident in her attractive stride. With a little flick of hair, she opened the editor's door. The man inside seemed surprisingly young. After a muted conversation with two or three looks his way, she stepped back out.

"Quintin says come on back."

Mike lifted the hatch on the counter and walked through. The editor stood to shake Mike's hand. The woman slid past him, a little too close, a hint of orange, or jasmine, maybe.

"Quintin Smith." A man who liked his food but not his exercise.

"Mike Carson."

"So, I gather. *New York Chronicle*, Mike Carson."

"Not anymore."

"You're kidding."

"I wish I was."

"That's a surprise."

"How about you keep it to yourself and I promise to tell you the inside story someday?"

"Hmm, decisions..." he smiled. "I'm kidding. Honor among thieves and whatnot. What can I do for you?"

"I need a press card."

"You want a *Times* press card?"

"Well, I could get a freelance one in a couple of days, but I'd rather be able to say I represent an actual publication."

"You're working a story here?"

"Not sure it's anything just yet. I need a day or two to dig."

"What's in this for us?"

"If it turns out to be a story, you'll have it first."

"What kind of story?"

"A friend has asked me to look into something, and I said I would."

"Look into what?"

"It might be nothing."

"You won't tell me?"

"Rather not, until I know more."

"You're asking me to trust someone I've never met, and given how valuable a *Times* press card is," he smiled again, "I think I need something more."

"Like what?"

"I'm one reporter down at the moment. We could do with some help."

"Doing what?"

"A couple of pieces a week. Maybe an occasional council meeting to give us a night off. Not too much."

Mike weighed it. It wouldn't hurt to keep his hand in.

"Alright. A couple of pieces a week."

"Excellent." The editor pulled a Nikon out of his desk. "Just need your photo for the credentials. If you come back around four, say, I should have them for you."

As Mike was walking toward the front, Quintin called.

"I should have said, the reason we're a reporter short is that we couldn't afford one. I can't pay you."

Mike laughed. The Liz lookalike was waiting for him at the hatch.

"I'm Cathy," she said, "Cathy Ross."

Mike shook her hand. "Nice to meet you, Cathy."

"Will we be working together?"

"Unlikely, I think. I usually work alone."

"Shame." She lifted the hatch and let him slide past her.

Mike parked off Bluebonnet Road and walked to the corner. It had been days now, but the scars on the ancient live oak looked really fresh. No tape or evidence markers. The crime scene guys had been quick.

The car hit high and slid down the trunk, dragging bark and splinters with it. Shards of shattered glass lay in the grass. Oil and other fluids had soaked into the ground. There were drag marks through the dirt where the vehicle was pulled back to the road.

It was an achingly familiar scene. Another tree, on a different road. The one that killed his brother, Andy, at Piney Creek, the humpback corner notorious for tossing speeding vehicles into oncoming traffic or the woods. There had been no blood at Piney Creek and there was none here at Bluebonnet. He started searching for cartridges, not expecting to find any. The crime scene guys had probably scooped them all. He was raking through some longer grass with his fingers when he saw the tuft shift and heard a rustle. Rustle or rattle? *Oh crap.* He felt the warm coil move beneath his hand and turn in his direction. *Oh shit, shit, shit.* Snake. *Big snake, damn big snake, pissed off snake.* He scrambled backwards like a fleeing crab until he hit the tree. He saw a flicker of movement away from him and exhaled. Rat snake. Not venomous, but still, it could so easily have been a rattler. Snakes coiled around his nightmares. He wiped the sweat out of his eyes and steadied his breathing.

Mike started to get up, but his shirt snagged on one of the splinters and snapped him back. He was trying to unhook himself, head twisted at an awkward angle, when he caught a glint of brass, then another, in the grass by the ditch. He tugged himself free, ripping a hole in his shirt, and picked them up. Short cartridge, bigger than a .22, smaller than a 9 mm, not something he was familiar with. The location of the cartridges suggested a shooter on the road. Mike measured his steps back to the tree. Seventeen—about fifty feet. A long way for a small round. He followed the line, past the live oak to the smaller trees and brush beyond. On the third tree he spotted a tiny hole, then noticed shredded leaves, and small holes in other trees, at least seven in all. He didn't have a knife, but he was sure there was lead in there. A full clip for any pocket pistol.

CHAPTER
TEN

DUKE MCMILLAN HAD LOVED Scroggin's Drug Store since he was a kid. It was the oldest operating business in Taborville. Established in 1890 by Albert Scroggin, it had gone through four generations, and every generation tried to maintain its history, making only those changes to the building that were absolutely necessary for the survival of the business. Little had changed in 130 years. The exterior of the single story, flat-roofed building, seemed identical to photos from the early 1900s, although brick had replaced the original wood fascia. The drug store had survived the fire of 1903 and the tornado of 1924 and was painted a traditional golden ochre as it had been for a hundred years.

The building stretched back an entire city block and was divided into thirds. Inside the double doors, a soda counter took up one entire wall in the first third of the building, with a row of 1950s chrome stools topped with red seats begging for service. A mirror ran the full length of the wall and reflected part of the ornately stamped-tin ceiling with its floral design. The range of ice creams, sodas, and milkshakes ran to seven double-sided pages on the articulated metal menus sprouting at regular intervals from the counter. On the wall opposite, before the long wooden rows of ancient, narrow drug drawers, was a magnificent Wurlitzer Victory Model 950, glowing in glass and burnished wood. The same forty tunes had been available since 1977.

The pharmacy counter sat at the rear of the public store. Behind it, hidden from public view, was the compounding pharmacy, and beyond that, a large storeroom.

The same tinkle on the doorbell announced Duke's arrival these many years later. He sat on one of the soda fountain stools. The young server in her pink-and-white-striped shirt with a red bowtie and paper soda jerk hat approached, but the owner, Joshua Scroggin, waved her away.

"I'll look after Mr. McMillan."

The server skulked away, no doubt annoyed because Duke McMillan was a big tipper.

"What will you have, Duke?" Joshua asked in a voice meant for public consumption.

"I'll take a sarsaparilla.

Joshua busied himself making the soda and McMillan waited. When the store was empty, he said in a voice only Joshua could hear, "Don't you ever speak to my boy like that, understand?"

"Maybe if your boys weren't such screw-ups, I wouldn't have to."

"What did you say?"

"You heard me. Your boys are putting all of us at risk, especially Karter."

"You need to watch your mouth."

"Yeah? You need to remember who got all of us into this mess—you and Taylor and that damn Magnolia Trails—and remember who is getting us out of it. All of you are up a creek without me. So, I'll have a little respect. Thank you very much."

"And you are in the hole without me."

"Correct. So, coming in here and giving me shit doesn't help our cause."

"Joshua, I'm serious. If you mess with my family, this fine old store will be just a memory, lost forever." He blew into his fist and his fingers scattered in the air.

"You'd better make sure you keep them under control, then."

McMillan took a sip of the sarsaparilla.

"You've lost your touch, Joshua. This is crap."

He pushed the glass away and put five dollars on the counter.

"For the girl."

The bell tinkled his departure.

In Houston Memorial Hospital, Zane McMillan's driver, Rafael Garza, ascended from unconsciousness with no clear memory of the accident on I-10. He remembered the crushing pain in his chest, knifing down his left arm, his left hand slipping from the steering wheel, useless. Rafael remembered gasping for breath and thinking he needed to get the Horny Toad Couriers truck off the interstate but couldn't figure out how. He remembered hearing metal screeching, but nothing more. Now he heard gentler sounds. Whooshes and beeps, quiet professional conversations, air conditioning, little echoes. He cracked his eyes open to see a smiling face. Not a kindly doctor, or a happy nurse, but a man in a blue uniform with a badge that read "ICE Officer."

"Welcome back, Mr. Garza. You're a fortunate man. That

was a narrow escape, they tell me. Must have been your lucky day. Not so lucky for the others and maybe not so lucky for you, either."

Garza followed the agent's eyes to the bracelets clamping his wrists to the bed.

"Two people are dead, Mr. Garza, killed by your truck. A truck you should not have been driving since you should not be here in the United States. You are now detained by ICE until a judge can make a determination."

Garza struggled to speak; his mouth felt so dry.

"What will happen?"

"It depends on the courts, but I imagine it will be prison here for vehicular manslaughter, illegal entry, forged documents. It's a pretty long list, to be honest. Eventually, deportation after what I imagine will be a lengthy sentence, back to where you've come from. Mexico, I'm assuming."

Things in the room beeped more rapidly, and a nurse hustled to the bed and motioned the ICE officer to leave.

"Wait."

The officer paused.

"What if I have information?"

"About?"

"Drugs. A lot of drugs."

CHAPTER ELEVEN

THE MEDICAL EXAMINER for Tabor County was based in San Antonio. The diabolically distorted muzak ebbed and flowed on the phone—little waves of acid dissolving Mike's patience. *Just the thing for a throbbing head.* A calm recorded voice regularly assured him she valued his call and the next available agent would answer him. As if.

"Hello," said a live, male human voice. "Medical Examiner's Office."

"Mike Carson, *Taborville Times.* I've been holding for thirty-seven minutes, by the way. I'm looking for the autopsy report on Adam Polley in Tabor County. Killed last week."

"Sorry for the wait. We're short-staffed today. Polley, Tabor County, right? One moment."

More muzak.

"Here we are. Cause of death gunshot wound."

"That's it?"

"No, there's more, but I can't give you the full report. Details are being withheld because of an ongoing investigation."

"It's a public record."

"Correct. And in due time, the full report will be available but, under Texas law, police can withhold some information in an open investigation. Stuff only the killer would know. I'm sure you've seen it on TV."

"I have. Can you give me anything else? Single gunshot? Multiple gunshots?"

"Cause of death, gunshot wound to the head. That's all I can give you?"

"Small caliber?"

"Eh, no, there are three other calls holding. I have to go."

The gunshot that killed Adam Polley was not small caliber. Two guns must have been involved. Mike sat back on the newly delivered sofa in Uncle Harold's den and thought about the implications. Rooms To Go had gone, and he had checked out of the Holiday Inn. He constantly expected to hear the familiar chesty wheeze, and the house seemed lonely without it, but he was glad to be moved in. The place was livable but still not saleable; nothing that a contractor couldn't solve when he could get around to hiring one.

There was a loud knock, followed by a more urgent rapping, before he could get to the front door. He opened it to an agitated woman.

"There's a rat in my backyard," she said, her voice close to a shout, face flustered.

"Do you want help?"

"No. It's gone now."

"OK?"

"It came from your yard, from that criminal eyesore you have out back."

"I'm sorry. Who are you?"

"You know damn well who I am. I'm your neighbor."

"Back or side?"

"Your next-door neighbor, dammit. Right there," she said, pointing to her ranch-style home. "Sofia Navarro."

"Right, sorry about that. Nice to meet you, I guess. Mike Carson." He extended a hand. She looked at it like it was rancid.

"You better get that toxic dump cleaned up right quick or I'm calling the council. And believe me, you'll be in big trouble." She turned away but apparently wasn't finished. "I know people."

"I'm sure you do."

"And you had no right to throw away my sister's yard signs."

"I don't think Texas property law would agree with that assessment."

"You want to go to court? Bring it on. I'm ready."

"Look, I think we're getting off on the wrong foot. Your sister's yard signs are—"

"Clean your mess," she said and marched her ample butt across his driveway. "Damn health hazard."

He heard her door slam and quietly closed his own.

Mike parked outside Tabor Trust Bank just before Holly walked through the doors a little after six. He caught up to her before she climbed into her truck.

"Holly."

She turned, glanced around, nervous.

"Mike. Hi."

"Hey, if you have a second, I need to ask you a few questions."

She looked around again, a little furtive. "Sure, but maybe

not here. The manager is a bit, I don't know, creepy, I guess. Let me go home and change. I'll see you at Longhorns in, say, thirty minutes?"

She'd swapped the banker suit for dark jeans and a black shirt when she walked up to the booth.

"Are we going to eat?" She looked at her knock-off Rolex smothered in fake gemstones. "I've only got about an hour."

"How come?"

"I have a second job in the kitchen over at the chicken place."

They ordered chicken fried steaks, which came with gravy, mashed potatoes, and waterlogged green beans.

"You have questions?" she said after a few bites.

"Was Adam a fast driver?"

"No. He was careful. Always drove the limit and never got a ticket in his life."

"You're sure he was clean?"

"Completely. Absolutely. Totally. Hand to God."

"What did he drive?"

"An old Crown Vic he picked up at a police auction real cheap—$400, I think. He had a beautiful truck before but it was repo'd."

"Crown Vic, that's interesting. Repo'd because of drugs?"

"It was gambling. He had this thing—a condition the doctor called it—apophenia. Saw patterns even when they weren't there. Thought he could see the patterns in card games and, boy, was he wrong about that."

"The drugs?"

"He was always in pain from Iraq. Purple Heart. In the damn chow hall, of all places. Thought he'd be safe as a cook. He got hooked on that oxycodone they kept pushing at the VA. But the policy changed, and he couldn't get it anymore. Thank God it all stopped when he met the healing hand of Jesus."

"You're sure he stopped gambling?"

"We were on the right path, Mike. He went to GamAnon and NarcAnon meetings every single week in La Grange. You can check. And he wouldn't even take a paracetamol. I know his arm still hurt like crazy, but he just prayed and toughed it out. We had to sell the house and a bunch of other stuff to pay down the debt. Rented a double-wide out at Lakeview instead, crappy but cheap. We were doing everything we could."

"The thing is, Adam was hauling ass when he hit the tree. He might have been running from something, or spooked, or both. I don't know."

"Running from what?"

"No idea yet. Maybe he was in the wrong place at the wrong time. Driving a Crown Vic. Maybe someone thought he was a cop."

"Oh God, I never thought about the car."

"Did they give you any details about the shooting?"

"Just that he was shot. Why?"

"I'm trying to work out if he was hit before the crash or after. If it was before, that's probably why he crashed, but I think it was after the crash."

"Why do you say that?"

Mike opened his hand and showed her the cartridges.

"Because I found these at the crash site."

Her face trembled, tried to rebuild, and failed as the remains of her meal absorbed her tears.

Mike sat, unsure of what to do. *When in doubt, shut up.* He waited. She dabbed the tears with her napkin, irritated.

"I'm sorry. Just keeps happening."

"No need to apologize. I hate asking this, but he wasn't making a buy for you, was he?"

"Wow. Come straight out with it, why don't you? No, I

don't do drugs, don't drink either. No need to ask you, though. I can see it in your face."

Mike looked out the window.

"Nothing to say about that, huh? I can see it in your eyes, in your skin, in your hair, on your breath. The booze."

She put ten dollars beside her plate. "I have to go."

He pushed it back towards her.

"I pay my way, mister. And you know what? Maybe you should just forget this."

"What?"

"I don't need to be around drunks." And she left.

Mike paid the check and drove to the house. The echoes mocked his loneliness as he walked to the kitchen and took a glass from the draining board. *Big mouth. Had to come out and say it, didn't you?* But what were the options? It was a question that had to be asked. He had to check. *Yeah, like everything got checked, right?* He opened a kitchen cabinet. *Could have sworn there was half a bottle in there.* He started hunting, cabinet by cabinet. Nothing. He opened the fridge. Hidden behind the gallon of milk sat an unopened bottle of Bulleit 95 Rye Frontier Whiskey. Aged twelve years and no longer in production. Fire alarm whiskey. Break glass only in an emergency. He reached for it. *Wait. Wait one second.* He remembered now. He went to the TV cabinet and there it was—half a bottle of Jack Daniels. *Phew.*

Two drinks later, Charles Coolidge was back. Hanging in Mike's head again. He'd never met the man but knew every researchable detail of his life. The only child of privileged parents who'd never worked a day in their lives, both minor heirs to family fortunes made in railways and construction.

Charles had gone to law school but migrated to money, not that he needed it. He was an intensely private man with a public conscience, donating to multiple charities and rights organizations. *I'd have really liked him,* Mike thought, *if I hadn't killed him.* Words. *Dangerous things,* Liz had said. He sometimes wondered if it might have worked out better between them if he'd focused on the feelings between the words. The trouble was, no matter how hard he tried, his attention was drawn away from the negative space to the need for a well-constructed sentence and the feelings floated away freely, unrecognized.

Each career success carried with it corrosive little seeds of destruction. He loved the recognition, the validation, the approval. He loved it more than anything, even more than the work itself, and the more he got, the more he needed it. Liz grew distant after he was nominated for a George Polk Award.

"Why can't you be happy for me?" he'd asked.

"Do you think I find comfort," she'd said, "when I'm in bed alone at night, for weeks on end, knowing my husband is God knows where, pretending to be God knows who, and doing God knows what to protect his cover story? Do you think *your* award is a comfort to *me*?"

He didn't have an answer.

"You bring it back with you, little bits of it, stuck to you—little bits of the other lives. Some of it's nice, the caring parts. But some of it is really dark."

"I'm not sure what you mean," he'd said.

"There's a veil in your eyes now. Did you know that? I used to know exactly how you felt just by looking into your eyes. Now...."

He'd had no answer for that, either. They'd sat in silence.

"I have a question for you," she'd said finally. "What good is the truth if you have to lie to get it?"

"Sometimes it's the only way."

"And you're very good at it, aren't you? Living the lies. I wonder sometimes if the real you is out there, in the story, or here with me." She'd stared into his eyes. "I'm not sure I could tell if you were lying to me anymore. I just wouldn't know."

He'd picked up his glass of bourbon.

"And what's in there that you can't find with me?" she'd demanded.

He'd thought for a long time before answering.

"A chance to forget the stuff I can never tell you."

CHAPTER TWELVE

THE BENIGN LITTLE man on Mike's doorstep smiled as the door opened.

"You are Mr. Mike Carson," he said, with the hint of a question.

"Yes."

"You need help." This was not a question. "I am Señor Salvador Alvarez. You will call me Juan. I will call you Mike." He gestured behind him at the minivan and a line of men, women, and children in the driveway. "My family."

Good God, Mike thought, *how many of them are there?*

"How did you know?" Mike had never called the number. It was still in his notebook.

"Maria Elena." The little man did a bounce on the decking. "We will start here. This is not safe. When the woodwork is done outside, we will paint. Think about the color. Then we will move inside."

Mike had never been steam-rolled so softly.

"How much will all this cost?"

"What is fair and just. You will afford it." He smiled again. "I will need a key and a credit card."

"I don't lock the door. Nothing here to steal."

"Just the credit card." He held out his hand.

Mike had trusted no one so soon or so completely. He turned over his Mastercard. Señor Salvador Alvarez, whom he would call Juan, held the card in both hands with reverence and nodded.

"We will return with materials and tools."

The family climbed into the minivan when Juan turned to join them. Mike looked at the empty space in his wallet where the Mastercard had been. He could always tell the bank he lost it.

Shauna, the receptionist at the police station, recognized Mike as he entered the lobby.

"You're that reporter fella who was here before."

"That's right," Mike said, brandishing his new press card. "I'm looking for Sergeant Green."

"Can't help you there. He's on patrol."

"Do you think the chief could spare a moment? He knows me."

"He's always busy, but I can check."

She buzzed him in a few minutes later with a severe warning that Chief Gates was pressed for time. She escorted Mike to his office.

"Mr. Carson," he indicated one of the two chairs in front of the remarkably tidy, institutional desk. Nothing in, nothing out, nothing pending. Behind the desk, a bookcase reached almost to the low ceiling. Books on law enforcement, reports, a signed baseball and mitt, pictures of the chief looking deadly on a SWAT course, beaming with a huge catfish, and posing on a golf tee with the governor and attorney general. There were no family photos anywhere.

"Thank you, Chief, I'm with the *Times* at the moment."

"I heard."

"I had a few questions about the Polley killing."

"Not much I can say; ongoing investigation."

"I drove out to the crash site. It surprised me there was no incident tape preserving the scene."

"It's been processed and recorded. We're efficient here, and thorough."

The cartridges in Mike's pocket begged to differ.

"Indeed. The speed of your ballistics impressed me."

"In what way?"

"Less than twenty-four hours after the shooting, you could link it to suspects from San Antonio. Presumably the bullets matched some shooting or shootings there?"

"Like I said, we're efficient."

"The autopsy must have been done immediately, then?"

The chief didn't answer.

"I'm trying to get the timeline down. The scene was processed, the body would have been removed after an initial look-see by the medical examiner and the coroner or maybe a justice of the peace. Then the body would have been transported to the morgue in San Antonio. The autopsy had to happen to recover the bullets. Then they would have to be matched through the national ballistic info network over at ATF."

The chief was stony faced. Mike flipped through his notebook.

"And you released your statement at, let's see, eight thirty, in time for the ten-o'clock local TV news. To get the statement prepared took, what, thirty minutes, maybe an hour? That's a lot of ground to cover in thirteen hours. Very good going."

The chief's eyes narrowed.

"Like I told you, we are efficient and thorough."

"Can you confirm that a gunshot to the head killed Mr. Polley?"

"Who told you that?"

"Medical examiner's office."

"That's not a detail they should have released, and you'd best not write it. It could impede our investigation."

"And how is the investigation going? Any closer to identifying suspects?"

"I've given you everything we can release at the present moment, Mr. Carson. Now, if you will excuse me, I have a lot to do."

Not according to your in-tray, Mike thought as he rose.

"You will stay out of trouble, Mr. Carson, won't you?"

Mike called Frank Wolfe in Philly.

"Skippy," Wolfe said, cheerful as ever. "How's thang's goin' down thar in the Lone Star State?"

"That's a truly awful accent."

"I'm offended. You know I got a prize for drama, right?"

"Could have fooled me."

"Swear to God, stack of Bibles. My parents still have it somewhere. 'Course it was in the sixth grade, but a prize is a prize, my friend. So. What's cooking?"

"I'm working."

"That's great. Who's the misinformed editor who hired you?"

"I didn't say they hired me. I signed on with the local paper. Guess I could put my expenses down as charity since I don't get paid."

"I knew you'd get bored."

"More like a favor for a friend. Remember, I told you about

the murder? Turns out the guy married a girl I knew in high school."

"Oh, man."

"Yeah, and she was getting the runaround from the local constabulary. So, she asked me to help."

"And you couldn't resist. Is she a looker?"

"Thing doesn't add up, though."

He ran Frank through the timeline he had outlined to the chief. "You've got way more crime desk experience than me. Does this make any sense?"

"I'll tell you for a fact, Skippy, you're being fed a mountain of bullshit. No way there was a bullet match in that time. No way."

"Yeah?"

"Absolutely. I just did a piece on this. ATF dragged in a training center in Huntsville to help them out, and they've been boasting they return results in forty-eight hours—on cartridges, mind you, not bullets."

"That's what I thought."

"No problem. By the way, try to get paid. It's a profession, not a spiritual calling."

Mike laughed and hung up.

When he got to Uncle Harold's, he had to park out back on the grass. His driveway was full of pickups parked next to a freshly delivered dumpster that was already close to overflowing. Juan and two other men were screwing boards into the decking. One front rail was new and the other was being demolished by two teenage boys. An older woman and someone who appeared to be her daughter were schooling four younger children on the lawn. The women sat cross-legged. The kids sprawled but seemed attentive. Piles of wood siding were stacked neatly around the house. A generator burbled and charged a large array of tool batteries.

Mike's boot left a dark footprint on the fresh wood of the porch steps. Juan got off his knees as Mike approached. All work stopped instantly.

"We are keeping everything that is not rotten. It is good to keep the house original. So much history. So many stories. We will work for one more hour, then we will go to eat. You will come with us."

He introduced his brother and a cousin, then a son and a nephew.

"I'm not sure I can keep all the names in my head."

"That's OK. We know who we are."

Exactly an hour later, the generator stopped, tools were packed, offcuts stacked or trashed, and the children swept the deck. Mike smiled. Literally all hands on deck.

Twenty minutes later, Juan tapped politely on the door.

"We will go now to Nuevo Comenzo for dinner. You will join us."

The only thing new about Nuevo Comenzo was the name. The building was 1960s basic with painted Hardie board siding and a low slanted roof that looked like it had wanted to be higher but could not make the effort. It sat two-tone tan and brown in one corner of the decaying parking lot of Taborville's oldest strip mall, like an afterthought.

Inside, the place was humming, almost completely full of extended families sharing carnitas and conversation. Overly large brown horseshoe booths lined the window walls. Four and six-top tables filled the space available in the center and surrounded a fake stucco-walled fountain whose pump had long since failed and was now trailing faded plastic bougainvillea. The service doors to the kitchen banged constantly as servers hurried steaming plates of enchiladas and tamales, flautas, and fajitas to the hungry tables.

Juan selected an open booth toward the back. The family sat in practiced order, leaving Juan and his wife, Rosa, on the ends of the horseshoe. There was no room for Mike. He pulled a chair from another table and sat on the end to the obvious annoyance of the waitstaff who had to ballet dance around him.

It's just as well they know each other, Mike thought, looking at the packed bodies. Two large baskets of chips and salsa landed quickly, along with eight large glasses of ice water and four smaller ones for the kids, who perched on parents' laps. Juan ordered for the entire family. Mike asked for chimichangas, beef and chicken. The family chatted happily in Spanish while he sat mute and clueless.

"Today has been a good day," Juan said. "You are happy with the progress." If there was a hint of a question in his voice, Mike could not discern it.

"Oh yes, very."

He sipped his water, wishing he could switch the chlorine taste for something stronger, but it didn't seem appropriate to order beer. The food arrived quickly and when all the white oval plates crowded onto the table, the family joined hands.

Oh, here we go. Do you have a personal relationship with Jesus?

Juan extended his right hand, Rosa her left, and he had no option but to take them or risk offense. Everyone bowed heads, and a surge of calm energy hit him like a shock. Mike could almost smell the fire around which the ancient people sat, feel the wings of eagles in their flight, and hear the voices echoing off canyon walls in chant. But this family spoke no words, no prayers or invocations, just a quiet connection with some unseen power. Then, the current broke as hands busied themselves with food. Mike's palms rested on the table as he tried to rationalize what had just happened.

"You will be fine; you do not need to worry." Juan said and crunched into a flauta.

I guess this is what they mean by a close-knit family, Mike thought, looking at the interactions between fathers, uncles, mothers, sons, and daughters. *Not at all like my family.* You could drive an eighteen-wheeler through the gaps between the Carsons. Juan and Rosa seemed to float above it all, connected to everyone by some spiritual gossamer, steering the family dynamic with nods and smiles. Gentle folk. The sound of excited chatter, the laughter and the gentle teasing was pleasantly alien and distracted him from the food. Mexican had never been his favorite—something to do with the refried beans and how they looked like cow splat on the plate.

Mike excused himself for the bathroom before the check arrived, intercepted the server, and handed her a Visa to pay for all the meals.

"Mr. Mike bought our food," Juan said when Mike returned. The family, in unison, put their palms together, bowed their heads, and offered namaste, a gesture that touched a place somewhere in Mike's heart he thought had long crusted over.

"Tomorrow we will do walls."

Mike sat in the Sentra, unsure of his next move, until eventually the car drove itself to Joe's Liquor Store.

CHAPTER THIRTEEN

FAMILY ALVAREZ STARTED nail gunning at eight o'clock. Mike dived out of bed. For a fraction of a second, he was back at the Intercontinental Hotel in Kabul, the night of the Taliban attack. He got to his feet, embarrassed and relieved.

He dressed quickly and stepped onto the porch. School had started under the fan. Rosa and her mother smiled at him.

"I'm going to grab some breakfast," he told Juan. "Can I bring something back for you?"

"No, Mike, thank you. We have eaten. Now we work."

Mike ordered his usual at Longhorns.

"Mike? Mike Carson?"

The guy seemed vaguely familiar, standing there, smiling, expecting Mike to know him.

"It's Jimmy." Not much help. "Jimmy Hughes," as if that should explain it. "We sat beside each other in tenth grade."

"Of course. How are you?"

"Doing good." He sat down, uninvited. "You?"

"Fine, thanks."

"I never thought I'd see you in town again. Not after the class reunion."

"Right. Not one of my better moments."

"It was eloquent, even though you were loaded, but you were always good with words. '*You think you are legends with a legacy, but what you really are is a league of lamentable losers.*' I never forgot that, maybe because you fell off the chair right after."

"It was pretty harsh."

"I used to think so but, you know, I'm not so sure now. All those football jocks are still talking about high school games 'cos nothing better ever happened in their lives."

"Still. Pretty harsh."

Jimmy owned a dry-cleaning store and was divorced, had two kids who had grown and gone and never called.

"But you, you've been all over the world doing those big stories. People might not say it, but I think we're all sorta proud."

"Shame I'm such an asshole."

"Yeah. Well, I need to go. It was great to see you."

Mike's phone vibrated.

"Hi Mike, Quintin Smith. At the *Times*."

"Yeah."

"I was wondering if we could call on your services tonight."

"That was quick. You're not wasting any time. What do you need?"

"It's city council."

Mike groaned.

"I know. Boring. It's my father. He's had a stroke. I have to drive to Dallas."

"Sorry to hear it. Are you at the office?"

"For about thirty minutes."

"I'll come right over. You need to talk me through the coverage you want. It's been a long time since I did meetings. Long time." *But a deal's a deal.*

Quintin had pulled raw copy from the last three meetings by the time Mike got to the office.

"Unless there's something really unusual, this is the normal coverage. We're the paper of record so we have to write the boring stuff, even if it doesn't set the world on fire. We tweet the meeting in real time."

"I don't tweet."

"It's not that hard."

"I don't tweet."

"Seriously, it's just a running commentary. Meeting's opened, this passed, that passed."

Mike fixed him with a killer stare.

"I. Don't. Tweet."

"OK. I'll see if I can get Cathy. She's covering another meeting that overlaps. Maybe she can come after."

He handed Mike a key to the building, made his apologies, and left, slinging a heavy leather bag over his left shoulder and pulling a small carry-on behind him.

The logo for Sisters in Arms firing range was a pastiche of Norman Rockwell's Rosie the Riveter. The rivet gun had been replaced by a .50 caliber machine gun, the sandwich by Dirty Harry's .44 Magnum. The haughty smile was just the same.

Mike was not a fan of guns, not after killing his one and only deer as a kid. The horror of the life he snuffed out far outweighed one of the few times his father had been proud of him. Still, he practiced and was proficient. It was Texas, after all. His time in Afghanistan cemented the aversion. He had seen, in gruesome detail, the appalling damage done to the human body; had seen soldiers bleed out, innocent bystanders splayed and broken.

He turned into the dirt driveway and followed signs to the office. A field of sweetcorn to his left faced a series of gray metal buildings on his right. Reports from large caliber rifles interrupted the crack of pistol fire. The range seemed busy for a weekday.

The office had no windows. Above the double glass doors, a steel roll-down waited to secure the building. Mounted high on the corners, arrays of cameras covered every angle.

The lines of gun-racks and illuminated cases stretched a full 200 feet to the main counter where a tall and muscled woman stood. Her cropped hair was dyed silver, and her T-shirt read "Gun Control Because Criminals Follow Laws, Right?" She had intersecting female symbols tattooed on her right forearm. She seemed cheery.

"What's your pleasure?"

He produced one of the cartridges he'd found at Bluebonnet Road.

"What kind of cartridge is this?"

".380 ACP. Why?"

"I found it. It seemed kinda small, and I wondered what kind of gun would shoot it."

She walked over to one case.

"Any of these."

There were a surprising number of small pistols and revolvers on display. Lots of names Mike recognized and some he'd never heard of.

"Are you looking to buy?"

"I'm not sure. Thinking about it."

"Do you have a concealed carry permit?"

"No...they look so small."

"They're a close-up weapon, kind of last resort, but if you shove one into your attacker and empty the mag, you will definitely neutralize the threat."

"That close?"

"Some folks who practice can get pretty accurate up to fifteen feet, but the sights don't really help, and the grips are pretty small."

"So, it's a pistol cartridge?"

"What is this? Some kind of quiz? Are you going to shoot or just shoot the shit?"

Mike laughed.

"Sure, I'm going to shoot. Why don't we try the Glock and the Taurus?"

"Good choices. I have some rentals at the front. Of course, if you want some real .380 fun, you want to shoot the MAC 11, 1,200 rounds a minute."

"A machine gun?"

"Machine pistol."

"Do you have one?"

"Of course." She grinned. "What good is owning a place like this if you can't have all the toys?"

"Can I try the MAC too?"

"If I come out to the range with you."

She had not been kidding about the rate of fire. The machine pistol had a suppressor, which she told Mike to hold in his left hand. With the stock extended, Mike squeezed the trigger on full auto, counted one thousand and one in his head, and the mag was empty. The thirty-two rounds all went down range, but he did not know where.

"You're not here to buy a weapon, are you?" she said.

"No. I'm doing a bit of research." He paused. "For a novel."

"You should have said. That's exciting. What's your name?"

"Mike Carson."

"Have you written anything I would have heard of?"

"I don't think so."

She unscrewed the twelve-inch suppressor, collapsed the stock, and replaced the empty magazine.

"I haven't shot this sucker in a while," she grinned. "Time to go all Scarface." She held the MAC in her right hand like a regular pistol, stood side on to the range, squeezed the trigger, and channeled her best Al Pacino.

"Here comes the pain."

Spent cartridges flew and bounced. Mike knew, in that moment, someone on Bluebonnet Road had emptied a MAC into Adam Polley's Crown Vic but failed to kill him.

CHAPTER FOURTEEN

THIS CITY HALL was new to Mike. The architects had attempted to keep the building consistent with the city's more historic structures but had missed the mark. It was more barn than building, more impotent than imposing.

The brightly lit lobby led to the council chambers on the left and offices on the right. The chamber had seating for a hundred, arranged in neat rows of gray chairs, facing a raised pine dais. Along one wall were plastic tables already half full of city staff. Mike recognized the police chief immediately, hunched over, reading his phone.

Eleven spectators sat in the audience, spread around the room. The mayor and council members milled about, their animated chat occasionally broken by soft laughter. The city manager sat at one end of the dais and looked like he was asleep, his tiny, bald head reflecting the harsh fluorescent lighting.

The mayor, Bill Pryor, stopped his glad-handing a few minutes after 6:30 p.m., got everyone seated, and formally opened the meeting. Mike jotted notes by rote, consulting the agenda and waited, pen poised to cross out item numbers as they came up. He had spiked his large bottle of orange Gatorade with vodka. Things could be worse.

The somnambulant city manager's report was written in formal technical language and read without inflection, punctuation, or energy. At "Item (H)—Financial Matter," the lifeless recitation came to a halt.

"Council Member VanDorn asked me to include this item, but I don't know what it is," the manager said.

There was a tiny murmur from the audience. Nadia Navarro's head snapped up. *Striking woman,* Mike thought, *shame about the sister.* Other council members looked uncomfortable. The mayor and Xander VanDorn sported little smiles.

"Council Member VanDorn," said the mayor.

VanDorn was in his mid- to late sixties, with a full head of snowy hair and a neatly trimmed beard. If it wasn't for the ratty eyes, he might have been considered handsome. His voice was surprisingly soft. "Thank you, Mayor."

"Can't hear you," yelled a voice from the audience. "Microphone."

Mike glanced over his shoulder. Mr. Hodge, his old English teacher. The man must be in his eighties now. Still crazy about civics. The world could do with more like him.

"City Manager, the reason I asked you to bring this up is because of a previously unreported excess in the general fund," said VanDorn.

The city manager shuffled through his notes, shifted in his seat.

"Yes, $374,483," he said, "I was—"

"Thank you," said VanDorn. "I raise the issue because I have become aware of an opportunity to further secure the city's future water needs. A private consortium is about to drill a new well in the aquifer that could supply the city with an additional 10,000-acre feet of water every year. The consortium is offering the city a participation in the well. A kind of public-private partnership, if you will. About $350,000 towards the drilling costs, and a contract to supply water when the well is operational." He beamed. "It's a great opportunity."

"It's highly irregular," said Navarro. "This should be on the agenda, not buried in the city manager's report. Citizens have had no advance warning and have a right to comment."

Council Member Isaac Brook took his cue.

"I would like to make a motion that this council allocates the additional monies discovered in the general fund to—"

"To what?" demanded Navarro. "You don't even know, do you? We can't invest public money without the public being given an opportunity to speak, and we know nothing about this consortium."

There was a sincere fieriness to her, Mike thought, a centered righteousness. Brave, foolhardy, maybe both. He had images of lances and windmills in his head. Taborville City Council had never been very concerned about the public's opportunity to speak. He suspected it hadn't changed in the years he'd been away.

Everyone in the chamber was paying attention now. VanDorn leaned forward and activated his mic.

"Mr. Mayor, if I may, the consortium is being led by a familiar figure to us all, Mr. Duke McMillan, who has done so much for this city. I notice Mr. McMillan is in the audience tonight. Perhaps he could fill in some details. If you think that would be helpful to the council?"

"It certainly would," said the mayor. "Mr. McMillan," indicating the podium.

"I'll do my best, Mr. Mayor and council, but I have nothing prepared. I was not expecting to address council tonight," McMillan said.

"I'm sure you'll be fine."

Mike leaned back in his chair as McMillan talked. This was a good 'ol boy classic. One for the books. The mayor, VanDorn, Brook, and McMillan, who just "happened" to be in the audience, were in on it. He wondered how many more.

Seven minutes into McMillan's rambling explanation, Navarro interrupted. "Mr. Mayor, we have exceeded the five-minute time limit for public contributions."

"Come on now, Nadia, why don't you hear the man out?"

"It is Council Member Navarro, Mr. Mayor, and the speaker has exceeded his time."

"I propose we suspend the five-minute rule, Mr. Mayor," said Brook.

"Second," said VanDorn.

"All in favor?" The mayor counted four votes. "Against?"

Navarro held up her lonely hand.

"Carried. Continue, Mr. McMillan."

Thirty minutes later, Duke McMillan sat down, but by now the chamber audience had doubled, summoned by texts from friends at the meeting. Mike overheard one woman behind him.

"I was in my damn pajamas, having a glass of wine. Had to get dressed again."

A line formed in front of the city secretary, who handed out speaker request forms. The mayor called a five-minute comfort break.

Cathy Ross slid into the seat beside Mike a minute later. That hint of orange and jasmine again.

"Sorry, got here as fast as I could. What item are we on?"

"Manager's report."

"My God. What's going on?"

She edged her chair closer and Mike filled her in as a growing buzz of dissent spread around the room. When the meeting resumed, Navarro put up a spirited fight to prevent a vote on allocating the monies, encouraged by growls from the audience. The mayor was forced to postpone action until the next meeting. Two items later, in Citizens' Comments, he ruled everyone out of order who wanted to comment. Citizens' Comments, he said, were restricted to items not on the agenda, and this item had been contained in the city manager's report, which *was* on the agenda. Despite the ensuing uproar, he maintained his ruling. The council went into executive session at 10:30 p.m. Mike and Cathy left.

"What's the deadline for this copy?" he asked Cathy.

"Latest noon tomorrow to get through the system."

"Wanna drink? I sure as hell need one."

Gold Spurs was the only place still open. They grabbed a table away from the noisy bar. The server ignored them.

"Maybe we need to be at the bar this time of night," Cathy said.

They slid onto two of the stools and still got no recognition.

"Excuse me, could we have some drinks here?" Mike said in a loud voice. The server left the bar and went through a door at the back. Moments later, a manager appeared.

"Hi," Mike said, "could we have a double Jack on the rocks and a white wine, please?"

"I'm afraid not, sir, and I would be grateful if you'd leave."

"Excuse me?" Mike said.

"What's the issue?" Cathy said.

"The gentleman is not welcome in this establishment. We are happy to serve you if he leaves."

"This is about the other night," Mike said.

The manager addressed Cathy. "This, eh, gentleman,

started a fight with other customers last time he was here. The police had to be called. As a result, he is...."

"Barred." Mike said.

"No longer welcome," said the manager. "Now, if you would please leave."

Nadia Navarro slammed a clenched fist on the tabletop. The mayor jumped.

"Just what in the hell are you up to, VanDorn? What's that crap you were trying to pull?"

"Now, Nadia," said the mayor, "calm down. I won't have language—"

"I'll use whatever the hell language I like. What's going on here? What are you people up to?"

"You're an unstable person, Nadia," VanDorn said. "I've told you this before, Mayor. The woman is out of control. Radical."

Her voice dropped several tones and slowed. Her eyes narrowed and her teeth gritted. "Don't you dare try to demean me like that. Don't. What is this little scheme? Who's in this water consortium? Are you, Xander? You, Brook? You, Mayor?"

VanDorn settled back in his chair and smiled.

"And what if we are?" he said.

"It's a conflict of interest."

"If something is good for the town and happens to be good for a few private individuals, we have still served the public good."

"That is rarely the case around here," Nadia said. "And I think the citizens will have a very different view from yours."

"The citizens won't be hearing about it, Nadia. We're in

executive session, remember? Confidential information. You daren't breathe a word outside this room."

Cathy's apartment was small by Texas standards, but comfortable.

"It's just a little two-bed, but it suits me," she said. "I'm hardly ever here."

Mike picked up the glass of Scotch, not his favorite, but it was no time to be picky. Cathy nestled onto the sofa beside him, tucked her legs, and took a big swig of Sancerre.

"You're not from here," Mike said.

"No, I'm from Oregon."

"What brought you to Texas?"

"School, I went to UT."

"Me too."

"I know, you and Walter Cronkite."

"Hardly in the same league. They don't have a journalism school in Oregon?"

"Sure, University of Oregon, but I wanted to get out of Roseburg to a big city and, anyway, I'd rather cheer for Longhorns than Ducks."

They laughed.

"Do you mind if I ask you a personal question?" she said.

"Sure."

"Why are you here? I mean, what's the real reason? Quintin told me some bullshit story about you taking a sabbatical from the *Chronicle*."

"And you didn't believe it?"

"Not a word, and anyway I know when Quintin's lying. He always scratches his ear."

"The *Chronicle* and I had a parting of the ways, the same

time my wife and I had a parting of the ways. I'm taking a bit of time and distance to figure out the future."

"Do you think you'll be here for a while?"

"I don't know. Depends on how long it takes to sell my uncle's house. This is not my favorite place in the world."

"I hope you do. Stay, I mean."

"Why?"

She poured them both a second glass.

"I'm hoping you might mentor me. I want to move to one of the big papers, maybe even TV, but I'm not learning anything from Quintin. He's barely hanging on."

"I'm not sure I would have much to teach you."

"Oh, Mr. Modest Pulitzer Prize, I'm sure you are wrong about that."

"What do you want to know?"

"How about how you got the Pulitzer, for a start?"

"I did an expose of private military contractors, went undercover in one of them—DRI, Dynamic Reaction International."

He told her about the training at DRI and the deployment to Iraq; the scandals he'd uncovered, the drugs, the arms sales, the child prostitution, the excessive use of force. He spoke of almost everything he'd written in the series of articles, but not the other things—not the things that wandered through his dreams.

"I know you didn't want to be covering council meetings, so you must have needed that press card badly. It's got to be something exciting. What you're working on, right?"

"I'm having a look at that murder."

"The Polley shooting."

"Yeah. He was married to a friend of mine and there's something off about it. Like way off."

"Really. Maybe I can help?"

Mike wrestled with the thought for a while before he answered. "That might be useful, actually. Local knowledge."

When she poured the third glass, she was practically on top of him. He wondered if she'd eaten anything. She was getting very happy.

"What's that?" she took his hand and stroked the tattoo. "Hmm, question mark."

"Something I should have paid more attention to."

"I don't get it."

"It means a lot of things. Mostly stuff I learned from my Uncle Harold. Question everything. Take nothing for granted. Are your facts straight? Should this story be written?" He sagged into the couch, let his head fall back till he was looking at the ceiling. "Some stories shouldn't be written, no matter how good they are."

"Bullshit."

"It's not, you know. There are consequences to what we do. Real consequences."

"It's not our job to worry about consequences. We report the facts. The chips land where they land."

"I used to think that," he said, feeling old, "but there's more to it, believe me."

"Hey, don't go all melancholy on me."

"It's nothing that another whiskey won't cure."

She poured him another glass.

"Seriously, though—"

"I don't want to be serious," she said.

He took a big swallow, lay back, and stared at the ceiling again. He wondered about the unknowns. How many anonymous innocents had he wounded by his clever words? There was no telling. He closed his eyes, but Charles Coolidge was there, accusing. Before he could open them, her cool hand was on his forehead, stroking. God, he missed that. The comfort of

Liz's touch, a woman's caress. Cathy kissed his eyelids softly. Soothing. She traced the outline of his jaw with her fingers and then kissed him on the mouth. A gentle, healing kiss. When he returned the softness, her lips became more urgent, her hands more needy, her body more demanding. He dissolved into her desire and was overwhelmed by his own. It had been so long. She moved his hand to her breast and all of him knew what she wanted and needed. He needed the same.

Afterward, she observed him on one elbow, smiling and glowing.

"So, what happened?"

"What do you mean?"

"To you, what went wrong?"

"Who says anything went wrong?"

"Oh, come on. You didn't have a 'parting of the ways.' They fired you, right? What went wrong?"

"I don't know. A lot of things, I guess. Disillusion mainly. You do all these stories, hoping, believing you're making a difference. But you're not. There are more homeless now than ever. Old people are still being abused in care facilities, private military contractors have grown exponentially, etcetera, etcetera, etcetera. In the end, you're only selling newspapers."

"Wow, there's a pep talk. Thanks."

"You asked. It was that—and pressure. You try to make everything as good as the story that won the Pulitzer, but you can't. You try to make the lightning strike again, but pretty soon you realize it's the gods that make the lightning and you are just a man."

"Savior complex, huh?"

"Maybe."

"I read that most men get over it when they get to thirty-three. What age are you?"

"I should go."

"You could stay. Get to know each other...again."

"I have that piece to write for Quintin."

"At this hour?"

"I enjoy writing in the quiet of the night, and I know if I don't do it now, it won't get done in the morning."

She kissed him deeply at the door. "That was fun," she said. "We should do it again sometime. Soon."

Nice to know.

Raul was on his usual perch as Mike walked home.

"Hey, Raul,"

"Hey, Jack man."

"No Jack tonight, sad to say." Mike sat.

They contemplated the empty street.

"I was wondering if you knew where a guy could score?" Mike said.

"Goddamn Federales."

"No, my friend, I'm not a cop. Honest."

Raul spat into the gutter. "Bad business. Pharma-shooticals. Might as well take a gun to your head. Save yourself time and trouble and a whole lota pain, from what I seen."

"I know, but if someone was that stupid, for argument's sake, where would they go? If they were in pain."

"You think I know?"

"Yeah, I do. You're a smart man, you see what's going on. A guy I know was killed. I need to find out why."

"A man in town told me once, 'There's no pain when you walk up bluebonnet.'"

"Where can I find this guy?"

"In Pinegrove Cemetery. These days he got no pain."

"Are you talking about Bluebonnet Road?"

"'No pain when you walk up bluebonnet,' is all he said."

"Ever hear anything else?"

"I got talking to another guy at the food pantry one time, casual, and he says, 'You ever go up there to the post office, you know, to get well?' and I don't know what he's talking about but I say, 'The post office,' and he says, 'Yeah, near the big house on the corner but you gots to watch for the cameras, see everything they do.' So, I finish my chicken, and he says, 'Man, you gots to be careful. They got it covered. For real.' And then he got kinda spooked by me and shut up."

"What did he mean?"

"I got no idea. You can't trust them drogadictos."

CHAPTER FIFTEEN

DUKE MCMILLAN TRIED Xander VanDorn's office line. VanDorn screened all calls on his cell and Duke didn't want to leave messages. Xander picked up on the second ring.

"Have you seen the paper?" Duke said.

"No. I've been in the office all morning working on a report."

"Well, it's not good. 'Council Uproar' is the headline."

"Front page?"

"Above the fold, and it's not just a report on the meeting. He's done follow-up interviews. He's talked to Navarro, and that crazy water rights guy, and to the city manager."

"Manager better not have said a damn word," said VanDorn.

"He didn't really, but it's the way Carson has written it. *The city manager was reluctant to discuss the issue but emphasized that council's responsibility was to set policy, and the manager's to run the city. When pressed, he admitted the way the issue appeared in his report was, quote,' unusual.'*"

"The manager is skating on thin ice, but it doesn't sound all that bad."

"Until you get to this. Quote: Nadia Navarro appeared to be the only council member taken by surprise when the issue was raised. Multiple sources confirm Duke McMillan is not a regular attendee at council meetings. According to Navarro, he only shows up when it's in his interests, unquote. Next sentence; 'Discussion of an item in advance by three council members would constitute a quorum and would be a breach of The Texas Open Meetings Act.'"

"Dammit, we don't need Carson getting his teeth into this. Not now."

"He's all over the Polley thing too, according to the chief."

"I wish you'd kept that boy of yours on a tighter leash," VanDorn said.

"Carson is a bigger issue now. We don't want him getting too comfortable here."

"I'll make a few calls, see what's possible," said VanDorn.

The hammering and sawing were so loud, Mike had to leave the house and cross the street to hear the call from Quintin Smith. Looking back, the speed of transformation amazed him. Uncle Harold's was taking shape again.

"Quintin, how's your dad?"

"No improvement, sadly. Great piece on the council meeting, thanks for that."

"You sent me to a good one."

"You didn't think to tell me you were working on the Polley murder?"

"I was just about to call you. Did you hear this from Cathy?"

"You talked to her and not to me?"

"Sorry."

"I would have appreciated a heads-up. I didn't need to get my ear chewed by the chief."

"I was going to call you."

"The chief says you were pretty insulting, sarcastic. Rude."

"Did he? Maybe a bit of sarcasm, I'll admit, but I was praising the department's miraculous efficiency."

"You know every paper needs good relations with the police. It's symbiotic. We help them, they help us."

"Of course, I know that, but in this particular case, they are talking crap. Something's wrong. The drug angle just does not stand up."

"How much of this is personal?"

"It's a story."

"You're not using this paper because of a personal relationship with Polley's wife? An intimate relationship?"

"Wow. An intimate relationship?"

"It has been suggested."

"By the chief?"

No answer.

"I know Polley's wife. We were in high school together. I hadn't seen her in sixteen years, then I heard her husband had been murdered. So, yes, I know her, but I'm not in the habit of trying to bed the wives of murder victims."

"There's something else, a suggestion that you are trying to discredit the police because of pending assault charges against you."

"Here we go. I tried to help a young lady who was being harassed at Gold Spurs a few nights ago, got hit in the head with a beer bottle and kicked in the face by Karter McMillan, and yet somehow the police decide to give him a pass, arrest me, and threaten to charge me with assault."

"You didn't know Duke McMillan owns Gold Spurs?"

"Not then."

"Benefit of local knowledge."

"And now what? Quintin, you know this confirms what I've been saying. Discrediting the journalist is step one in the playbook."

"I hear you."

"And?"

"Alright, I believe you."

"You've been here a couple of years now. Is Bluebonnet Road associated with drug dealing?"

"I've heard rumors, but nothing concrete"

"I'm going to find out."

"Don't blindside me again. It's not something I can afford in this community."

Mike drove to the crash site again, up the full length of Bluebonnet Road, pulled a U-turn, and went back. There was only one big house on a corner. The two-story porched mansion was antebellum and faced a row of ranch-style homes on the side street. He parked on Bluebonnet, opposite the house, and waited. A battered Ford Econoline slowed beside him and then took off. Ten minutes later it was back and repeated the procedure, even came back a third time.

Over the next two hours, two sedans and a pickup mirrored the behavior. He decided to follow the next vehicle that showed up, but it turned out to be the Taborville Police Department SUV. It pulled in behind him. He placed his hands in full view on the wheel as his old pals Green and Brown approached.

"We got reports about a suspicious vehicle," said Sergeant Green. "What are you doing?"

"Just sitting, observing nature. No law against that, last time I checked."

"Some people might think, people who called 911, for example, that you were casing a house and maybe intended to rob it."

"I don't remember Taborville being so full of suspicious people. Of course, you wouldn't know, since you're not from here."

"Why don't you move on down the road, where your nature observing won't bother folks?"

"I'm not sure the nature I was observing will be as visible down the road. But I'll try it."

"We'll stay here a while to make sure."

Mike fired the engine and moved off. He remembered the house now. There was no side turn when he was a kid. The Scroggins owned all the land on that side of the street back then. They must have sold some off for the row of ranch houses. The Gerlich family owned and farmed all the land on the other side of the road, but then old Mr. Gerlich died and his kids sold the farm to The Lignite Mining Company.

Times must have been really hard to force the Scroggins to sell land. They'd been accumulating it for generations. Maybe it was time for Mike to get a soda.

Scroggin's Drug Store hadn't changed except the server wore less makeup. Pop had never taken Mike for a soda. He'd ask Andy, and Mike would tag along in defiance, knowing both of them would rather he didn't. They sat at the counter, talked about football, and ignored Mike's attempts to chime in. He would sit, swinging his feet, observing all the other action in the mirror.

Old Miss Johnson, with her ivory handled cane, looking for her bunion cream; red-faced young men buying condoms and chewing gum; Mrs. Guthrie, the preacher's wife, complaining loudly about hot flashes, and waving air into her fiery bosom; sad women with trails of snotty kids, counting out their coins to pay for medication. Old Mr. Scroggin knew everybody's ills and lots of their secrets, useful information for a man who wanted to be mayor.

Mike walked past the soda counter to the dispensing area.

"Hey, Mr. Scroggin."

Old man Scroggin's son, Joshua, was maybe fifteen years older than Mike, not as much as twenty. His hair had thinned and grayed. The mustache on his lip looked out of place. A touch of Clark Gable on a face that was more Jack Elam. He probably hadn't been the one who summoned the cops to Bluebonnet Road. It looked like he'd been here for a while.

"You probably don't remember me, Mike Carson. I used to come here as a kid."

"Oh, I remember you coming in with your brother and your daddy."

"Back when your daddy was the mayor," Mike said.

"That's right. How can I help?"

"I'm going to be in town for a while and I'd like to switch my prescription here."

"That won't be a problem. What medication?"

"Statin for cholesterol. Family inheritance."

"Just call your doctor and have it switched to this location."

"Will do. How is your daddy?"

"He's out in Longview at the care home. Alzheimer's, unfortunately."

"Sorry to hear that. And the family?"

"They're fine. Eldest daughter is at college in Colorado. She plans to take over this place after me. My other son and daughter are here. I'd best get on. These prescriptions won't fill themselves."

Mike left. He'd never liked sodas much, anyway.

When Mike got back to the house, Juan approached.

"Have you thought about color? We get paint in the morning."

Mike hadn't, but instinctively knew. He came back a few minutes later with a Kodachrome framed photo of a proud Uncle Harold posing outside the house with his wife and daughter. The walls were pale yellow, the porch and window woodwork painted white, framing a stained oak door. The tin roof was an aged copper green.

"I'd like it to look exactly like this again."

As Juan studied the photo, Rosa detached herself from the children and joined him. She reached for the photo and ran her fingers gently over the soft-focused family, tracing their outlines. She held the print and bowed her head for a moment. When she looked up, there was the glisten of a tear rolling across her eye.

"May we keep the photo for now?" Juan said, "We will get these colors tomorrow. Please eat with us tonight."

Juan's and Rosa's smiles were irresistible.

What is it about these people?

At the restaurant, Mike ordered carne asada. The excited chatter subsided when the food arrived. *Here it comes, the joining of the hands.* He wondered if the last time had been some kind of weird aberration. This time, he could swear his heart stuttered and missed a beat, but then instructed every muscle in his body to relax. Juan studied him for a moment and then focused on his food.

One boy was talking about Mike, kept looking in his direction and questioning the adults. Rosa hushed him but need not have bothered. Mike couldn't understand a word. Juan was stifling a little laugh.

"What's going on?" Mike said.

"Please don't be offended. Christophe wants to know why your father did not teach you how to fix things."

"Good question." Mike grinned. "Mostly because he didn't know how himself. He was useless round the house."

Juan translated to the nodding heads. The boy spoke again.

"Christophe says his father, my brother, could teach you, if you like."

"Me?" Mike mimed hammering a nail, missing the nail, and landing on his finger with a howl. The table erupted. Little Christophe spluttered food back on his plate.

As they finished eating, Juan announced something to the family in Spanish and said to Mike.

"We will move to another table. You. Me. Rosa."

When they were re-seated, he fixed Mike's eyes with his fully present stare.

"I do not know what you believe, or if you believe at all, but you must listen now. You must listen with your heart. It is important."

Rosa took his hand, looked into his face as a mother might, if she was expecting her son to be executed, maybe. She spoke, slowly and earnestly in Spanish, then paused and took the photo of Uncle Harold's family from her purse.

"Rosa has had a gift from the time she was a child." Juan said.

"What kind of gift?"

"She receives messages."

Mike tried to pull his hand away, but Rosa would not let go. She started speaking faster now, pointing at Uncle Harold with her other hand.

"What's she saying? This is crazy."

"This man says he loves you. He says you can find everything. The answers are not far away, but you can never find them by looking through the glass."

"You know, this is cruel, making up crap, and pretending it's from my uncle."

Rosa spoke briefly to Juan.

"He told her you would not believe. He gave her a word. She does not know what it means."

She squeezed Mike's hand hard, trying to force faith and belief. Her brown eyes burned. "Remington."

Some days after school, Mike would find Uncle Harold pounding on his Remington portable typewriter, two-fingered hunt and peck. He typed with intense ferocity, as if he could push the words right through the paper into people's brains. The Camel cigarette dangled from his lips, forgotten. His eyes scanned the spiral notebook. Proper Gregg shorthand. Hands circled over the keys; forefingers extended like a pair of hunting eagles while his eyes danced around the words inside his head. His whole body was in motion, head swiveling back and forth between the notebook and the page, shoulders forward and back in perfect rhythm with his circling fingers. Then, he would freeze, sentence now composed and strike hard and fast. Letters smacked down on the page.

Uncle Harold liked to tell people the Remington had been to Vietnam—which was true—if folks assumed he was with it, that was up to them. Mike thought he would have been a good soldier. He was big, like all the Carson men, and would definitely have been brave, but he had shattered his knee playing football and couldn't run—"4F, unfit for military service," Pop had said. "A hard tackle is a curse, but sometimes a real savior. Lucky break, you might say."

"How did you get the typewriter?" Mike had asked one afternoon.

"Friend of mine from Houston went. Francis Neely. Reported for UPI."

"UPI?"

"United Press International wire service. He never saw much action, I don't think. Mostly stationed in Saigon. Anyways, when he got back, he needed money. He sold a bunch of stuff to get his truck fixed, and I picked up the Remington. Best ten bucks I ever spent. That thing has told some tales."

Mike had gone through the house after the funeral and was surprised to find no trace of the Remington. The battered typewriter was one of the few earthly possessions his uncle claimed to love. It had disappeared.

Mike looked up at Juan and Rosa's anxious faces.

"Remington. It's a typewriter, my uncle's typewriter."

"Maquina de escribir," Juan said.

"Ah, maquina de escribir de su tio. Entiendo." Rosa seemed satisfied with the explanation.

What the hell is going on here, Uncle Harold?

CHAPTER SIXTEEN

CATHY ROSS GLANCED up when the door of *The Taborville Times* office rattled. *Oh gawd, him.*

"Mr. McMillan, how can I be of help?"

"I wanted to place some advertising, and I had a few questions about pricing and discounts."

"I can help you with that. Let me pull up the rate cards. Come on through."

McMillan sat in the captain's chair in front of her desk and laid down a thick folder. The chair used to be hers, but it killed her back. She spent her own money on an ergonomic office model, thinking she could claim it back on expenses, but Quintin had refused. Wouldn't even go half. Cheap bastard.

She talked McMillan through the rates and all available discounts. "It really all depends on how many ads, how often, and how much space."

"Interesting. Tell me, do you get a commission on the ads you book?"

"I do. It's not very big, but yes."

"If I were to book a lot of ads with you, rather than Quintin, that would be money in your pocket."

"Yes."

"And if my business acquaintances were to do the same, that would also be money in your pocket."

"Yes. I'm not sure what you are getting at."

"Oh, I'm just getting the lay of the land, so to speak."

"I see."

"I'm a little confused," he said. "I thought you were a journalist."

"I am, but on a small paper you have to multi-task. Report, sub-edit, layout, advertising, digital. All part of the job these days."

"A matter of survival, I suppose."

"Indeed. And did you wish to place some advertising today, Mr. McMillan?"

"That rather depends. The paper seems to be taking a more critical stance towards me lately. The city council report was rather inflammatory, I thought."

"I'm afraid you would have to take that up with the editor. We try to keep the editorial and commercial separate."

"A Chinese wall. A rather flimsy one, if you ask me." He slid the folder off the desk. "In my position, it's a little difficult to justify parting with my money when the paper hires someone like Mike Carson." He smiled. "The man does not have the best interests of the town at heart. His kind of journalism is destructive. It's bad enough in a big city but catastrophic in a town as small as this. Adverse publicity could undo a lot of the good work I've done. Now, if I had some insight into what he's planning to write, I might be more comfortable about the spend."

"I don't think that would be proper."

He shifted in the chair. "That's a shame, Cathy. It is Cathy, isn't it? Not Katie."

Her tongue wouldn't move. She looked him in the eyes, and

the hard twinkle confirmed he knew. But how much? She tried to interrogate his eyes and Duke McMillan laughed.

"You have so many questions, don't you, Katie? How does he know? How *much* does he know? What's he going to do with the information?" He adjusted his baseball cap a little. "Relax. Nobody needs to know anything."

Maybe she had a chance. She steeled her throat.

"People change their names all the time," she said.

"They do. John Wayne is so much better than Marion Morrison. I guess there are lots of reasons to change. Your daddy being a convicted, white supremacist murderer would be one of the more unusual, wouldn't you say?"

Shit. Shit. Shit.

"Not your fault. Not at all. We don't choose our parents, Miss Magruder, and the sins of the father, etcetera, etcetera. No. You shouldn't be ashamed of that."

What then?

"What you should be ashamed of is taking the name and accomplishments of a fine young lady who met a tragic end and passing them off as your own."

Goddam it, he knew it all.

"But no one needs to know you flunked out of college and you don't have a degree in journalism. Nobody in town needs to know about your daddy's racist murders. Folk don't need to know you stole the life of a dead girl. I mean, it wouldn't do *you* any good, would it? And what good would that do for *me*?"

Her head dropped, shoulders sagged, breath escaped.

"The real question is, what can *you* do for *me*?"

She looked up, opened her mouth, but had no words. He smiled as she stayed silent.

And defeated.

"There are many ways you can be of help," he said.

. . .

Mike spotted Duke McMillan exit *The Taborville Times* building, get into a BMW, and drive away. He crossed the street. Cathy was at her desk behind the counter. She seemed startled when he walked in.

"What was that about?" Mike said.

"What?"

"Duke McMillan. I just saw him leave."

"Oh, he wanted to place some ads for his businesses and happened to mention how helpful it would be if we were to run a piece on the opportunities his new water well would present to the city."

"What did you say?"

"I said I would ask Quintin, and I was sure he would give it his serious consideration."

"I'll call Quintin."

The editor answered almost immediately in a voice devoid of energy and hope. His father was no better. He would need to stay in Dallas.

"It's not the worst idea in the world, Quintin. I'll interview him and do a piece. Give me a chance to figure out what he's up to." Mike said.

"You would only piss him off, after the council report, and this thing between you and his son."

"Come on, man, you could do with the ad revenue. You can't write it, being in Dallas. Cathy is sprinting to keep up with all she has on her plate. And remember, I write for free."

"You're a conniving bastard."

"Are you only figuring that out now?"

CHAPTER SEVENTEEN

SONNY BELL WAS twitchy walking into the county courthouse. He didn't like the law—cops, courts, any of it. He had been summoned here by a judge. Okay, it was a county judge, a kind of mayor for the county, but he hated the word "judge" and he had good reason to.

The message left on his business phone had been friendly enough, but he didn't know why he was here, and that bothered him. He thought about not coming, just ignoring the message, but that would eat away at him. Better to find out what was going on.

When he walked into the office, two large, agitated women, dressed identically, blocked his view of the secretary.

"I tell you, they're missing," one of the women said. "Seven of them, gone."

"Could they have been misfiled?"

"Oh no. Poor Adam was meticulous about his filing. Meticulous. And we have gone through all the land registry cabinets for the past three hours."

"We have," chimed the other woman, "every single cabinet. They're gone."

The secretary stood and indicated Sonny should sit in the waiting area. "Give me a moment, sir."

She disappeared behind the wall of flesh again. "Right, ladies, I'll let the judge know that seven of Mr. Polley's files are missing. Thank you."

The middle-aged twins turned and left the office.

"The judge will be with you shortly, Mr. Bell." She went back to her keyboard.

Sonny sat facing an eagle. It sat above the lone star carving on the door of the judge's office. There was a mess of carvings. Armadillos and bluebonnets, white-tailed deer and 'possums, largemouth bass, and catfish. But the damn eagle was mean looking, like it wanted to rip you to pieces. He glanced away. The judge's secretary clicked away on her keyboard, paying him no mind.

"Any idea what this is about?" he asked.

"I'm sure the judge will tell you." She didn't even raise her head to look at him. Rude. She could do with a lesson in manners. He could teach her a few, get her to show respect. Some dark night. He grinned at the thought. A light flickered on her phone.

"The judge will see you now."

She walked round the desk, tight-assed, not much to grab hold of, though, and swung the door open. "Mr. Bell, Judge."

The room was dark, even though it was the middle of the day, blinds drawn on all the windows. The judge sat behind a big desk. They looked old: the desk and the Judge. The only light was a brass desk lamp. Made him look like some weird horror movie guy, half in and out of the light.

"Take a seat, Mr. Bell."

Sonny sat.

Silence ticked by.

Sonny liked silence. Keeping quiet was always a good idea

in his business. Loose lips, like they said in those old World War II movies.

"Well?" asked the judge.

"Well, what?"

"What do you think?"

I'm not telling you what I think, not till I know what the hell is going on here.

"Do you understand why you're here?"

Sonny said nothing.

"Oh, I apologize. I thought this had been explained. You're here to talk about your bid."

"What bid?"

"For janitorial services, for the courthouse."

"I never—"

"Every few years we think it is prudent to issue RFPs—requests for proposal—to ensure we have the best contractors."

"I didn't—"

"You operate a cleaning business, correct, Bell Cleaners?"

"Yeah."

"This would be quite a lucrative contract, if awarded."

"I never got a request thing."

"No, you were recommended."

"Who by?"

"Our chief of police, Walter Gates."

A hand grabbed Sonny's guts and twisted, then twisted again. That creepy bastard Gates.

"I see, from your face, you know him, from some time ago perhaps. The chief tells me he has been monitoring your progress over the years."

"Yeah, I know him."

"He believes you would be an excellent fit for the county." The judge slid a couple of sheets of paper across.

Sonny turned them around. The form was all filled in with

his company name, description of services, and the amount of the bid.

"Of course, you should submit it on your own letterhead."

Sonny nodded.

"You understand what I'm saying?"

Sonny nodded again.

"I feel good about your prospects of winning the contract. Now, the chief tells me you also supply specialist cleaning services, that you have a method of neutralizing hazardous, eh, material?"

Sonny didn't move.

"We may have occasion to require those services. Contracted separately, of course."

Mike knew not to approach Holly at the bank, so he discreetly followed her home, out past the city limits to Tabor Lake, and down the neglected county asphalt roads. Single- and double-wide manufactured homes were interspersed with trailers. Rusting cars and trucks sat in fender-high weeds and were mown around.

Loose dogs chased Holly's truck before turning their attention to his rental. Two miles in, she turned onto a dirt track, up a small hill, and parked outside a sagging gray double-wide. She turned, fright-faced, as he pulled in behind her.

"What are you doing here?"

"Holly, we need to talk."

The home was old but tidy. The living and dining area were recently painted, and evangelical posters festooned the walls. *In Love With Jesus, Tell the Devil Not Today, John 3:16.* A collection of crosses fought for wall space with the posters. Crosses with trendy designs, the crucifix as fashion accessory rather than excruciating, execution device. She gestured at a small dining table, and he sat.

"I'll be just a minute."

She came back barefooted in sweatpants and a T-shirt.

"Tea?"

"Sure."

She placed two ice-filled glasses on the table.

"I'm sorry I was upset at Longhorns," she said.

"Understandable."

"I didn't like you coming to the bank like that."

"I didn't have an option. You never gave me your number."

"I didn't, did I?"

"The thing is, I'm running into the same brick walls you did. The chief is lying about what happened, but there is some drug connection to Bluebonnet Road. When Adam was buying oxy, where did he get it?"

"He would never tell me. But there are people at my church who should know. Tell you what, this Sunday you and me will go rolling."

"Rolling?"

"Holy rolling."

"Right."

Holly didn't know when the medical examiner would release Adam's body and Victim's Services had not contacted her. She had no updates on the investigation. It appalled Mike.

"I don't need support from the police," she said. "I have my support from Jesus and my pastors."

God, I need a drink, Mike thought. "Of course. Were you asked to identify Adam?"

"No. One of the officers did it. They said it would be hard for me to see him."

"Which one?"

"Catch Washington. He does security at our church most Sundays. He knew Adam well."

"Catch Washington, right," he wrote the name in his notebook, and stared blankly at the page. *Pretty weird, not having a family member do the identification. Of course, if someone wanted details hidden, then...even a beer would do right now.*

"You know the Lord sees you, Mike, even if you don't see Him. He knows your unhappiness, He knows every hair on your head, He can help you change your path. All you have to do is ask Him and praise His name."

"What makes you think I'm unhappy?"

"Happy people don't drink like you do. Here you are in Taborville and you are alone. Something bad happened in New York, didn't it?"

"I don't want to talk about it. It was all my own fault and now it can't be fixed. Any of it."

"The future is not written."

"I suppose not."

"Jesus loves you; He sees the man you are. And the man you could be."

"You seem very sure."

"I am."

"I appreciate your faith, Holly, in God, in me." He gestured around the walls. "I just don't think this is me."

CHAPTER EIGHTEEN

THE GUY at Mike's door was short, overweight, and sweaty. He had been looking around at the work materials—the Alvarez family didn't work weekends—and jumped when the door opened.

"Help you?" Mike said.

"Sorry, I wasn't sure if anyone actually lived here yet. I am Antonio Gonzalez. I am running for city council."

"Who are you running against?"

"I don't like to think I am running against anybody, but my opponent is Nadia Navarro."

"And what's wrong with her?"

"I don't understand."

"Is she not a good representative?"

"I wouldn't like to say such a thing, but there are people who believe she has brought a lot of division to the city council."

"I see. And what would you bring?"

"I would like to see civility and dignity returned to council meetings, less division, less controversy."

"Doesn't strike me as much of a platform, if you don't mind me saying. Do you stand for anything else?"

"Mr., eh...."

"Carson."

"Carson, yes. Mr. Carson, I think the city works best when the council is unified. That has always worked for us in the past."

"Keep the status quo?"

"Exactly, exactly. May I ask for your vote?"

"Yes."

"Thank you, and would it be OK to put a sign in your yard?"

"No, it would not. I'm a journalist. I write for the local paper here, these days. Can't afford to support any candidate in an election."

"I understand. But I can depend on your vote?"

"No. I said you could ask for it, but how I vote is not something I ever share. I'll say this though—maintaining the status quo in these parts is not a great platform, in my opinion. Thanks for dropping by, and good luck with your campaign."

Mike was waiting when Officer Catch Washington came out of the police station after his shift and got into a Jeep Cherokee. He tailed Catch to Sonic, pulled into the next slot, then made a great show of spotting him, tooting his horn and waving. Catch smiled and waved, then went back to looking at the menu. Mike got out and walked across the front of the vehicle to the side window. It slid down slowly.

"Hey, Mr. Carson. How are you?"

"I wanted to thank you for just giving me a warning the other day."

"I could hardly bust my babysitter now, could I?"

"I wondered if I could buy you lunch, maybe at the steakhouse?"

"You don't have to do that."

"It would be my pleasure, and I really want to hear about your brother. We were pretty close in school."

Catch thought for a second.

"What the hell, a steak sounds real good."

The steakhouse had once been a hay-barn and now had a huge Texas Lone Star flag painted on the roof above its red walls. The parking lot was gravel, large enough to cut a tire, or twist an ankle and dust every patron's shoe with white. Ceiling fans hung thirty feet from the roof and quietly moved the tepid air.

Catch ordered a T-bone with all the trimmings. Mike went for a small filet. They drank iced tea, and Mike quizzed Catch about his older brother. It was no surprise Sam had two master's degrees now, in criminal justice and psychology.

"I told him I ran into you. You should call him. He said to give you his number," Catch said.

"That would be great. We had a good time at school, even though I didn't play ball, as you know. I guess you took after him."

"I like to think so."

"I ran into another friend, Holly Kingston, Adam Polley's wife. Your name came up, said she knew you from her church."

"It's not my church. I go to Calvary Baptist, but I do security for Way of the Lord most Sundays. Their services start a bit later."

"You know Holly?"

"Sure."

"She said you helped her out when her husband was killed, identified his body, so she wouldn't have to see."

"I did." Suspicious now.

"She was grateful, but now she's wondering, you know, trying to figure out how bad it was."

"Pretty bad. What's this to you?"

"She's a friend, just trying to help her out. She's not getting any information from the department. Her head is flying with all kinds of crazy thoughts. She just can't understand why someone would want to kill him."

"You're a journalist, right? You know I can't talk to you about a case without getting into trouble with the department. They have a press officer."

"Totally off the record here. I'm just trying to help my friend, and there's a distinct scent of bullshit from the press officer."

Catch laughed in spite of himself.

"My brother says you're a good guy. I hope he's right, because I'm taking a chance here. Adam Polley was shot up pretty bad. Got hit by five or six rounds in the legs and chest, and then one shot to the head, larger caliber, .357 magnum would be my guess, took off almost half his head. She didn't need to see that, not till a funeral director could work some magic."

"How come you did the identification?"

"I was on earlies, got called to the scene. I recognized the car, and I recognized him."

"Seems to me the scene got processed really quick."

"Look, I appreciate the food, and that you are helping a friend, but this is getting real uncomfortable for me. I have a duty to the department, and I want to keep my job."

"I'm sorry, I get it. No more questions."

"Thanks. I'll say this. If it was my family, I would have questions."

They talked about football. Catch was really proud of his

brother's high school and college careers. His own NFL ambitions ended in his senior high school season with a bad ACL tear.

"You know they still talk about your brother, Mr. Carson. Every locker room speech. Andy's a legend. His picture's right there like an inspiration. I really wish I could have seen him play when I was old enough to appreciate it."

"He was special, saw everything, processed it so fast. He had a sort of sixth sense, could tell what everyone was going to do before they knew it themselves, and that's when the magic happened. Impossible throws to space no one knew would be there except him, and maybe the guy who caught it."

"Man, that must have been something."

"It was. But that kind of magic sometimes comes at a price. You wouldn't want to be the kind of asshole he could be."

CHAPTER NINETEEN

MIKE PULLED on his pants and opened the door. Holly.

"Don't tell me you forgot. It's Sunday, the Sabbath. We're going rollin.'"

"Sorry, rough night."

"You've got five minutes, mister, then we need to roll."

"Help yourself to tea, or whatever."

"I'll just wait here."

Mike did a quick wash of pits and bits, pulled on a clean shirt, and climbed aboard her ancient pickup. She barreled down the road, trailing clouds of black diesel.

"This truck needs a tune."

"I know that. Just haven't gotten around to it. Have a few things going on."

"Sorry."

"You need to get your mind right for this morning. Go with the flow. Open your heart to the spirit while you are there."

The Way of the Lord Church looked like a huge warehouse with three towers on the front. A police cruiser blocked one lane on the highway to give church goers unfettered access to the ample parking area, which was filling steadily. Catch Washington was directing the traffic.

Way of The Lord was painted in giant lettering on both sides of the roof. *All the easier for God to pick it out from His vantage point above*, Mike thought. A crowd of hugging, gripping well-wishers quickly surrounded Holly, and he understood why she felt comforted here. There was genuine concern, unlike the polite platitudes he'd seen in his own church as a child. Holly introduced him to the pastors as an old friend, which he supposed he was, and led them to their seats.

The large altar had two big video LED screens hanging from the ceiling on chain motors. Arrays of flown speaker stacks flanked the screens, and two matching bass stacks framed the floor. A Christian rock band was set up on the left facing a tiered bank of singers in matching blue on the right, more concert than church service. Mike wondered where the money came from.

The congregation was mostly young and white. Almost everyone was under forty. A lot of poor faces, marked by the subtle signs of inadequate nutrition, and missing teeth. Other emaciated drug faces contrasted with the unhealthy sweat of junk food obesity. The eyes changed from lost to breathless anticipation into pure joy as electric guitars filled the room with triumphant celebration and rocked into "Go Tell It on the Mountain."

Everyone got to their feet, clapping to the beat, following the lyrics on the screens. The atmosphere kicked up another rung and became ecstatic as the band segued to "Run into the Arms of Jesus." Blissful bodies started to canter, arms out, unable to control their exuberance, and did circuits of the aisles. Mike thought a slow walk to the emergency room would better serve some of them.

The air tingled with the static of electric belief. Hope and love were airborne on a bouncy castle of happiness—a sanctuary from all the daily disappointments and ruthless realities of life. Holly was fully in it but kept checking on him from the corner of her eye. She need not have worried. Everything here was infinitely preferable to the hypocritical rigidity of the Catholicism he had been born to, disputed and abandoned.

When everyone had run into the arms of Jesus, the band came to a punctuated halt, and the pastor walked to center-stage like a rock star to deafening applause and led the prayers.

Hannah, the female pastor, started a long homily about her recent vacation in Europe, complete with holiday photos on the screens. She loved the quaintness of the buildings, the narrow cobblestone streets, and the spires reaching towards the heavens.

"But the spires are disappearing, and are being replaced by domes," she warned.

There were gasps and groans from the congregation, not happy about mosques and Muslims.

"Christians are being overwhelmed by immigrants. They'll soon be outnumbered. And do you know why? Do you know why? Because Europeans are aborting their babies."

Mike was trapped, stuck beside Holly, with no alternative ride home, and he needed to stay to talk to her friends, who might have information about drugs on Bluebonnet Road. He wanted to stand up and yell or get up and run. Instead, he folded his arms and sank lower in the pew.

When the last loud hymn had ended, Mike stood with the rest of the congregation.

"You didn't like it. Too much?" Holly said.

"The music was ... good. Lively. Uplifting."

"But?"

"But nothing. I can see why you find comfort here."

"And the message?"

"It's not my thing. Now, what about those folks you said could help us?"

There was a community room at the back of the church where they served cold drinks with coffee, cake, and cookies. Holly waved at two guys sitting on a wooden bench and led him over.

"This is my friend, Mike, the one that's helping me."

They nodded greetings.

"Tyler and Saul are friends of Adam's from NarcAnon. They all found Jesus about the same time. Tell Mike what you told me about Adam."

"On my mother's grave, he was clean, man, working the steps," Saul said. Tyler nodded his agreement. Mike believed them.

"Before, back when you guys were using, did you go out to Bluebonnet Road?"

"Sure," Saul said, "that's where everybody goes."

"I thought as much, but I can't figure what the system is out there."

Tyler shrugged. "It's pretty simple—"

He was distracted by Saul, who was staring intently at something over Mike's shoulder. Saul nudged Tyler with a sharp elbow.

"We gotta go, bro."

Mike and Holly turned to see Zane McMillan approaching, gripping and grinning through the sea of lost souls.

"Holly, is that you? I was so sorry to hear about Adam. Terrible tragedy, I wanted to convey my condolences. Mike, I didn't think you were a churchgoer. Have you finally found Jesus?"

"Didn't know he was lost, Zane." *Don't pretend you're interested in me. We both know different. You never once said sorry after my brother died. None of the McMillans did.*

"Funny. You know what I mean," Zane said.

"I'd say that's between me and my creator."

"Oh, touchy subject, apparently. Of course, you Catholics are all about the guilt, and the angst, and the dark confessionals, aren't you? Sorry for your loss, Holly. May the Lord bring you comfort." He took her hand. "If there's anything my family can do, please don't hesitate to ask." Zane walked away, then stopped. "Oh, by the way, Mike, I heard you met my brother. Karter."

"I did indeed, down at Gold Spurs, briefly. There's a place that has changed."

"There have been a lot of changes around here, Mike. Things aren't what they used to be."

"I'm beginning to figure that out. Manners, for example, aren't what they used to be. He doesn't say a lot, your brother. Has a nice pair of boots, though. I got to see them up close."

Zane laughed and continued on his way. "Good one."

Holly shuddered. "He gives me the creeps."

"Is he a regular here?"

Zane was doing the rounds, shaking hands, clapping shoulders, with all the fake sincerity of a politician or a realtor.

"Fairly regular. Turns up for the afters, mostly. Supposedly, the McMillans donate to the church. That's what I heard, anyway." She checked the room for Saul and Tyler, but they had left. Holly drove him home and said she would try to contact them later.

The wolf howled from Mike's phone. His Frank Wolfe ringtone.

"Skippy, how are things?"

"Good," Mike said.

"You know, for once, I think you might be telling the truth."

"Screw you."

"Listen, we've developed a great contact over at NIBIN. Want me to check if your local yokels ever checked the ballistics you were talking about?"

"Abso-freaking-lutely."

"Has anyone ever said you have a way with words?"

"It has been mentioned."

"They were lying. Shoot me over the details and leave it with me. Laters."

"Did you just say 'laters'?"

"It's not my fault. I have a teenage daughter."

The intersection of Bluebonnet and Weimar roads was nothing special. Two old wagon trails ran into one another in the woods one time and got paved over. There had never been houses on Weimar Road, something to do with unstable earth movement. Mike remembered the road being blocked from time to time by fallen trees. The live oaks had never been replaced, leaving holes in the tree line. He pulled off the road into one of the gaps and waited. He had thought about bringing some bourbon, but his interactions with police were far too frequent to take the chance.

The air was loud, with insects and animals going about their nocturnal business. Waves of cicada calls crescendoed and diminished, to regroup for second verses. The night was crystal studded with a billion diamonds. A gleaming moon cast pale, earthly shadows of twisted trees and branches, embracing each other in the slow dance of ages. Sound and light played with the landscape, toying with perspectives, having fun with humans.

His eyelids were resting before the first headlights hit the startled trees. A small dark Toyota pickup slowed and turned onto Bluebonnet Road. Mike fired the engine and followed. Before he left the house, he'd removed the fuses for the running lights. Without lights, he held back a discreet distance. The pickup stopped near the Scroggin house and parked on the Lignite Mine side of the road. A passenger climbed out, walked into the bushes, returned seconds later, and the truck moved away. Mike eased forward, keeping the taillights in view. They turned left on Flores Trace and left again on Weimar Road. They weren't in a hurry. Mike's speedometer flicked back and forth around thirty miles an hour.

The pickup followed Weimar Road and turned left onto Bluebonnet Road again. It pulled into the same spot. The passenger repeated his trip into the bushes, and the truck headed back to town. Mike returned to his station at Weimar Road and tried to make sense of what he'd seen.

Thirty minutes later, an older model Honda repeated the procedure. This time, the driver was alone. Mike tailed the car from a distance as it slowly completed the same circuit. The driver retrieved something from the bushes and drove away. Mike decided to follow him to town. The Honda accelerated hard and was soon doing sixty. Mike kept pace and was grateful for the moonlight.

He heard a low rumble increase to a ferocious roar. In an instant, the road lit up like a nuclear explosion. His night vision was obliterated, blinded by the intensity of the light in his rear-view mirror. In shock, he grabbed the steering wheel hard. *Please let the road stay straight.* He was so disoriented it took him a second to realize it was a large truck behind him with light-bars and spotlights. The glare eased slightly as the truck pulled alongside on his left. He had a brief glimpse of a male passenger before one spotlight turned and pinned him like a butterfly in a case.

Mike accelerated, but the truck kept pace. The road was brilliantly lit, but he couldn't see a thing with the spotlight blasting through his side window. The spotlight crept closer. He eased the car to the right. The truck continued to press him. He turned the wheel and felt his right-side tires moving onto dirt. The truck kept coming. Mike braked sharply and pulled farther to the right, all wheels on dirt now, not slowing. Thumps and bumps of rocks, the swish of foliage, and then the Sentra hit something hard. Airbags exploded in his face, and he was back in darkness.

The airbags deflated. Mike's face and chest had been hit hard. A heavyweight punch that made it hard to breathe. His left elbow felt broken, although it probably wasn't. The side bag impact had come fast.

The silence was broken only by the ticking of the cooling engine. He pushed at the driver's door but couldn't shift it, so he climbed across into the passenger seat and got out. He grimaced as he checked the range of motion of his left arm and elbow, and then the night turned to day again. The truck was coming back, fast. Mike limped quickly into the comforting concealment of the trees.

Three figures got out of the huge crew cab and went to the car.

"No one here." Male voice.

Female voice: "Karter, turn the lights this way."

Two high-powered beams from the truck carved through the darkness. Mike took a chance and peered around a tree.

The silhouettes moved in his direction. Karter, apparently, and a shorter girl, the same build as the one who bottled him, and another taller, skinny looking man.

"Where the hell is he?" The voice could be Karter.

"Go get the tac lights." The female voice, authoritative. "He's got to be here somewhere."

Mike moved quietly through the trees, away from the beams of light. He stopped behind a large trunk and closed his eyes for twenty seconds to restore some night vision, then moved on. The three powerful tac lights stabbed into the dark places. Mike continued to move in the opposite direction, then....

Crack.

A dead branch snapped under his foot.

"Hear that?" The female again.

Mike froze for a second, and then slid behind another trunk as the flashlights sought him. He wondered about doubling back or trying to skirt around them. The lights were more organized now, sweeping before them in a line, but the woods were dense.

"Stop, stop." The other male. "Listen."

Brush rustling. The beams swung towards Mike.

"There."

The expectant silence was shattered by gunfire, shots cracking in rapid succession, shredding leaves, thunking into tree trunks, dropping branches. Getting closer.

CHAPTER TWENTY

MIKE CLIMBED FARTHER up the live oak and hugged the trunk a little closer. He flattened his head against the bark. The firing stopped. Something charged through the brush. A deer.

"Goddammit, Karter. What the hell is wrong with you? We can't go shooting at random strangers," the female said.

"They were snooping, you saw that."

"Whatever. We're supposed to scare 'em, not kill 'em."

"We gotta go," the other male said. "Someone will have heard that."

The three hunters turned back towards their truck. The flashlights converged on the rumbling pickup and then snapped off. Mike heard doors closing, and the lights moved away towards Weimar Road. He counted a full five minutes before he climbed down. Slumped at the base, he was angry and aching. Karter McMillan and that girl, Jess, from Gold Spurs. Again. Along with a random skinny guy.

He limped back to the stricken Sentra, and something blinked on a branch overhanging the road. Maybe it was nothing. Or maybe it was something....He stared at the silhouette framed against the moonlight and there it was, again. A little red blink.

'You gots to watch for cameras, man.'

Motion activated, probably.

The Sentra fired up but wouldn't move—in drive or reverse. Mike shone his iPhone under the car. It was beached on a tree stump, both front wheels a couple of inches off the ground. He got back to his feet and dialed. A tired voice answered. A loud TV in the background.

"Tabor Yard and Lawn, etcetera."

"Levi?"

"Yeah."

"Mike Carson. There's been a wreck with the rental. Can you come and get me?"

"Are you hurt?"

"A little banged up, but OK."

"What happened?"

"Just east of Flores Trace on Bluebonnet Road, as soon as you can."

Ten minutes later, lights crawled towards him from the Trace. Mike waited in the trees to make sure it wasn't the pickup returning, and when he was sure, stepped into the road. Levi brought the Escalade to a halt.

"Oh man, you look like hammered hell. Where's the car?"

"Back there a way. Please, just take me home."

"I should take you straight to the ER."

"Please, just take me home."

They rode back in silence. When they arrived outside the house, Levi asked again.

"Are you sure you don't need to be checked out at urgent care?"

"Certain. I just need to sleep. And I'd appreciate it if you could keep this to yourself." He reached for his wallet. Levi gave him a knowing look.

"Forget it. This one's on me. And I get it. A little under the weather. No need for the cops."

Mike walked straight to the bedroom, peeled off his clothes, and lay down carefully. It was the first time he had gone to bed completely sober in ten years.

Getting out of bed was a struggle. He managed it once in the night but had wimped out twice already this morning. Ribs, arm, hip, and ankle all waited patiently to stab him if he moved. A million small octopus tentacles unsticking told him the Alvarez crew was using paint rollers on the outside walls. He rolled cautiously on his right side and levered himself into a sitting position. His left ankle protested as it touched the floor. Must have been slammed against something in the crash, maybe the side of the brake pedal.

Dressing was a challenge, and the effort left him sweating. *How the hell did NASCAR drivers climb so nonchalantly out the window of their wrecks after they bounced and flipped and flew at insane-miles-an-hour?*

Mike thought about breakfast but knew he could not walk to Longhorns in this condition and limped to the kitchen to make coffee. He downed a handful of ibuprofen and within minutes regretted it as the pills started a revolt in his empty stomach and forced him to the bathroom. Dry retching did not improve his chest pain or his mood, but Listerine and coffee got the taste out of his mouth.

He eased himself into an armchair and dialed Alamo. The agent took it in her stride, like it happened every day, happy it wasn't a fault with the car. After establishing there was no issue of a lawsuit, she asked if he was OK and, since he had taken all insurances, assured him there would be no problem. Would he like another vehicle?

"We have nothing on the lot right now but will have some returns this afternoon. I'll hold one for you and call when it's ready. I have your number on the rental agreement."

Levi Forrest arrived with the Escalade fifteen minutes after Mike called. Rosa and her mother fussed over him in Spanish when he came out. Juan came around the corner in well-used painter's overalls.

"Mike. We did not know you were home. No car. What has happened?"

"There was an accident last night. The car was wrecked."

He climbed into the SUV.

"You still look like hammered hell," Levi said. "Where to?"

"The urgent care. I think you were right. I need to get checked out. I have a few other things to take care of. Think you could stay with me for a while?"

"Yeesss," Levi said hesitantly. "I'll need to make some calls, get a few things in motion."

Mike hadn't thought about health insurance until the receptionist asked him for it. He handed over the insurance card he'd had at the *Chronicle*. She tapped the keyboard with the flat of her finger pads. The meticulously painted, ridiculously long fingernails made anything else impossible. Mike wondered if her knuckles were double-jointed.

"Did you know this expires in a couple of days?"

"Sure," he lied, "but it's good for today?"

"Yes."

He wished he could see George Kleinberg's face right now

and shoot him the finger. Kleinberg was the business manager at the *Chronicle* and had been instrumental in firing him. As Mike waited for the doctor, he called the *Times*. Cathy Ross answered.

"Mike, how are you?"

"Alive. Someone ran me off the road last night."

"Oh my God, are you OK?"

"I'll survive. I'm over at urgent care getting checked out."

"I'll come over."

"Not necessary, please don—"

She'd hung up.

Small world. Dr. Charlene Baily, MD, had been in his class. Mike thought she was genuinely pleased to see him. Her cool, delicate hands scrutinized him, and then she sent him for X-rays of chest and ankle. He waited in the empty, sterile treatment room for results. There was a small tap on the door and a smiling nurse.

"Someone to see you. Says she's a friend."

Cathy's head bobbed out from behind the nurse and snuck a look.

You didn't need to do that, he thought. *That's nice of you.*

"It's fine."

Cathy came in and closed the door.

"Oh my God, you poor thing, what happened?" She embraced him, started kissing his cheek and forehead, fussing.

"Careful," he winced. *But it was nice to be fussed over, even if the jasmine was a little overpowering.*

"Sorry, sorry. What the hell happened? Why didn't you call me?"

Mike filled her in on his night's clumsy detective work.

"They must have seen me the first time I came down the road tailing the Toyota and been ready when I followed the Civic."

"Any idea who it was?"

"Karter McMillan, for sure, his girlfriend—at least I assume she's his girlfriend—

and some other lanky kid."

"And they ran you off the road?"

"Not just that, Karter shot at me."

"Did you call the police?"

"No, I don't trust anyone over there. I swear there's a drug pick-up in the bushes outside the old Gerlich place on Bluebonnet."

"You didn't see it."

"No. I think they have that road wired with cameras. Probably were watching. I don't suppose there are any computer geniuses in town?"

"It just so happens, I know two real nice gamer nerds who run the electronics repair shop."

"Good. I'll need their help. Actually—"

Another discreet knock and Dr. Charlene was back. Cathy excused herself.

"Well, good news. There's nothing broken. You have a tiny crack in one bone in your ankle. You can see it here, but it should heal on its own. Your ribs will be sore for a while. I'd recommend a boot for the ankle if walking on it is sore. I'll write you a script for the pain."

She noticed Mike's fingers were absent any rings. "You're not married?"

"Not anymore. You?"

"Tried it. Didn't like it much. My daddy told me not to marry a jock, but I didn't listen. He was wiser than I knew."

She handed him the script.

"Get this filled and try to rest, but keep the joints moving, elevate the ankle, and ice it three times a day. You should feel a lot better in a couple of days."

Levi had the Escalade running when Mike came out. He climbed into the cool.

"Where to? I can stay with you, made my calls."

"Scroggin's. I have to get this script filled."

Mike handed the script to Joshua Scroggin, who seemed a little surprised to see him.

"You look like you're hurting."

"You're not wrong."

"What happened?"

"I got in a wreck, close to your place, actually, on Bluebonnet Road."

"I'm so sorry."

"Thanks."

"Grab a seat. I'll have this for you in a couple of minutes."

"Dad," a female voice said from the back room.

"Yeah."

"Where's that new delivery of Percocet?"

"Third shelf on the right, near the middle."

He couldn't see her, but he didn't need to. The voice. It was her. *We're supposed to scare 'em, not kill 'em.*

"Your daughter?" Mike said.

"Jess, my youngest."

Mike sat on one of the stools at the soda counter. *The McMillans and the Scroggins together. Interesting.*

Mike opened the bottle of pills in Levi's car and swallowed two with a swig of water from the cooler. Then two more.

"Joshua Scroggin's kids, you know 'em?"

"Yeah. Amber, she's the one in college. Then there's Peter and Jessica...Jess."

"Jess, is she, like, a little thing?"

"Short, yeah."

"And what about the brother, Peter? Wouldn't be a skinny, lanky kid by any chance?"

"Yes, athletics team, long distance. How come?"

"I'll tell you in a minute. What's Jess like?"

"Pretty wild, from what I've seen. Booze and boys, and maybe other stuff. Hangs out with Karter McMillan and his crew."

"I'm pretty sure Jess and Karter and Peter were in the truck that ran me off the road last night."

"You were run off the road?"

"Big crew cab with a ton of light-bars and spotlights. I think it had a lift kit. It was really high."

"Did you see the color?"

"I couldn't see a damn thing. They had massive light in my eyes the whole time. Ran me into the trees and then came back looking for me."

"Hey, Mike, this is serious. You need to take this to the police."

"That's the last thing I need to do. Karter McMillan is protected."

"Those damn McMillans—shit slides right off. Time I showed you Magnolia Trails, if you're up for it?"

CHAPTER TWENTY-ONE

MAGNOLIA TRAILS WAS a little out of town on the Flatonia Road. A huge sun-faded sign read, "Magnolia Trails, Planned Community, Nature's Noble Beauty, Homes from the $250,000s." The Escalade turned in. A screen of trees hid the development from the road and not a magnolia among them.

"Good God," Mike said, "it's huge. How many houses?"

"The plan was for 400. There's 300, almost finished."

They cruised around the network of unused asphalt roads past a variety of home styles and sizes, all with similar stone frontages.

"Almost 300 built and not a one sold." Mike hadn't heard Levi sound bitter before.

"What happened?"

"*Field of Dreams* syndrome, I call it. Build it, and they will come. But it was greed. Greed, greed, and more freakin' greed. The financial crisis killed it off. The development company went down the pipes with enormous debts; investors lost everything."

"Who were the investors?"

"Almost everyone in town who had some money. All the

good ol' boys—VanDorn, Brook, Scroggin, Wally Gates, all that crowd and, of course, Duke McMillan and Christian Taylor—they were the developers. And then there were all the damn fools like myself who didn't think it was a gamble and couldn't take the hit. Bank owns it now."

"Which bank?"

"Duke McMillan's bank, Tabor Trust."

"Wait, I don't understand. I thought you invested with Duke."

"I did. Magnolia Trails Development Corporation was his company, his and Christian Taylor's. When it collapsed, the bank was the biggest creditor and took it over." He looked around at the houses. "They got this. We got nothing but a crappy memory."

"Duke must have lost money, too."

"I guess he must have, but it doesn't show. He's been buying up downtown for the last five years."

Mike picked up cash for the Alvarez family from his account at Wells Fargo and invited Levi to lunch, but he declined. Levi dropped him at the *Times*. Mike and Cathy went to a little taqueria on Main Street with room for only five tables in the courtyard. She kept touching him in a slightly disconcerting, possessive way. The tacos were divine, exploding in the mouth.

"I know who the girl was last night," Mike said.

"Yeah?"

"Yeah, she's Joshua Scroggin's daughter, Jess."

"How do you figure?"

"I heard her voice in the drugstore, recognized it, although I couldn't swear to it in court."

"I've seen them hang out. Are you sure it wasn't just kids doing drunk, crazy stuff?" she asked.

"It was deadly serious when the shooting started."

"McMillan, Scroggin, and drugs."

"Kind of makes sense when you think about it," Mike said. "Having a compounding pharmacy would be a brilliant cover for a little side dealing."

"Why would they take the chance? The drug store does good business."

"The Scroggins owned all the land on their side of Bluebonnet Road when I was a kid. Now they don't. Something made them sell. Seems many people lost serious money in this town."

"Before my time."

"I might go down to the land registry office, see what I can find about those sales, but what I really want to do is see what the hell is going on in those bushes. Kind of hard to do when they have the road wired with cameras."

"After lunch," she said, "we'll go talk to my guys at Kryptonite." She slid her hand over his again and squeezed reassuringly. "I'll look after you."

"Thanks."

The guy behind the counter at Kryptonite Tech Systems had the look of a New York bicycle courier without the attitude or fitness—or those grown men who still used skateboards, ten years after leaving high school. The store was a mix of sales and service, repairs and refurbishments, but the repair department was winning the battle for space. Dismantled desktops whirred in one corner, laptops lay in careful pieces awaiting new motherboards or screens, a dozen iPhones and Androids were plugged into a charging station. On one section of the wall, a stack of four shelves displayed a small selection of used devices for sale.

Counter guy wasn't much of a talker, except maybe on a gamer microphone in pitched cyber battles in the dead of night, but he brightened up when he saw Cathy.

"Ryan, this is my friend and colleague, Mike Carson."

"Hey, nice to meet you." An educated voice. Slow and gentle.

"I'm not looking to buy anything, and I don't need repairs. I'm looking for advice, but I'm happy to pay for it."

"He's doing a story and needs some tech help," Cathy said

"I have a theoretical challenge," Mike said. "Suppose there's somewhere that has a lot of camera surveillance. Would there be a way of disrupting it for a few minutes?"

"If the cameras are using Bluetooth connections, you could use a cell phone jammer. But that would be a federal crime."

"Theoretically, again, what if someone has placed surveillance cameras monitoring a public road, checking everyone who travels on it? That might be illegal too."

Ryan called for his partner.

"Steve, what do you think? In theory."

Steve emerged from a room in the corner. Average height, jet black hair cut short, he filled his T-shirt, had muscles where Mike only had ambitions. All the looks of someone who had served.

"Hey, Steve," Cathy said.

"Hey, Cathy. Jamming the Bluetooth can be done with a cell phone jammer, but as Ryan says, it's a federal crime. Not something we can help you with. Even owning a jammer is a federal offense."

"Suppose someone wanted to have a look at the folks who are doing this potentially illegal surveillance. Is there some kind of camera that could be placed inconspicuously, not on private property?"

They both liked this better.

"There is," Steve said, "and it's pretty genius. A camera in a very ordinary-looking rock."

Ryan was the computer guy, Steve was something else, an electronics engineer, and much more besides. Mike had guessed right about his service. U.S. Army, Cyber Command. A plan was forming.

Back at the *Times,* Mike asked, "What's a Cyber Command guy doing in Taborville? Guy like that could have his pick of jobs in Silicon Valley, you'd imagine."

Cathy laughed. "Why do most people end up where they do? Love. Steve had a very high-paid cyber security job in California, but his husband didn't like the big city, so they moved here."

"Steve and Ryan, they're—"

"You got it."

Levi collected Mike up at the *Times,* and they drove to Alamo to pick up another car. A Hyundai Elantra this time.

"I was wondering, Levi, if your lawn service has contracts for any properties out on Bluebonnet Road, by any chance?"

"I do, why?"

"I would love to get your help."

Mike outlined his plan.

"I don't know. That sounds pretty sketchy."

"Levi, it's all tied to McMillan. I'm almost positive. Folks are dying from opioids all the time. When they're not getting shot at."

"Yeah, I know that. But this is damn risky. If anyone found out I was involved...."

"Think about it, will you?"

Mike opened his laptop, settled into Uncle Harold's armchair, searched for Duke McMillan, and dialed his office number.

"McMillan Enterprises." Efficient, cool.

"May I speak with Duke McMillan?"

"Who's calling?"

"Mike Carson, *Taborville Times*."

"Regarding?"

"A feature article on his water well."

"One moment, please."

Mike waited. The music was classical, soothing.

"Mr. McMillan is away from his desk right now. May I have your number for a return call?"

Mike gave his number and wondered what would happen next. He didn't have to wait long. He answered the phone to Quintin Smith.

"Hey, Mike, I just had a call from McMillan."

"I'm not surprised. I just called his office."

"He wants me to do the piece. When I told him I was out of town, he asked for Cathy."

"And?"

"And I told him it wasn't everyday someone in Taborville got to be interviewed by a Pulitzer Prize winner and he should be happy."

"Did he sound happy?"

"Not a bit. But he'll see you in his Main Street office at ten in the morning. Please remember we depend on local advertising."

CHAPTER TWENTY-TWO

DUKE MCMILLAN'S office occupied a discrete, single-story building in the middle of Main Street. Two arched windows framed a navy-blue door in the center of the gray painted stucco. "McMillan Enterprises" was etched into both glass windows, a subtle ostentation in an otherwise ordinary historic building.

A woman sat inside the door to the left. She was attractive, politely efficient, wore a sober suit of charcoal gray, conservative jewelry, and a forced smile. The sign on the desk read "Executive Assistant."

"Mike Carson for Duke McMillan."

She indicated a seat opposite.

"I'll let Mr. McMillan know you're here."

She walked to a paneled office at the back, which sported one window with blinds. Mike studied the main room. Two young men and a woman tapped at desktops, heads down. The walls were full of framed publicity photographs, photo-shopped to perfection. Oil wells, delivery vans, breaking ground ceremonies with gold shovels, huge commercial machinery, a strip mall, and aerials of what Mike presumed had been the early development of Magnolia Trails before they built any houses—a little Texas empire. He was about to meet its Duke.

In all the years he'd lived in Taborville, Mike never got more than a cursory nod from Duke McMillan, even though Andy and Zane were close friends. Duke always stepped in to hug Andy after football wins, to Pop's obvious annoyance. In the world of Taborville football etiquette, only the coach was entitled to embrace a footballer before the player's father. These courtesies did not apply to The Duke, a man who made rules for others but none for himself.

Mike stood waiting beside the executive secretary's empty desk and counted the minutes. This was chess. McMillan was sitting in his private office, looking at the clock as often as Mike surreptitiously checked his watch. He had prepared for this, had been through it many times with difficult interviewees in the past. Some predators like to play with prey. Uncle Harold taught him never to bluff.

"In any negotiation, you decide the absolute least you will settle for, when you won't concede even one cent more. Find that place and you have total confidence to bargain."

Mike had decided on seven minutes. Five was understandable for an unseen circumstance, six was rude, seven shifted the balance of power, and became demeaning. Exactly six minutes and thirty-seconds after ten o'clock, he rose and coughed. One of the young men looked up from his busy keyboard.

"Could you tell Mr. McMillan we will need to reschedule?"

"Mike, I'm so sorry. I got stuck on a call, forgive me. Damn state regulations, bureaucrats, you know how it is." McMillan stood in his doorway, all starched jeans and barrel chest in his blue floral western shirt, smiling like he'd spotted his favorite prize bull. Overhead, lights bounced off his bald head. The executive assistant walked slowly back to her desk, theatrics now completed.

"Come on back." Duke waited for Mike to reach his office, stood to one side, and patted him on the back as he entered, then shut the door behind him. "Welcome, I feel I've known you forever, although I guess we've never had a proper conversation." He went to a sideboard. "Coffee? Water? Tea?"

"Actually, I'm fine."

McMillan settled behind his large mahogany desk. A silvered oil drilling bit sat at one side, posing as an oversized paperweight. Awards from state and local chambers occupied the other. A series of photos behind him showed McMillan as hero, entrepreneur, philanthropist, and friend.

"Are you well, Mike? You look a little rough around the edges, if you don't mind me saying."

"A minor argument between a rental car and a rock. The rock won."

Duke faked a laugh. "After all your exploits, I'm surprised to find you back in Taborville."

"Well, sometimes it's nice to come back home."

"Especially when it's a voluntary break from the big time. It is, isn't it, voluntary?"

"I'm not here to talk about myself, Mr. McMillan."

"And I'll be delighted to answer your questions, in the public interest, of course. I just like to know who and what I'm dealing with."

"Believe me, so do I."

Mike pulled out his notebook and asked his questions, which were respectful, and designed to allow McMillan to boast about his accomplishments—which he did with growing enthusiasm. Mike started with philanthropy, then moved to McMillan's vision for historic downtown, including his restoration and investments in the neglected buildings. He had

McMillan take him through his entire business history and enterprises. The Duke tried to step over the failure of Magnolia Trails, saying it was tragic, but nobody could have foreseen the property and financial crash. There were casualties everywhere. Someday, his vision for Magnolia Trails would come to fruition.

After the extensive history, Mike got to the water well, McMillan's latest venture.

"This will guarantee water for the future, and is critical to our growth, our development, our very survival." McMillan was passionate.

"I thought the city had already secured water rights for anticipated future needs?"

"They have made some provision, that is true, but there are those on council, experts in this field, who believe the city has under budgeted its needs, and could be in serious trouble down the road."

"Like who?"

"Xander VanDorn for one. Xander was CEO at Wichita River Authority for many years. There's nothing he doesn't know about water. Isaac Brook is another."

"Brook, the realtor?"

"Yes, Isaac has studied future water needs extensively as they relate to property development and growth. Our consortium can bring a guarantee of quality supply going forward. You may not be aware, but there have been problems with the city in recent times. Contaminants in the wells, which are not deep enough to withstand our cyclical droughts. We've had boil water notices every couple of years. Our well will be deep enough to guarantee excellent water quality."

"You said 'our consortium.' Are they involved?"

"I was referring to my investment partners in the project."

"So not VanDorn and Brook?"

"Well, that would be improper."

"It would. So, who are these other partners?"

"Tabor Trust Bank has a stake."

"Your bank?"

"I'm one of the founders, but it is hardly my bank."

"And who else?"

"There are several angel investors who prefer to keep their involvement discrete for the time being."

"Is that going to be a problem for you?"

"Certainly not. We will supply the city with all the information it requires at the appropriate time, and to be clear, what we are offering the city is a gift for the price of its investment."

"So why would your consortium be offering gifts?"

"I thought that would have been obvious from this interview. I love this city. I want to guarantee its future."

Mike thanked him and turned to leave.

"Oh, I wanted to ask, how's your son, Karter?"

"Fine."

"Glad to hear it. I was afraid I might have damaged his foot with my jaw."

He strode through the door. He had all he needed. For now.

Xander VanDorn worked from an office at his house, a large sprawling affair that dominated an acre at the edge of the historic district. The pale blue home had started as a modest Craftsman but had four extensions, and now boasted a swimming pool, guest house, outdoor kitchen, jacuzzi, and sauna. Xander's office and man cave consumed one entire wing, with a separate entrance on the side street. He opened the door himself to Mike's knock. His pale green, ratty eyes studied

Mike with dispassion, like a hangman, calculating how much rope to allow for the drop.

"Thank you for seeing me."

"Duke asked me to."

The anteroom to the office was a museum of firearms from a bygone age.

"I see you're a collector."

"In a small way, yes. Guns that won the West."

All the important Winchester rifles from 1866 to 1886 sat side by side on a single rack. The collection of sidearms included the Colt Paterson, the iconic 1851 Colt Navy and the 1860 Colt Army. There were many others Mike didn't recognize.

"I could wax lyrical about these all day, but you didn't come to talk about the West."

They sat on either side of a large coffee table with matching red leather sofas. A Remington cast of *Coming Through the Rye* sat in the center of the table. Three of the four horsemen pointed their bronze six guns at the ceiling fan revolving slowly above them.

"You're not from here?" Mike said.

"No. I grew up in Amarillo."

"What brought you to Taborville?"

"My wife's family, the Milburns, had property here. But that has nothing to do with why you're here. You came to talk about Duke."

"That's right. How long have you known him?"

"Going on twenty years."

"How did you two meet?"

"At an oil and gas convention in Vegas."

"I thought you were a water guy?"

"There's a lot of water in hydraulic fracturing. I had an interest."

"And how would you describe him?"

"A talented and resolutely determined businessman, one who sees opportunity early, seizes it, and has the stones and wherewithal to see it through. A man of vision, a community leader, and a great friend to the people of this city."

"That's quite a tribute."

"Well, he's quite a man."

"I'm wondering how this opportunity for the city came about. I was at the council meetin—."

"I'm fully aware you were there. Equally aware of the snide, potentially actionable, insinuations in your reporting. We're used to some criticism from the *Times*, but this New York-style yellow press is extremely unwelcome. To hint that the city council is breaking the law—"

"I documented what happened. Any inferences are in the minds of the readers."

"The way you presented the facts caused misleading inferences. The meeting was perfectly proper."

"How do you explain why people were upset at the meeting?"

"There are a lot of small-minded people in this town, Mr. Carson. You would know that better than I. Plodders who would squander opportunity through excessive caution and a lack of imagination. This opportunity is time limited. I did not want it wasted."

"Council Member Navarro wasn't too happy about the way it was raised."

"That woman is clueless. She's a hysterical reactionary liberal."

"Can I quote you on that?"

"I'd rather you didn't, but whatever. She is what she is. It wouldn't come as a surprise to her to hear it from me."

"How did you hear about this golden opportunity? Did Mr.

McMillan approach you? Wouldn't this have normally gone to the city manager?"

"No. It wasn't like that. As a director at the Tabor Trust Bank, I'm familiar with a lot of Duke's business. "

A telephone interview with an equally pissed-off council member, Isaac Brook, revealed much of the same. He had known Duke McMillan for fifteen years and thought highly of him. He, too, was a founding director of Tabor Trust Bank. Mike made a note to get a list of all the founding directors and investors.

Mike heard similar accolades from the Taborville Chamber of Commerce, the Taborville Tourism CEO, and the mayor. Duke McMillan, it seemed, was an all-around good guy who was putting his money where his mouth was and helping Taborville in many ways. Looking through his notes, Mike didn't believe a word of it.

Council Member Navarro said she'd like to meet in person. She suggested the English Tea House downtown. It was an anachronistic little place, all New Age and chimes, bottle trees and windmills, little water features and painted frogs. The owner claimed descent from British aristocracy, although no one could prove it. Her one and only offering was full English afternoon tea with watercress sandwiches, scones with jam and clotted cream, and Earl Grey tea, of course. When Mike arrived, she was bustling about in Victorian dress, with a lace collar and black patent shoes as an old Victrola scratched out well-worn tunes from the 1920s.

Mike joined Nadia at one of the three tables in the tiny room, which was full of chintz and dust and efforts at nostalgia.

"Thanks for meeting me," Mike said, and shook her hand. It was warm, the grip firm and assured. A confident woman.

"It's my pleasure." Her voice had a natural laughter that warmed the room.

"You look a lot happier than you did the other night."

She laughed and leaned in. "I don't have my armor on today. I hope it wasn't a mistake." She laughed again, and Mike grinned.

"I don't think you have anything to fear from me."

"I hope that's true. You seem like a nice person, in spite of what my sister says. You shouldn't pay attention to her, by the way. She's always angry about something. You're just the latest target."

Mike laughed now, a little shocked by her directness.

"She does have a point about my outbuildings. I need to get something done about that."

"You should tell her. Actually, though, don't bother. She probably wouldn't listen. Tea?"

"Sure." He sipped some tea, picked at the bland watercress sandwich, ate a bite of the scone, which was too dry for his liking. A large gray tabby cat tried to jump on the table, but he discouraged it with his foot.

"You don't like cats?" she said.

"Not on the table. Not at all, really. I'm more of a dog person."

"Me too. What's your favorite breed?" Her face lit up.

"I grew up with German Shepherds, but I had a Schnauzer once that I really loved. I'd get another if my lifestyle ever settles down enough. You?"

"I have a Bijon, who's dumb as a rock but very affectionate, and a couple of Chihuahuas that I'm fostering at the moment.

We have a good dog rescue here. I've been able to get funds for it from the council—bit of a pet project, pardon the pun."

She was an odd mixture, Mike thought. Tough as nails and warm as summer sun.

"Duke McMillan, local hero and savior of the town. That's the gist of your story?"

"Yes, more or less. So far, no one has a bad word to say about him."

"I'm not surprised. He's a complicated man, McMillan. He makes a big contribution, is generous to our charities, helps raise funds for good causes. But it is all transactional. He expects a lot for his generosity."

"Like what?"

"Preferential rates in our business park, variances in zoning, fast-track processing for his planning applications, lots of public infrastructure funding for his developments. I imagine you've heard of Magnolia Trails. The city lost big on that misguided venture. The man has an influence over virtually every ordinance that might benefit or hurt his business interests."

"That's a lot."

"It is, Mr. Carson."

"You can call me Mike."

"Mike," she studied him. "You look like a Mike."

"I do?"

"Strong, direct, no frills. It suits you."

"Thank you."

"Well, Mike," she smiled, "McMillan bends this town to his will. The candidates he supports for city council have almost unlimited funds through him and the people he influences."

"You're not one of those people?"

"Are you kidding?" She laughed loud and hearty. "No, definitely not."

"How did you win your seat?"

"I did the one thing they didn't expect. I did the work, walked every street, knocked on every door, asked for every vote, promised I would represent people honestly. McMillan and his good ol' boys were so used to winning, they put up yard signs and presumed anyone they endorsed would automatically get elected. Of course, I got help. There are some brilliant and talented women in this city. They rolled their sleeves up and came on board."

"What made you run?"

"I hate bullies. And I hate unfairness, always have, all my life."

"Why are you so opposed to McMillan's water deal?"

"First, the process. When someone tries to sneak a vote on council for a substantial amount of taxpayers' money, without proper notice, you can be sure it stinks. Second, officially we don't know who is in this consortium. Have you found out?"

"No, McMillan hasn't been forthcoming."

"Off the record, I'm hearing the land they intend to drill on is owned by a felon, a man who has been convicted of fraud. Is that the kind of person the city should do business with? I don't think so. Xander VanDorn knows only too well that the city's future water supply is guaranteed for the next fifty years. We've been doing deals for the last two years. Why is it so important to him and McMillan that we buy this extra water? I have a feeling—and my feelings are rarely wrong—that there's some self-serving interest here."

"You will vote against it?"

"Yes, unless they can prove the deal is good for the city and everyone involved is legitimate."

"Can I quote you on that?"

"You can say I am opposed to the venture until a full

proposal, including the names of all the players, is put before the council."

"And a quote about Duke McMillan? For my piece."

"Duke McMillan does a lot of good for this community, but does even more for himself... Can I trust you, Mike? Will you respect a confidence?"

"Of course."

"OK," she said, "you can't attribute this to me, and you'll have to verify independently, but it will point you in the right direction. The mayor, VanDorn, and Brook are all involved in the consortium."

"How do you know?"

"They told me."

"Wow."

"Said it in executive session. Practically boasted about it."

"I thought executive session discussions were secret."

"Not unless there's a specific ordnance passed by the city thanks to a legal opinion by our esteemed attorney general. Taborville doesn't have a specific ordnance. I've tried to get one in place but no takers. So I am in the clear."

CHAPTER TWENTY-THREE

MIKE WAS STILL THINKING about Nadia Navarro when he got to Paolo's Pizza & Pasta. She was such a conundrum of combat and compassion, like she'd hack you down, without mercy, to protect the vulnerable but would then tend to your wounds.

Ryan and Steve were waiting, slightly awkwardly, at the table with Cathy. There were no outward signs of affection between the two men. Taborville seemed to have a "don't ask, don't tell" policy. Everyone ordered pastas of various flavors.

"Thanks so much for coming, guys. I appreciate it." Mike said.

"We came for Cathy, to be honest," Ryan said.

Cathy gave Mike a playful elbow in the ribs. "See?"

"What's so special about her?" Mike said and got a harder elbow.

"She wrote a brilliant piece about Kryptonite when we opened the store. Got us off the ground."

"Guys, I need your help, and I can't ask for it without putting you in the picture. I'm investigating Adam Polley's murder."

He told them what he'd found so far, stressed the potential danger, explained how he'd been forced off the road, and his suspicions of a drug dealing drop.

"This is about drugs?" Steve said.

"There's definitely some drug connection, but I'm not sure exactly what. Polley had been a user but was clean when he was killed. The cops still say it was drug related."

"What kind of drugs?" Steve asked.

"I'm not a hundred percent on all of it, but opioids for sure."

"I'm in."

"Hang on a second, Steve," Ryan said. "Into what? You don't even know. Cathy?"

"You guys might not be aware, but Mike is a pretty well-known investigative reporter, used to work for *The New York Chronicle*, won a Pulitzer. He has a nose for this stuff. I trust him, and I'm helping where I can."

Steve put his hand on Ryan's. "It doesn't matter. If it's opioids, I'm in. You know that." He looked at Mike. "I never went to Afghanistan or Iraq. My war zone was a keyboard and a terminal but two of the guys I trained with, real friends, did multiple tours, survived the Ali Babas and the Hajis but ended up dead because of that crap. Two in all the twos. Two hundred twenty-two OD deaths every single day this last year. Did you know that? Over 80,000. Who are the bastards behind this?"

Mike outlined his suspicions about Karter McMillan, Jess Scroggin, and her brother Peter.

"Guess I'm in too, then," said Ryan quietly.

"How come?" Cathy asked.

"Ryan got sucker punched by that homophobic asshole Karter six months ago, outside Gold Spurs. If I'd been there, the little prick wouldn't be walking around now." Steve smacked the table hard enough to make other diners look over.

"We don't need you in jail," Ryan whispered.

"Sucker punching is his style, for sure." Mike told them about his own tangle with Karter, and when the food arrived, he outlined his plan.

"Let's be clear," he said as they waited for desserts. "We could all end up in jail. Just thought I would mention it."

When Ryan and Steve left, Cathy suggested going back to her place for a nightcap. It wasn't the nightcap she was after, Mike thought, flattered but puzzled by her enthusiasm. Maybe she just liked older men. There was an urgent warmth to her and it was comforting to feel wanted, desired, attractive. When she told him she'd bought a bottle of Blanton's bourbon, she tipped the balance firmly in her favor.

Next morning Mike dialed Frank Wolfe in Philly.

"Skippy, what's going on?"

"Nothing much, except someone tried to kill me."

"What now?"

"Yeah. I got run off the road, smashed into the woods, and shot at."

"You, OK?"

"Just bruises."

"They shot at you?"

"Nowhere close, fortunately."

"How come?"

"I was up a tree."

"I guess you must be onto something, Tarzan."

"I was checking out a place I'm pretty sure is a drug drop. I'll know for sure in a couple of days."

"Always with the dangerous stuff. You're some kind of adrenaline junkie."

"Someone's scared I'm getting too close, but I don't know what I'm getting close to."

"You be careful, Skippy. It's actually good you called. Saves me the trouble. I heard from my guy at NIBIN. Your police chief is lying. They haven't run a search for Taborville Police in over a year."

"Thought so."

"Don't you think that's dumb? I mean, why lie about something that is so easy to check?"

"They didn't figure on anyone checking, would be my guess. But what are they trying to hide? If the out-of-town shooter angle is a lie, then we're looking at something local. Whoever shot Polley is probably still in town."

"Sounds like it. Anyway, try to not get your head shot off. And if you need something, holler."

"Do not say 'laters.'"

"Laters."

That afternoon, an old Ford F-150 chugged along Bluebonnet Road, puffing little clouds of black smoke. The long, metal trailer hauled two ride-on mowers. It had an array of weed whackers in racks on one side, and leaf blowers on the other. Just past Flores Trace, the truck shuddered to a halt. The driver popped the hood and peered in at the engine, scratched his head, and took out his phone.

"Nosotros estamos aqui," he said, when Levi answered.

"Bueno."

Seven minutes later, the Escalade pulled up on the opposite side of the road, leaving just enough room for a vehicle to negotiate the chicane they'd created. Levi climbed out, walked to the tailgate of his Escalade, and pressed the sensor. He reached into the trunk space and pulled out a large metal toolbox. As he walked across the road to the stranded pickup, another figure slipped out in black fatigues with a small backpack and melted into the woods.

Mike sat in the back seat, protected from view by the tinted windows. Steve said he needed ten minutes. Mike watched as Levi disconnected leads and then had his driver fire the engine several times, without success. As the last seconds of the ten minutes counted down, Levi walked to the SUV, started it and moved farther up the road, looking for enough space to turn. He pulled onto the shoulder, decided he couldn't pull a U-turn, and settled on a three pointer instead. Reversing on the second point of the turn, he missed the brakes and backed off the road to the edge of the woods. Steve dived inside the tailgate, Levi hit the door-close on his dash, and completed the turn.

The Escalade drove to the front of the forlorn pickup. Levi opened the tailgate again and searched for his jumper cables. As he moved towards the pickup, the rear passenger door on the driver's side opened and Steve darted into the trees, screened by the door and Levi to complete his mapping of the Bluetooth cameras.

The charade of the broken motor continued for another eight minutes. When Steve reappeared in the trees and gave a thumbs up, Levi reconnected leads, and, miraculously, the engine fired right up. He disconnected the jumper cables and returned them to the Escalade. Steve slid between him and the door into the SUV. He was smiling like a bull in a cow barn.

The pickup hauled the trailer away.

"Well?" said Levi, as he got back behind the wheel.

"Mission accomplished."

Levi started laughing, loud and hearty.

"Now that was some James Bond shit, right there."

Steve glanced up from the laptop.

"Haven't had this much fun since I left the service. Let's see what we got."

What they had, an hour later back at Kryptonite, was a map showing the geolocated positions of all the cameras and their Bluetooth identifiers. Ryan had headphones on, which leaked gangsta rap as he worked methodically on his keyboard, following digital breadcrumbs into the cloud. They could not be sure video footage was stored there, but it was probable. The dealers would be able to identify anyone who ripped them off, and the footage would give them opportunities to blackmail people who'd like to keep their drug habits secret. Ryan said not to wait for him. It would take a while.

Steve took Mike into the back office, unlocked a large metal cabinet, and produced a plain brown cardboard box. He pulled out the most realistic-looking plastic rock Mike had ever seen. It was about nine inches tall and a foot across at the base. A tiny pinhole camera seemed like a blemish on the stone. Steve turned it over and unscrewed the metal base.

"It's battery operated, six-month continuous life, has digital recording, and has its own transmitter, so we can livestream. The camera is extreme low light, will get excellent pictures at night, which we can also computer enhance if necessary."

"This looks like Special Forces stuff, or CIA."

Steve grinned. "I couldn't possibly say," and with an even broader grin said, "Oh, you have my assurance, sir, this is perfectly legal."

He fired up a laptop and connected it to the camera. The image of Mike looking at the rock was sharp and color accurate.

"Auto focus, auto exposure, controlled by a minicomputer. Motion detectors trigger it to record. We'll get some unwanted wildlife footage, but it will capture everything that moves. When do you want to plant it?"

"As soon as I can figure out how to do it without tipping them off," Mike said.

CHAPTER TWENTY-FOUR

THE FROSTY EXECUTIVE secretary answered "McMillan Enterprises" on the first ring.

"Duke McMillan, please," Mike said.

"Mr. McMillan is not available presently. May I be of help?"

"Maybe. Mike Carson from the *Times*. When I interviewed Mr. McMillan the other day, he didn't mention the name of the water consortium corporation, and I forgot to ask."

"I see."

"Can you tell me?"

"Reflow Logistics."

"And who are the directors?"

"I'm sure you'll be able to find that information from the Texas Secretary of State's office or one of the business directories."

"I could, but it would be so much easier if you told me. Save me a lot of trouble."

"I have another call holding, if there isn't anything else."

"I guess n—" The line went dead. Friendly type.

Mike spent the next two hours getting nowhere. The

company was so new it wasn't included in most of the Texas registers. When he finally tracked down the directors, they turned out to be two Houston-based lawyers whose firm specialized in setting up corporations. McMillan was taking care not to reveal his investors.

The story was infuriating to write. He could only report facts from the public record, and he couldn't confirm what he'd been told by Navarro. At face value, Duke McMillan and his consortium appeared to be a good thing for the city, despite objections by Navarro and the Texas Water Conservation League. It frustrated Mike that he couldn't warn the *Times* readers there was a huge conflict of interest and possible corruption on the council. He conveyed as much concern as possible, while keeping the coverage technically neutral. After a couple of rewrites, he emailed the piece to Quintin Smith.

Holly looked exhausted when she opened the door. Her face was shiny from moisturizer, eyes red from lack of sleep or too many tears, or maybe both. She'd changed out of her bank uniform into a T-shirt and jeans. She poured them both iced tea at her little dining table, sat back and waited for Mike to talk.

"I'm making progress, and I hope to know a lot more before long. The chief's been lyin'."

"I knew it."

"They never did a proper ballistics check. The out-of-town shooter story is bogus, which means whoever shot Adam might be local."

"But why?"

"I don't know. I'm pretty certain there's drug dealing at

Bluebonnet Road. Someone wants it kept secret enough to shoot at people."

"Shoot at people. How do you know?"

"Because people took a shot at me." He told her about the chase through the woods.

"Thank Jesus you weren't hurt. Mike, I didn't think this would put you in danger. Maybe we should leave it alone?"

"Not now. I'm going to see it through. We will get to the bottom of this."

"We?"

"I've got some help, but we are going to need a little more. Can you get hold of Saul and Tyler again? I need someone who's a user or was one."

Holly made the call. "Saul can come over."

Saul's ancient Jeep Wrangler wheezed up the hill ten minutes later and parked beside Holly's truck. Mike wondered if his demeanor had always been so furtive. Saul's eyes never stopped moving but not like the Special Forces guys Mike knew who constantly scanned for threats, more like a cheese-stealing mouse keeping an eye out for cats.

"How come you took off so suddenly on Sunday?" Mike said.

"Zane McMillan."

"What about him?"

"I work for McMillan's courier company. I didn't want him to see me talking to a reporter."

"Why not?" Mike said.

"They're real strict about con-fid-ent-iality."

When Mike outlined his plan, Saul shook his head vigorously.

"No way. No. I'm not going back into temptation." He thought for a minute. "You know, Pete Baker still uses. No judgement. He might do it." He gave them Baker's number and left.

"Real nervous kind of guy," Mike said, "especially where McMillan is concerned."

"He struggles," Holly said. She looked around the room. "I need to get this place cleaned up. People from the church will want to come around after the funeral." She paused. "You'll come on Saturday?"

"Sure, of course. Look, I'm going to head out, see if I can get to Pete Baker tonight.

Pete Baker had two Purple Hearts, although he said the first one didn't really count. He'd been hit by friendly fire in a brief skirmish with the Taliban during a village foot patrol in Helmand.

"We had this Haji local with our patrol," he told Mike. "Someone opened up on us, and we all get to cover. Damned if this freakin' Haji doesn't squirt off a whole mag. Sprayed it in all directions. One round ricocheted off a wall and got me in the butt." He laughed. "Some folks are butt ugly, but me, I've got an ugly butt—double pucker, you might say." He smiled again and then grimaced. "The second time. That's the one that really screwed me. IED, just outside the Green Zone. I had eight surgeries, but they couldn't get all the shrapnel out. I've still got some in my knee, my shoulder and a few small pieces in my head. Hurts all damn day, every damn day." He picked up a bottle of pills. Oxycontin. "Used to get these from the VA, but then they started saying I was dependent and stopped prescribing, but without them, I wouldn't be able to do shit."

"They look like regular prescription."

"That's the beauty of it. They look no different from what I got at the VA."

CHAPTER TWENTY-FIVE

PETE BAKER TRIPPED AS he walked into the bushes at Bluebonnet Road and appeared to have trouble rising, but when he did, the inconspicuous camera rock was positioned perfectly. He approached an old, crooked mailbox with the abandoned farmhouse behind it, slipped his order and payment inside and drove away. Mike lay in the back seat of Pete's Sonata, out of sight.

"OK, let's drive the circuit," Mike said.

Ten minutes later, Pete stopped at the mailbox again and picked up his pills. As the car pulled away, he dropped one of the two standard brown plastic containers into Mike's hand.

"Drop me off at Weimar Road," Mike said.

Steve was waiting in his van with a computer on his lap.

Mike climbed out of the car. "Pete, please be careful with those pills. Stay well."

"Don't worry. I got this handled."

I wish that were true, Mike thought, *but nobody has addiction handled.* Steve was beaming.

"Have we got a picture?" Mike said.

"Crystal clear, and you will not believe what just happened."

He reversed the recording and hit play again. The rock camera image shook and was a jumble of angles.

"That's him falling over."

The image settled and centered on the lopsided mailbox. Pete walked the few steps to the box, then walked out of frame. Mike waited, breathless, to see who would retrieve the order.

"Check this," said Steve.

Mike gasped. The mailbox simply disappeared. Steve moved the video backwards, frame by frame, and the mailbox rose in increments from the earth.

"They've got some kind of underground operation," he said

"We need to see what's back there, but how the hell we do it with all the camera surveillance?"

"Let's go back to the store," Steve said. "I've got a few more goodies in the cabinet."

At dawn the next morning, a drone rose and flew across the trees to Bluebonnet Road. Mike and Steve stood at the back of Steve's van, watching monitor pictures as Steve guided the Mavic 2 Quadcopter. When the Scroggin house appeared, he slowed and turned across the road. The roof of a small farmhouse appeared between the treetops, foliage surrounding the front and sides, right up to the walls. Steve descended the drone for a better look and slid across the front at treetop level. The house looked abandoned.

"Let's have a look at the back," Mike said.

The rear of the house was a different matter. A well-worn track across a short field led to a garage at the back. The drone descended again, and they could see the tracks were fresh.

"Follow the tracks," Mike said.

The quadcopter rose, flipped through 180 degrees and cruised across the grass, following the tracks to a small copse of trees. The copter climbed above the trees and continued to follow a route, cut through the brush, to a rusted metal gate on Flores Trace.

"So that's how they get in and out. Let's go back to the house," Mike said.

"This thing can do forty miles an hour." He hustled it back to the house and halted it with a gentle flick on the joystick. It crept in for a better look at the rear of the building.

The camera snuck close to a dirty window, but they couldn't see anything inside. The drone moved away from the window, and Steve said, "Uh-oh."

The garage door was rising rapidly, revealing jeaned legs, a red plain shirt, and then a ski-mask.

"Crap." Steve put the drone into a steep climb.

The shrinking figure brought a shotgun to his shoulder and fired. Less than a second later, the picture died.

"There goes $1,600," Steve said, throwing the useless controller into the back of the van. "We need to get the hell out of here. Right now, they'll know we have to be close."

The van sped down Weimar Road, back towards town.

"They are going to know something's up when they examine the drone," Steve said. "It's not a kid's toy. Best we can hope for is they think it's DEA or law enforcement. We need to be real careful."

"I'll compensate you for—"

"Damn right, you break it, you buy it."

Steve and Ryan had an intense, whispered argument in the back room when they got to Kryptonite. Ryan returned to the front desk. He handed a USB stick to Mike.

"Look at this. Try to figure out what it tells you, but you can never say where it came from. You can never mention us. Not me, not Steve, not Kryptonite. We appreciate what you are trying to do, but this is where we live, where we do business. We can't afford to be involved. Not anymore. I hope you understand."

"Of course. I'm sorry, Ryan, I really am. Didn't think things would turn out like this. I'll write you a check, as promised."

"No, we can't have a paper trail. It has to be cash. We bank at Tabor Trust."

"OK, cash then. I'll drop it off."

"Mail it. I don't want anyone seeing you at the store."

When Mike got back to the house, the family Alvarez was in full swing, putting a second coat of paint on the outside walls. Kids were being home schooled on the porch while teenagers painted the surrounding woodwork. A small transistor radio played salsa at the back of the house. Juan approached when Mike pulled in.

"We will finish the walls and windows today. I have walked on the roof. It is still strong. The rust is on the surface, not serious. There is a special paint we have used before. I think it will be good for your roof. We will paint the roof tomorrow."

"Great."

Once inside, Mike placed Ryan's USB stick in his laptop, and the files surfaced on his screen, but he was interrupted by a rap on the door. Sofia Navarro from next door.

"You have done nothing about that mess."

"It's in hand."

"I warned you I'd call the council."

"Look, I said I'm doing something about it, and I am. Just look around you. Work is going on here. I will deal with it. Chill for a bit."

"Don't you tell me to chill, mister, my sister is on city council. I can get you in a lot of trouble."

"Is that supposed to scare me?"

"You don't want my sister on your case. She's a fighter."

"Look, lady, I told you I will deal with it. I've met your sister, and I really liked her, but you need to know...if you want a fight, I'll give it to you, both of you if necessary and when I fight, I win, no matter what. Understand? Now please get off my porch. You're interrupting the work." Mike closed the door in her face.

When he heard her stomping off, Mike quickly returned to the laptop. The USB had date-stamped video of the surveillance cameras on Bluebonnet Road the day Adam Polley was killed. Ryan had tracked them down on the cloud. The grainy black-and-white images showed Polley's old Crown Vic driving slowly down the road and pulling in opposite the Scroggin house turnoff. The car sat immobile for a few minutes. It wasn't clear what Polley was doing. Then it accelerated hard onto the asphalt, fishtailed slightly, and sped away. The frame stayed empty for almost a minute and then two vehicles turned onto the road from the turnoff and followed fast.

He did not recognize the late model Mustang but gasped as the second vehicle entered the frame, a black-and-white Dodge Charger painted in the colors of Taborville Police Department. The vehicles hurried after the Crown Vic.

Ryan had edited all the cameras surveilling Bluebonnet into one video. The footage overlapped, but it was clear the Mustang and Dodge Charger were closing the gap to the Crown Vic as they raced along the narrow road.

The last images of the Crown Vic showed it swerving off the road, at speed, for no apparent reason. Moments later, the Mustang and Charger appeared in the frame and braked hard to a halt. Mike didn't recognize the man in the Mustang, but he knew exactly who got out of the Charger. Police Chief Walter E. Gates. The men exchanged a few words, then walked off the road together, following the track left by the Crown Vic. Two minutes later, they returned to their vehicles and drove back the way they came.

Mike hit fast forward on the laptop. Seventeen minutes farther on, another black-and-white pulled up. He recognized Catch Washington. More vehicles arrived in the following thirty minutes, a fire truck, ambulance, crime scene investigators, the medical examiner, and finally the police chief's Dodge Charger again.

The Crown Vic was never in shot, nor was any of the activity close to it. After two hours, the final shots of the video were of a wrecker coming through to retrieve Polley's car. The images proved one thing conclusively. Police Chief Walter Gates knew a lot more about Adam Polley's death than he was saying. He was there.

Mike drove to Walmart, bought five more flash drives, and copied the video onto each of them. He suddenly realized he was ravenous. He ordered a bacon burger at Longhorns and chewed over his options as he crunched on the overdone bacon. The images he had from the video were suspicions and conjecture. He could prove there were lies and disinformation from the police chief, but not what had happened to Adam Polley. Getting any closer to the drug operation would be dangerous, and he had already lost his allies. As he paid the check, a penny dropped. He rummaged in his wallet for the scrap of paper and dialed Sam Washington's number.

"Yes?" The voice was so cheerful it could light a room.

"Sam, it's Mike Carson."

"Mike Carson, as I live and breathe, the man, the myth, the legend." He laughed loud and heartily. It was infectious. Mike found himself grinning. "Jacob said you might call. Said he had to pull you over, you bad man. You're not doing any of that distracted driving right now, are you?" He laughed again. "I tell you, that little booger is dedicated, yes, sir. I hope he didn't give you a citation."

"No, just a warning. So how are you, Sam?"

"The finest. If I was any better, I couldn't live with myself." He chortled. "Mind you, Jacob says the same can't be said of you, my old friend. You've been getting into some trouble down there."

"Guilty as charged. But it's been for good reasons. Do you think we could get together, Sam? I'd like to catch up. And I could do with your advice."

"My advice. Good Lord, you must be desperate. What do you have in mind?"

"Could you do dinner tomorrow night?"

"So long as it's in Austin."

"Any suggestions?"

"Do you still like steak?"

"Is the Pope a Catholic?"

"Willie Nelson's Texas Roadhouse. It's on I-35, just by Slaughter Lane. Six o'clock."

"Done. Can't wait to see you. It's been way too long."

CHAPTER TWENTY-SIX

A SHAMBLING FIGURE of a man made his way slowly along Weimar Road, casting a short shadow under the early afternoon sun. Clothes hung from his body as if he had shrunk inside them. The brown trousers were too long and dragged on the roadway beneath his laceless sneakers. The navy blue hoodie sank his face into deep shadow. The gray sports jacket over the hoodie was at least three sizes too big. He carried a sleeping bag tied with rope on his back, and an ancient carryall dangled below the right sleeve of the sports jacket, held by an unseen hand.

He walked with the pace of a man who had no particular place to go, a being in purposeless motion. It was hard to determine his size, and impossible to tell his age, his face hidden deep inside the hoodie. The few cars who passed could not describe him in any detail. He was just a derelict on the road to somewhere, or nowhere. When the road was empty, he stopped and looked around, then moved into the trees, apparently to relieve himself, but did not reappear.

Once under the cover of the trees, Mike pulled down the hoodie and sought a good vantage point. He wanted a clear view of the rusty gate they had seen with the drone where the tracks led to the back of the abandoned farmhouse. When he found the perfect spot, he untied the sleeping bag, laid it on the ground, opened the carryall, and removed a new Canon digital camera with a long telephoto lens and a tripod. Notebook in hand, he sat comfortably with a thermos of coffee. The clothes and bags had come from Goodwill, the camera gear from Best Buy, and the shambling gait had been perfected years before in New York. He glanced at the tattoo on his wrist, the question mark, and felt the story buzz inside him, the dangerous adrenaline, the visceral excitement of chasing a hard truth.

Weimar Road was not well traveled, mostly locals going to and from town. The few vehicles that passed flashed by at speed until a Horny Toad Couriers van arrived, slowing right in front of him. He started to record. The rusty metal gate looked like it had not been touched in years. A heavy, rusted padlock secured it to a solid metal post. As Mike filmed, the entire structure, posts and all, slid sideways into the scrubby hedgerow. The van drove through and the gate slid silently back into position, looking as abandoned and unused as it had been. The green van with the cartoon horny toad logo followed the tracks across the field through the trees towards the abandoned house. Forty minutes later, it returned and went back the way it came. Although he got a good closeup of the driver, Mike did not recognize him. Horny Toad Couriers was one of the companies Duke McMillan boasted about in his interview.

"We've made it the most successful courier service in the whole of South Texas. Zane runs it now."

What Mike had seen could be an innocent delivery, but who delivers by courier, through a back gate, to an abandoned house?

Although the trees provided some shelter from the brutal heat, the humidity was high and Mike sweated heavily. As the afternoon dragged on in boring monotony, he thought frequently about calling it a day. There was Adam Polley's funeral tomorrow and he needed to be alert for that, to have some decent sleep. But he was done cutting corners. *Stay the course.*

He had counted six cars in the last hour, all traveling in the same direction. People on their way home from work. He was hungry now, and thirsty. He'd drunk the last of the CamelBak water fifteen minutes earlier. Dusk was descending like a forgetfulness. Best not want to walk this road in the dark. He rolled the sleeping bag, tied it with the rope and put away the CamelBak and thermos. It was such a disappointment. One solitary van, which could mean absolutely anything.

He adopted the same aimless shamble and made his way back to Walmart where he had parked the car. His thirst raged. There was half a bottle of bourbon at home, but he stopped at Joe's drive-through liquor window to pick up another.

He didn't make it back to the house. Holly called as he was leaving Joe's and asked him to come over. She had something to show him. When his lights hit the house, she stepped outside. She shook her head as he walked towards her. "What have you been up to? You look like a bum."

"That was the general idea."

Mike said he'd been staking out Bluebonnet Road. He decided not to mention the footage Ryan had discovered. It was inconclusive, and the funeral was just hours away.

"What did you want to show me?" Mike said.

She placed a yellow legal pad on the table. "We found this down the side of the sofa when we were cleaning. That's Adam's writing."

Mike examined the neat hand:

1. *All land size similar.*

2. *Each plot too small to build.*

3. *Only one has road access.*

4. *Plots owned by different people.*

"What do you think it means?" he said.

"It has something to do with his work, with land registry. Remember I said he saw patterns? He used legal pads to work them out."

"It could be something. I'll go by the courthouse on Monday. I wanted to check out ownership of the properties on Bluebonnet, anyway."

"You better not show up at my husband's funeral dressed like a bum."

Juan and Rosa were waiting for him on his porch when he got back to the house. Faint shapes in the spilled streetlight. He sat on the steps with them. If they noticed his clothes, they were too polite to comment.

"You're here late," Mike said.

"We came back to see you."

"About the house?"

"About the house and other things."

"OK."

"After we paint the roof tomorrow, are we done? I do not know."

"Actually, I need your help with the outbuildings. My neighbor is going nuts. We either need to fix them or tear 'em down."

"We know. She comes every day. We say nothing and she leaves. We can fix this. And the rooms inside must have new paint." Juan grinned and waved his arm at the walls. "The house has a beautiful new dress. It must not have dirty underclothes."

"Yes, we should do that."

"Rosa has been told a message for you."

Here we go.

"You must listen. She has been told there is much you do not know. The things you do not know will hurt you when you find the words. You must be very careful."

They stood and walked away; their duty completed.

ES—as if there was such a thing, but then again... she'd plucked Remington from somewhere. Mike stared at the night sky for half an hour and was no wiser, but a lot thirstier. He got to his feet. As he crossed the threshold into Uncle Harold's house, an involuntary shiver ran down between his shoulder blades. *Damn night air.*

CHAPTER TWENTY-SEVEN

THE FUNERAL SERVICE for Adam Polley was a relatively muted affair. Mike sat close to the back of the packed building. Holly was in the front row, hemmed in by church members. He glanced around but didn't recognize many faces. Just before the congregation burst into the first hymn, Mike caught the scent of orange and jasmine. Cathy slid next to him on the pew and squeezed his knee.

"You OK?" she said.

"Sure."

"It's just I haven't heard from you."

"Sorry, been busy."

"I heard. Steve told me about the drone."

"Yeah?"

The church band cut off further conversation. Mike wasn't sure what to expect: his only experience was the Catholic funerals he'd been dragged to as a child for the sake of appearances. Depressing affairs, too often conducted by priests who had never met the deceased; rituals completely detached from the life they purported to celebrate. The priests would have you think the deceased was a saint, but it could have been Lizzie Borden in the box, for all they knew.

Here people spoke of Adam's likes and ambitions, his passions and courage in the face of great adversity, his dogged determination to follow Christ, and his overwhelming love for Holly, the center of his universe. They prayed for Holly that she might find the courage in Christ to survive the tragic loss. They prayed for the perpetrators of this venal crime, that one day they might find Jesus too and forsake their evil ways. That they might be bathed in His blood of forgiveness and be placed on the path of righteousness.

"May the bastards fry in hell for all eternity," Mike whispered.

"Amen, brother. Amen." Cathy said.

Pastor Hannah introduced the last speaker, County Judge Christian Taylor. The man made his way to the altar. When he turned around, Mike gasped. "Jesus Christ."

People around him shot savage, scornful looks at his blasphemy. He lowered his head to avoid the eyes. There was no mistaking what he had seen. It was the same man who had stepped from the Mustang on Bluebonnet Road with the police chief and walked towards the wreck of Adam's car at the time of his murder.

"Are you alright?" Cathy asked.

"Yeah, yeah. Just got a bit overwhelmed."

He heard little of what the judge said but watched him walk over and bend down to console the grieving widow.

Holly nodded at Mike as she followed the pallbearers into the blazing heat outside. He waited for the church to empty from the front, examining each group of faces as they passed. The whole of city council. Cops filed by—Green and Brown, Catch Washington—in crisp dress uniforms.

Duke McMillan walked arm-in-arm with a woman young

enough to be his daughter, but who obviously wasn't. They were flanked by his two sons, Zane and Karter. All of them studiously avoided Mike, but Duke nodded at Cathy with a smile.

When all the pews had emptied, Mike and Cathy walked into the heat. People milled around and chattered in hushed tones, waiting for the hearse to load. A metamorphosing group of figures surrounded Holly, ebbing and flowing as men and women offered their condolences. The size of the group remained constant. Holly was well loved. The little cluster did not dissipate until the funeral director signaled and Holly climbed into the black limousine for the final ride to Pinegrove Cemetery.

"I need to get back," Cathy said, and pecked Mike on the cheek.

"OK, I'm going to the burial. See you later."

"Hope so."

Mike joined the long line of mournful vehicles, which turned slowly onto the highway and crawled away.

At the cemetery, Mike patted Uncle Harold's headstone and nodded to Andy's before walking up the hill to Adam Polley's grave. It had been dug in the shade of a tall pine. Without her microphone, only the first two rows could hear Pastor Hannah. Mike waited for the end of her spiritual drone. The coffin lowered, and the crowd began to disperse.

Mike moved as the police chief passed.

"Hello, Chief. Sad day. Any developments? Are you any closer to finding the people who murdered Mr. Polley?"

"This is hardly the time or place, Mr. Carson."

"I'm not sure I agree, Chief," Mike said, matching steps with him. "Wouldn't it be a comfort to the poor widow on this, of all days, to know you were close to finding the killers?"

"We are following all leads. Those responsible will be caught and held accountable."

"Very reassuring. These leads, are they still centered on shooters from San Antonio?"

"I'm not at liberty to say. Now, if you'll excuse me."

"Only, there's no record at NIBIN of any inquiry from Taborville PD about the bullets or cartridges used in this shooting. Nothing. Strange, don't you think?"

"What's strange is you claiming to have information, false information by the way, from an agency only accessible to law enforcement. How is that?"

"It's what journalists call sources, Chief. I'm wondering if you would like to revise your statement. You said ballistics pointed to a San Antonio connection, but there was no ballistic inquiry, was there?"

The chief stepped so close Mike could smell his gum. Peppermint.

"You don't know what you are talking about. And you sure as shit don't know what's good for you."

"I'm sorry, is that some kind of threat?"

"Take it however you want."

The police chief climbed into his Charger and hit the gas. Hard.

Sam Washington was the most cheerful person Mike had ever known. He was sitting in the back of Texas Roadhouse under the mural of the Highwaymen, Willie and Waylon, Johnny and Kris. Willie owned the place. It said so right above the door.

Sam was chewing through a handful of brined peanuts, discarding the shells on his side plate, as Mike approached. He still had an athlete's body, even all these years after his wide receiver days at Florida Tech. Sam dropped the peanuts.

"Hello, stranger."

The bearhug was long and strong.

"Sam, good to....Shit, what happened to your face?"

"Has it really been that long?" Sam fingered the puckered scar on his left cheek, then grinned and turned it into an extra dimple. "I got shot, dumbass, back when I was in Narcotics. Which means we haven't spoken in—"

"Eleven years. I'm sorry."

"I guess I could've picked up the phone."

"You did."

"I did, didn't I?"

"Come on, Sam, spill. What happened?"

"I was arresting this dealer, small time guy, name of Reggie Salinger. Out at Tabor Lake, you know, where the trailer homes are, and like a fool, I didn't clear the other rooms. Thought he was alone. Turns out he had a girlfriend staying. She steps out of the bedroom, all jacked up, and waves this nasty old Saturday night special in my face."

"Crap."

"I'm cuffing Reggie and I want to finish in case he runs, so I say, 'Why don't you put that down? You don't want to shoot a cop.' But it turns out, she did."

"Jesus."

"I'm thinking dammit, not like this, and—"

The server hovered.

"Could you give us a minute, please?" Mike said. "I've got to hear this story. And?"

"Weapon misfires. Cheap ammo, old as all hell. There's this dull pop, but the slug stays in the barrel."

"Lucky."

"I reach up to take it from her. Reggie's cuffed now. And,

man, if she doesn't pull the trigger again, but this time hits a good cartridge. The second round hits the first, and the piece explodes. Catastrophic damage to the weapon, and she loses her hand. They had to amputate." Sam sat back.

"What about your face?"

"Oh yeah, there was enough pressure in the barrel to push the first slug out. It goes through my hand, here, then through my cheek, takes out two molars, and lodges in my jaw on the other side."

"Mother of God."

"Yeah."

"This doesn't sound like you. Not clearing the rooms."

"Yeah. Stupid. Cocky. Of course, it was back when I was drinking."

The server returned. Mike reckoned from the way she beamed at Sam, she'd been eavesdropping. Of course, it could just have been his caramel good looks—the scar hadn't interfered with his chances of a movie career. After they ordered their steaks and sides, Sam looked him in the eye.

"Tell me how you lost your high-flying job and your gorgeous wife all at the same time?"

"Well, I, eh....you know—"

"No bull. It's me you're talking to."

"Truth is, I screwed up. Big time. Lots of times, really, but this last one did it. Liz told me something in confidence, and I used it."

"Wow. That was dumb."

"I know, I know, and the thing is, I didn't check it, either. Didn't check it, and it was wrong, but there it was, printed in the *Chronicle*. Things kinda went to shit after that. Long story short, this guy at Liz's work took his own life, and the *Chronicle* is being sued, and I didn't give them a leg to stand on."

"Damn."

"They'd reassigned me to the newsroom from features 'cos the last couple of investigations were busts, and there was this news editor, Brogan, who was a real hardass, always giving me shit about the Pulitzer, you know.... Anyway. Not that it's an excuse."

"But why would Liz—"

"It wasn't just that one thing. We were struggling for a while, you know, did the therapy stuff, all that. I guess the truth is we come from two different worlds, Rhode Island rich and small-town Texas hick. She liked the tuxedo me but not the guy who got the stories that took us to the award shows. Does that make any sense?"

"A little, maybe."

"I guess the real me was a little too... grubby for her."

"Grubby I get—sloppy, not so much."

"OK, I was doing a fair amount of drinking."

"Now drinking and sloppy, I understand."

"War zone whiskey. It keeps the edge off just a bit, you know, when the action starts you have just enough to hold steady and think this is not my day to die. And the other days when you've been digging and assembling and getting inside the story, you get home, and where's your sleep gone? All you have is adrenaline. There's no sleeping. And then there's pain. All different kinds of pain. Rejection pain and failure pain, fear pain, and fear of failure pain. And pain pain. I used to wonder sometimes if there was a different brand of whiskey for every kind of pain. In therapy, they said it was all about me trying to please my father, to get his approval, and of course Liz glommed onto that. It became all about that. Thing is, I don't want his approval. She thinks I can't enjoy anything, that I'm always trying to prove something—trying to expose bad guys to make myself feel better. To make up for all the crap my father did. And maybe some of that is true. But honestly, I don't want his approval—not that I'd ever get it. Or my mother's."

"Sounds like whiskey is running your life, Mike. I've been down this path. It doesn't end well."

Sam told Mike of one marriage lost, and then another. He shared stories of bungled investigations, leads squandered, and corners cut. He spoke of partners compromised and all the times he had faked being sober—until his rock bottom.

"I shot a kid."

"You did not."

"Two rounds in the chest. Thank Jesus, it didn't kill him."

"Drunk?"

"No, hungover, real bad, hurting, you know. I was getting out of the cruiser and this kid, Leroy Maynard is his name, points an AK-47 at me, and I didn't see it was plastic, and I just... I guess the training took over. Worst day of my life."

"When was this?"

"Seven years, five months, and thirteen days ago. Been sober ever since."

"Good for you."

"Yeah, but like every alkie, I'm just one drink from disaster."

Mike would have believed none of it had it come from someone else's mouth.

"You know you need help, Mike."

He nodded.

"Are you at bottom yet?"

"I don't know."

"Well, you've lost your job and your wife and your reputation. You wanna lose your life?"

"I almost did."

"Ah...huh?"

"But not the way you think."

Mike told him about being forced off the road, the shots fired in the woods, about Polley's death, his suspicions about the drugs, the lies in the police chief's statement, the false ballistics. He placed a flash drive on the table.

"The chief and the county judge were there, Sam, at the time Polley was killed. Right there at the crash site."

"You're kidding. There's video footage on here?"

"Yes, time stamped."

"Where did you get it?"

"A confidential source. Let's just say it was sitting on the cloud somewhere and we retrieved it."

"You want me to take a look at this?"

"Unofficially."

"I'll take a look, on one condition."

"Which is?"

"You come to a meeting with me."

CHAPTER TWENTY-EIGHT

MIKE'S SUNDAY was lost in an attempt to escape the inevitable. A day of solemn self-pity, a recitation of wrongs, and mysteries—the unholy secrets of the Carson family. Each slug of bourbon from the very first swallow in the morning had posed a question, and the questions mounted through the day in a maudlin miasma of misery. Why did his brother have to die and destroy his parents, and why had Mike not been good enough to fill the space left behind? Why had his sister run off and died, and why would his mother never speak of her? What had made his father resign abruptly and flee to Florida?

He wandered the house, glass in hand, demanding answers from the walls. Why was he so weak? Why could he not hold on to love? Maybe he didn't deserve it. Maybe they could see inside him. He wasn't worthy of a father's love, and he'd never known a mother's.

He cried a little and laughed a lot. Short, little savage tears squeezed from aching eyes. The laughter, sad and sarcastic, his own, superseded by his father's. Beatings with a belt were better than the derisive laughter following him up the stairs and the shouted questions. Who did he think he was with all these fine notions? Where did he think he was? Boston, New York, Washington, D.C.? No, boy. He was in Taborville, Texas, and had better get with the program, get realistic. This was not a place for dreamers. This was a place for men, real men, not namby-pamby library boys.

Mike passed out in the afternoon, head lolling on his chest, in front of a TV baseball game he cared nothing about. His iPhone vibrated on the side table and dinged its messages.

His urgent bladder forced him awake. It was dark now. The hunger pangs were distant and satisfied by a slice of bread and cheese. He thought about the tense meals at his parents' house; about secret excursions to Whataburger with Uncle Harold; the meals with Liz in the apartment, which had gradually turned into competitive contests of daily achievements as their respect for each other ebbed away. How could he have let it happen? He'd had loveshine in his hands and he'd let it seep away between his fingers.

He picked up the bottle. Bourbon would cure none of it, but it could help him forget. He sat and drank, and the voices hushed and crept away. Except one. Damn him. Sam Washington. The stupid things Mike had told him. Idiotic things. Horrible things. Things all horribly true. He looked down at himself in his stained white T-shirt and two-day-old jockeys and laughed aloud. He had a problem, alright. A problem he would have to face, and soon. But not this day, not while there was still bourbon in the bottle.

The vehicles rolled up silently just after 4 a.m. Six SWAT officers stood on the running boards of a black Chevrolet Tahoe, three on either side. They stepped down quickly as the Tahoe slowed, and single-filed to the building with rehearsed precision. More SWAT officers spilled from inside the SUV. Black-and-whites blocked the street on either side of the freshly painted house, another one parked at the rear in case of runners. Two more units positioned themselves to divert traffic should there be any at this hour.

When the full team was in position, the leader nodded and the breacher stepped to the door with his battering ram. On the leader's second nod, Mike's world exploded in ear-splitting shouts and noise. He only had time to swing his legs to the floor when the first of two masked, helmeted officers quick-stepped into the bedroom, both pointing weapons at his head, an M4 carbine, and a shotgun.

"On the ground. Now. Let's see your hands."

Mike lowered himself to the floor, and a kneepad punched his back, smashing his face into the pine boards. In a second, his wrists were zip tied.

"Get him up."

Rough hands dragged him upright and spun around to face the police chief.

"Get him out of here while we secure the scene."

They pushed him from the room.

"For God's sake, let me put some pants and shoes on."

"Whoa, son, you've been drinking," said one cop, waving the breath stench away.

Dressed, Mike was hauled into the street. Cathy Ross stood behind a police cruiser, Nikon in her hands. She looked shocked but took the picture anyway. They drove the cruiser into the sally port at the police station, took Mike directly to an interview room, and cuffed him to the metal desk. One of the SWAT team pulled down his mask. Sergeant Green.

"I formally request my lawyer, John McKinney, to be present."

"Understood."

The door slammed shut behind Green. Mike settled down to wait. He didn't think they'd be in a hurry to call McKinney, and he wasn't wrong, but Honest John kept them honest pretty damn quick as soon as he got to the station. Mike walked out at eleven o'clock on Monday morning nineteen minutes after his lawyer arrived. Everyone was very apologetic. The SWAT team had responded to a call about shots fired at his location. The call had been bogus. He'd been swatted. It was a thing. Politicians, election workers, and a bunch of celebrities from Miley Cyrus to Tom Cruise had it happen. Even Clint Eastwood, Dirty Harry himself, had been a victim. SWAT teams had to answer a "shots fired" call. They assured Mike every effort was made to ensure calls were genuine. Somehow, this one had fallen through the cracks.

Before Honest John climbed into his Cadillac, he turned and smiled.

"You know, I underestimated you. I didn't realize you were this talented. It takes someone special to upset an entire police department in the short time you've been here."

Mike looked at him hard. "Can I trust you?"

Honest John seemed offended. "Of course, you're my client."

"Yeah, I know, so?"

Two cops walked by.

"You'd best get in," the lawyer said. "Let's not do this here."

The office was more lavish than Mike expected. It occupied the ground floor of a two-story building on Corral just off downtown Main Street. There was a small reception, occupied by a pretty young lady in a business suit, and a large seating area surrounding a dark wood coffee table. Half the space was Honest John's office, which doubled as his law library.

The lawyer settled behind his desk. "Why don't you think you can trust me?"

"I don't know you, Mr. McKinney. I know nothing about you. If I'm really honest, you didn't sound too sympathetic when we first met. Sounded like you were siding with the McMillans and all that good ol' boy crap. And to be frank, I have to think twice about trusting anyone who has to put the word 'honest' in their marketing, especially a lawyer."

Honest John's laughter was loud and hearty.

"I guess that's a fair point. The thing is, I didn't give myself the name."

The way Honest John told it, he got the moniker during a trial in Midland. It was a tricky case, a man accused of fraud and embezzlement of a major local charity; a man he'd known from childhood, who had served with in the Army, was part of his regular golf four ball. The prosecution case was airtight. He had advised his client to plead guilty and take the best deal he could get. The client fired him and mounted his own defense. He called McKinney as a character witness. Although the judge was wary, he allowed it. After establishing the facts of their long relationship, the client asked him a question bluntly: "Do you think I am the kind of person who would do such a thing?"

McKinney responded this way: "I wish you hadn't fired me as your counsel because I'd have advised you not to ask that question, since I'm under oath. Knowing you as well as I do, I absolutely believe you are the kind of person who would do such a thing. Look how often you've cheated all of us at golf."

The man had gone to jail, and John McKinney had become known as Honest John. Mike looked around.

"Seems you do very well. You must have big clients to pay for all of this."

"The place is barely ticking over. I bought the building with my one big success, a class action suit for fracking damage."

"How come you're here in Taborville, and not somewhere bigger?"

"Complicated story."

"Which is?"

"None of your business. Enough of this. Attorney client privilege protects almost anything and everything you tell me. It's sacrosanct."

Mike nodded.

"So, Mr. Carson, do you have something you want to tell your attorney?"

"I'm being harassed by the police chief because he's lying about a murder, and I know it."

The attorney took a legal pad from his desk drawer and began writing. "Let's start at the beginning."

When Honest John dropped Mike at the house, the Alvarez family had lots of questions, which he answered with as little information as possible. Juan and his brother had already fixed the door frame. Mike agreed they should change the lock.

His computer had been moved, but he was confident its contents had not been seen. It was triple-password protected, and each document was individually locked. His iPhone was dead, so they probably hadn't accessed that either. The desk was a mess. They had definitely been through it. His notebook was still there but had probably been photographed. He ran backwards through the notebook, thankful most of the Polley story was in his head and not on paper.

He opened the right-hand drawer and ran his hand inside it anxiously. The flash drives he'd put there were gone. *Shit.* Now, they knew he knew. He went to his laundry basket and pulled out clothes until he got to the smelly sock at the bottom. He shook out two more flash drives. His theory that nobody wants to touch smelly socks or jocks had paid off.

As soon as his iPhone had charged a little, he fired it up to see a list of missing calls from Quintin Smith, Holly, and Sam Washington. He texted Holly, knowing she was at work in the bank, asking her to call as soon as possible. He returned Sam Washington's call and got voicemail, then he called Quintin Smith.

"Mike, what the hell happened? I tried to call you."

"I had the phone on silent. Didn't hear it. Why were you calling?"

"I got a tip off about a SWAT raid on a drug dealer. Nothing I could do from Dallas. Couldn't raise Cathy and I tried you. It went to voicemail, so I hung up, but Cathy rang me back."

"They told me a very different story. The version I got was a prank call about shots fired at my house. Big mistake, so sorry and all that."

"It's a problem for us. I'm coming under a lot of pressure to sever links between you and the paper."

When Sam Washington returned Mike's call, he already knew about the swatting. His son had been one of the black-clad, hooded officers on the detail. Sam was now convinced there were real issues in the Taborville Police Department.

"Mike, right now, you need to do three things in this order. First, come to a meeting with me tonight. Second, we go to the DEA tomorrow and then meet my boss. Third, be very, and I mean very, careful."

"Oh man, I've had no sleep. I could really do with an early night."

Sam's voice was as serious as a foxhole buddy waiting for an attack.

"Anything could have happened last night, and you were too far gone to notice. Catch said you smelled like a distillery. I'm not messing around here. This is not a negotiation."

They agreed to meet in San Marcos.

CHAPTER TWENTY-NINE

THE AA MEETING was held in the annex of an Episcopal church. Mike had not been sure he'd go at all, despite what it might mean. His friendship with Sam was tight, but wasn't always easy. Sam was not one to compromise, especially when the stakes were high.

Mike had seen him stand defiant, anchored to his principles, stalwart in the face of peer pressure, resolute against the attacks of teachers, and staunch even when membership of his beloved football team had been in the balance. Sam stepping between dickwads on the football team and Mike, their nerdy target, was how the friendship started. Sam was not a person to be trifled with.

Mike had special grace with him, a place in Sam's heart that he would never forget. Mike had told a lie that probably saved Sam's life and certainly preserved him from a beating. Sam had been seeing Clara Renick, the young white daughter of the Carsons' next-door neighbor. When a group of men confronted Sam right outside her house, Mike reacted to the shouting and understood the dreadful possibilities. He assured all the neighbors Sam had been there to visit him, to be assisted with his homework. Sam's pride almost killed the gesture. He was the smartest kid in the entire grade, by a comfortable margin, and everybody knew it, but he stayed quiet, and the angry men dispersed. Neither Mike nor Sam knew if they fully believed the lie, but it had been sufficient in that moment.

Mike drove to the meeting with a couple of minutes to spare. He had a full hip flask in his pocket in case of emergencies. Sam was waiting outside the building, looking at his watch. He propelled Mike into the room, almost like a suspect, which, in a way, he was. *This is Mike. I suspect he is an alcoholic. What is your verdict?*

As the meeting started, it was everything Mike feared. Earnest. Sanctimonious. A bit too much God, although they talked "higher power or God" as you understood him. In the tiny comedy club of Mike's head, he wondered if the "higher power" could be a giant bottle of bourbon. But his frivolity faded as the stories began.

Speaker after speaker stood and told their terrible tales of lives and families destroyed, jobs lost and hope with them, depths that none could imagine exploring, much less dwelling in.

Through the personal confessions, tiny fragments landed. Inside Mike's head, he nodded with increasing frequency.

Yes, I've done that.

Yes, I've thought that.

Yes, I've felt that.

All too familiar, all too real, but he could not bring himself to speak. He could not rise to utter the delusion-crushing words: "*Hi, my name is Mike and I'm an alcoholic.*" As the meeting closed and all the participants lined up at the urn to drink stewed tea and eat stale cookies, Mike slithered to the door, hoping Sam might not notice.

"You know this is for you. You need it." A voice said. "You

just can't admit it, and that's OK. But we will be here for you when you exhaust all your other options. I hope that happens soon because you don't look too healthy, brother."

Mike turned to see someone impossibly young and thought, *What the hell do you know? You're just a kid.* He headed for the parking lot.

Mike reached for the hip flask, unaware that Sam had padded out behind him.

"You really want to do that?"

Mike whirled.

"You can, if you like. Free country. But everything you are drinking to forget will be still with you in the morning, only a bit worse, and you'll be even less capable of dealing with it."

Sam grabbed him with the speed of an offensive tackle and hugged him, as if he was heading into combat. Mike tried to pull away, but realized it was futile. He relaxed and heard Sam whisper.

"You're not alone, my friend. I got you."

Truth lay heavy in the car as Mike drove back to Taborville. Truth and reality. Self-delusion had been getting thinner through the years. He'd swallowed all the red flags, dissolved them in fine bourbon, but like plastic ice cubes they wouldn't melt away. Now, he'd barfed them up, and they zipped through his memory like robots at a fulfillment center, pulling recollections one by one and placing them on a conveyor belt, each addressed to Mike's conscience.

Now every damn drink would have a red flag in it, like some bloody cocktail umbrella he couldn't ignore. Sacrilege—the sanctity of his forgetfulness was violated.

He shivered, shaken by the revelation. And by something else. A Horny Toad Courier van had just passed him, heading out of town. Mike immediately pulled a series of turns around the short city block and followed at a distance. The courier was heading for Bluebonnet Road. Mike stayed as far back as he could without losing sight of it. *Was it possible?*

It was—the van turned into Flores Trace. Mike stopped and counted off two minutes before he made the turn. As he got to the old, rusted gate, he could just make out the shape of the van, lights out, heading for the farmhouse. He drove on, pulled a U-turn, killed his beams, and waited in deep shadow, far enough away not to be a threat.

Just over an hour later, the van crept back across the fields and switched on its lights when it reached the road. Mike fired the engine and tailed it to the Horny Toad warehouse. After the metal roller door slid shut, he drove past and found a vantage point in the parking lot of another unit. He parked alongside a work truck, inconspicuous.

His eyes were drooping when he heard the engines. An odd rumble, like distant thunder, that grew louder as the warehouse door ground upwards, spilling fluorescent light onto the deserted forecourt. They came out in single file, vans and box trucks, fourteen in all. Mike looked at his watch—3 a.m. *Pick-up and distribution?*

When the door was fully closed and the vans were long gone, he eased out of the parking lot and drove home. He trotted up the steps and tossed his jacket on the sofa. *That was some damn fine investigating,* he thought. *I deserve a drink for that.*

CHAPTER THIRTY

THE DEA OFFICE in Austin was a nondescript affair, sandwiched between offices for engineers and environmental consultants. The agent they met was nondescript, too, but Mike figured he was an admin, not a field guy. Sam did the introductions, and Mike told his story. The agent sat quietly, listened carefully, and made notes until Mike finished talking. Mike handed over a copy of the Polley footage, the drone images, and his camera capture of the courier van on Flores Trace. The agent made a cathedral of his fingers.

"As Sam says, not much to go on, but it might be worth a look. I will make a few calls. See if Dallas or Houston have a couple of guys to spare for a few days. I'll get back to you."

Sam reminded him all the footage would be inadmissible in court, and the agent should forget how and where he got it.

"Confidential source. Understood."

The chief of the Criminal Investigations Division of the state attorney general's office comfortably inhabited the job, his office, and his gray suit. A white Stetson hung, lopsided, on a hat rack. He was already checking his watch as Sam ushered Mike through the door.

"I know you have a hell of a day, Chief. I'll make it quick. We're talking about possible corruption in Taborville PD, and in Tabor County."

That got his attention. "Taborville PD, remind me?"

"Chief is Walter E. Gates."

"Wally Gates, that SOB. What are we talking here?"

"There's footage of Gates and the county judge at a crime scene around the time a guy got shot to death. Then Gates shows up again, after units respond and knows nothing about it. A public statement that same day says ballistics suggest shooters from San Antone."

"Have they got Harry Potter doing ballistics down there? Damn. I don't like this. Where did we get the footage?"

Sam grimaced and inclined his head towards Mike.

"It dropped in from the cloud. Inadmissible and proves nothing, except they were both there, according to the time-stamp. Murder didn't happen on camera."

"What's your gut, Sam?"

"Something's off. They never ran ballistics. I checked."

"Alright, open a file." The chief turned to Mike, and all the warmth left his eyes. "Everything we've said here is confidential, off the record, unprintable. You were never actually here. Clear?"

"Crystal."

"Good. Thank you for your help."

Sam caught the same look.

"Sam, I don't let journalists in my office. Let's make this the one and only exception."

Mike thanked Sam in the lobby. "I have to write something."

"When's your deadline?"

"Six days."

"Oh man, that's tight. How much do you need?"

"Just the fact there's a state investigation would be enough to hang the story on."

"Leave it with me, no guarantees. Otherwise, how are you?" He looked at his watch. "Sober fourteen hours now."

Not really.

"How do you feel?" Sam said.

"Like crap." *Really.*

"It'll get better. Now get out of here before you completely ruin my reputation."

Mike and Juan looked at the mess of outbuildings. One had been a garden shed, one a workshop. The last was a Sunday house, which Uncle Harold's father had moved onto the property many years before. Germans built the Sunday houses in Texas, modest second dwellings close to a church, which they used when farms were too far distanced from the town for a day trip. The house had one small room at ground level, with a covered porch, and a half-story above for children's sleeping quarters, accessed by an exterior stair.

The shed and workshop were beyond saving, but Mike asked Juan to do all he could to preserve the Sunday house.

"I will do what can be done, but some wishes do not come true. We will see."

All three buildings were at the back of the property, embarrassed and hidden from the road, neglected for the last years of Uncle Harold's life, and all the years since.

Levi Forrest's original proposal to Mike had been for yard work and building maintenance. Mike limited the cost to the simplest of yardwork, and only those portions visible from the road. Surveying the decay, he regretted the decision, a choice born in the chasm between desire and duty, gratitude and guilt.

Juan organized the family with his usual quiet authority, and they worked with unhurried efficiency on the years of grotesque, unfettered growth and decades of decay. Chainsaws and loppers, weed trimmers, and rakes systematically chewed their way through the opportunistic chaos of shrubs and volunteer trees, vines, grasses, and creepers.

Juan called a temporary halt when they came upon poison ivy, which he and his brother removed with surgical precision, all gloved and sleeved, wearing bandanas on their faces in the humid afternoon air.

When general work resumed, even the smaller children weighed in, dragging lopped branches to a fresh dumpster installed in the driveway. By the end of the day, the buildings revealed their sad neglect. Walls eaten from the bottom up, crumbling in places to the touch. The territory of termites, untroubled for years. Mike was keen to look inside, but Juan cautioned against it.

"It is best to wait. Let the spirits depart in the night. We will look at this with fresh eyes and rested arms in new daylight."

Mike saw something slither close to the buildings. He shuddered and didn't argue with Juan's confident expertise.

Next morning, they discovered the contents of the garden shed were myriad and useless—broken leaf blowers, two rusted gas mowers, iron trowels, spades, forks, and shovels, which still bore the dried remnants of Uncle Harold's last attempts at gardening. Dozens of seed trays and a collection of empty yogurt pots, neatly stacked and ready for the seedlings he would never plant. Plastic sacks of fertilizers had split and spilled, and bottles of weed killer crowded dangerously on sagging shelves. There had been rodents in the shed; snakes and other creatures, too.

They removed the debris of an abandoned interest carefully. Each Alvarez signalled their entry to the space in case any creature or spirit remained. There was nothing to be salvaged and they knocked the structure down, smashing it into pieces sized for the dumpster.

The workshop had survived a little better at first glance, but termites had done their work, and winter rust had painted every metal surface. The shop was now owned by spiders, covered in their intricate traps, so richly filled with insects that many carcasses remained uneaten. Mummified creatures from another time. The tools were wooden handled, the kind once favored by collectors and bought by rustic restaurants for decoration. But the franchising of Cracker Barrel and other Americana eateries had created a thriving reproduction industry for the nostalgic tools and signs of yesteryear—when men were men, labor was manual, and all was well in the cozy dreamland of America. There wasn't a demand for originals anymore.

Mike told Juan he was welcome to all of it, but a sidelong glance at the Alvarez family's high-tech tool collection was enough to predict they would end up in the dumpster. The workshop building was also beyond saving. Mike was shocked how quickly it was dis-assembled, broken up, and carried away.

The Sunday house now stood alone, bracketed by two bare patches of dirt where its companions had once stood. The steps on this Sunday house could no longer be trusted to hold the weight of even a tiny child.

Three holes in the sloped roof overhanging the porch and decades of Texas weather had rotted out some of the flooring, but the boards to the front door seemed sound enough. The door was locked, but after a search of Uncle Harold's desk, Mike found and inserted an old key into the lock, which protested but released. Pushing on the door to open it, Mike snapped it from the lower hinges, and it hung drunkenly as he stepped carefully into the room.

A small fireplace sat oddly in one corner, as if added as an afterthought. There were small windows, both sides of the door, and one more on the left wall of the building. An old, overstuffed easy chair faced the fireplace at an angle. A small table and kitchen chair were the only other pieces of furniture in the room.

Beside the desk was a large metal trunk secured by an ancient Yale padlock. Mike tried all the keys, but none was a match. Reluctantly, he asked Juan to cut it. The battery-powered angle grinder made quick work of the steel, and Mike lifted the lid, cautiously at first, but faster when he realized what was in there. The Remington.

The typewriter, battered but unbroken, sat alongside stacks of files and a collection of leather-bound notebooks. Mike picked up one notebook and opened it with reverence. The pages were covered in confident copperplate, so neatly and beautifully written they could have been examples from an old schoolroom. These were daily journals. Mike ordered them by date. The oldest was marked 1980, the year Uncle Harold lost his wife and daughter.

When Mike was fourteen, he'd sat on the front porch with Uncle Harold, who had been preaching his journalism gospel.

"You know what happened on December 15, 1791?"

"No."

"First Amendment to the Constitution of these United States."

"Freedom of speech."

"Yes, freedom of speech, and religion, and assembly, and the right to petition all branches of government but equally important—the freedom of the press. You know what John Adams said? 'The liberty of the press is essential to the security of the state.' Think about that. 'Essential to the security of the state.' Why?"

"I guess people have to know what's going on."

"Exactly. Old Thomas Jefferson said freedom would be a short-lived possession if people weren't informed."

"The founders liked journalists?"

"Can't say they did. George Washington complained about the 'infamous scribblers,' but they knew the acts of the people we elect to govern should be examined and held to account. And that's why journalism is a noble profession, in Washington or right here in Taborville."

"It's what I want to do, but Pop is against it."

Uncle Harold scoffed.

"And what would he have you devote your talents to?"

"He wants me to be a lawyer, like him."

"A shyster, a pettifogger."

"Why do you always badmouth my dad? You never have a good word to say about him."

The silence dragged across the porch like a wounded ant. Uncle Harold walked into the house and returned with a fresh Shiner and a root beer.

"Do you know what happened to your aunt Lydia and your cousin Amy?"

"They were killed in a car crash."

"That's right, they were taken from me in a wreck, a head on collision. There are some who say it was an accident, but what is an accident? An unfortunate thing that happens. Happens unexpectedly, unintentionally, a terrible turn of chance." Uncle Harold took a long drag on his cigarette and let the smoke escape carelessly. He was no longer talking to Mike. "But what if it is not unexpected? What if someone actually foretold it? What then? Is that still an accident or is that something else?" He wheeled on Mike and demanded. "Well, is it?"

"I don't know. I'm sorry, Uncle Harold, I don't know what you are talking about."

The rage in Uncle Harold's face softened. "Of course, you don't. I'm sorry. How could you know? You were only a small child. What were you? Two?" He drank half the beer in one long swallow. "The man who drove the car that killed my Lydia and my Amy was a murderer."

"I don't understand."

"He murdered them, Mike. Might as well have slit their throats, took their lives along with his own worthless existence. Do you know who he was?"

Mike wanted to be somewhere else, even home, but he didn't know how to leave.

"No."

"Frederick John Michael Patrick O'Connor. Ever hear of him?"

"No."

"You wouldn't, would you? He was the eldest son of William O'Connor, senior judge of the Western District of Texas, a jurisdiction that covered fourteen counties, including this one. A man of power and influence. A man with connections. Not a man people in this small town would want to cross. You know that mansion, on the corner of Main and Redwood, the green one with all the outbuildings?"

Mike nodded.

"That's where they lived. And every time that feckless, worthless son of his drove home drunk, he got a pass. Three times he got stopped and failed the field sobriety test. One time, he couldn't even stand up. But every time those reports were sent to the assistant DA, he put them in a bottom drawer and they disappeared. After a while, the police didn't even bother stopping him. What was the point?"

Mike had seen Uncle Harold angry before, but not like this.

"Freddy O'Connor murdered my wife and my baby, but he was not alone. A whole corrupt system helped him. He should never have been behind the wheel of a car."

"I'm sorry, Uncle Harold. What has all this got to do with Pop?"

"The assistant DA who put those reports in his bottom drawer, the good ol' boy who toed the line, that was your father."

CHAPTER THIRTY-ONE

MIKE DIALED Frank Wolfe at *The Philadelphia Inquirer*.

"Frank."

"Skippy."

"I wish you'd stop calling me that."

"But it's so well earned."

Mike became Skippy in Afghanistan. He and Frank were reporting from a forward operating base in Kandahar. A Taliban attack with small arms fire started while Mike was having his morning evacuation. When an RPG exploded close to the latrine, Mike came hauling out, trying to pull up his trousers, while dodging rounds, spitting off the dirt. He'd ended up hopping like a kid in a sack race. A Sergeant Gregson gave covering fire and yelled, "Come on, Skippy, you can make it." That night Frank printed "SKIPPY" carefully in black marker on the back of Mike's blue press helmet, and the name stuck.

"I need your help," Mike said.

"How's the drinking?"

"None of your business."

"Since when?"

"Since always."

"I beg to differ. It was fine and dandy before—"

"Like I said, I need your help."

"With the drinking?"

"Come on, man."

"Tell me something good."

"I went to a meeting."

"Well, I'll be... And?"

"I didn't like it much."

"And?"

"I don't know."

"What don't you know?"

"I don't know. I guess I have an issue."

"And the skies opened, and a voice came down from above. This is my idiot son, in whom I finally have a modicum of hope. Good for you, Skippy. You should go back. What do you need help with?"

"The story I'm working."

"The murder?"

"Yeah."

"What's the problem?"

"I'm pretty sure I know what happened now, but I can't write any of it. It's all conjecture."

"I'm sorry. Who is this speaking?"

"What?"

"I thought for a moment there I was talking to a journalist."

"Hilarious."

"Skippy, you've been doing this deep undercover stuff for too long. Have you forgotten how the rest of us mere, non-Pulitzer Prize-winning regular folk do the job? Contacts, sources, people who give you information. And records, public records, remember?"

"I need to get this right. I can't afford...you know, another...."

Frank got serious. "No, you can't afford another Coolidge. When you need confirmation, develop sources. Have at least two for everything." Frank chuckled. "You remember how to do that, don't you? I have a book on my desk I can send if you're stuck. *The Complete Dummy's Guide to Journalism.*"

"Piss off."

"Glad to be of help."

An hour later, Mike got an anonymous call from a blocked number.

"Be at Taborville Police Headquarters at noon. Bring a camera," a female voice said, and rang off.

Mike parked at 11:45 a.m. and waited with his camera. Precisely at noon, three vehicles stopped directly outside the front of the police building—a Texas State Trooper sedan and two black SUVs with the Texas Department of Public Safety logos. It was a perfect shot. Mike got all three vehicles and the Taborville PD sign in the frame. Two troopers got out of the cruiser. Mike continued to fire off pictures as Sam Washington climbed out of the second vehicle, which was driven by a woman with aviator sunglasses and dark hair in a ponytail. Two Texas Rangers emerged from the third vehicle, resplendent in their Stetsons and cowboy boots, starched white shirts with badges pinned above the left shirt pocket.

All six lingered at the front as Mike clicked, and after a minute, Sam led them inside. The woman was last in line.

"Excuse me," Mike called, "can you confirm where you are from?"

"The Criminal Investigations Division of the Texas State Attorney's office, supported by Texas Rangers and State Troopers," she said.

"You're the one that called me, right?"

There wasn't the barest flicker in her eyes. No confirmation. No denial.

"Why are you here?" Mike said.

"You'll have to call the media office for that information."

"Thanks for the tip." She ignored him and walked inside.

The media office gave Mike an official statement which said it was policy not to make comments about active investigations. The term "active investigation" was enough.

Mike had submitted the piece less than five minutes before the phone rang, with Quintin Smith on the line.

"You're sure about this?"

"A hundred percent. You've seen the pictures."

"I know, but they haven't confirmed it's about the Polley murder."

"They can't, they won't. But it is."

"How do you know?"

"Impeccable source inside the investigation."

"I'm going to hold it for now and make a few calls myself."

"Don't trust me?"

"This is explosive, Mike. I can't take any chances. I'll call you back."

Ten minutes later, Mike picked up the phone again.

"You must be right. Wally Gates has just been called over to the city manager's office."

"I told you there was a story here."

"You did."

"So, we're good? You're going to run with this?"

"Got no choice now, do I? No matter how much flak I get, I have to print it."

Duke McMillan's executive assistant knocked gently on his door before opening it.

"Pamela."

"I know you said you didn't want to be disturbed, but I have the mayor on the line and he says it's really urgent. I said you'd call back, but he's insistent. Needs to talk to you right away."

"Best put the old goat through, then."

Mayor Pryor was agitated. "Have you heard about the chief —I mean, about what's going on?"

"Enlighten me."

"The chief's been suspended."

"What?"

"The city manager told me. He called him into his office just now and suspended him indefinitely."

"He can't do that, can he?"

"Sure. He's the chief's boss."

"What the hell is going on?"

"He says the state attorney general's Office has taken over the Polley inquiry, and insisted the chief leave the building until they're done."

"Does VanDorn know?"

"No, not yet."

"Call him. He might be able to do something."

Mike rewrote his piece for the *Times* website when the city confirmed Police Chief Gates had been suspended, pending the results of an inquiry into the handling of the recent murder of Adam Polley. He texted Holly.

```
Making progress.
Check Times website.
```

CHAPTER THIRTY-TWO

WHEN THERE WERE no further updates to be filed on the Polley story, Mike riffled through the plain manilla folders in Uncle Harold's trunk. They were files of his failures. The typewritten originals were rejects by the newspaper editor, each marked NFP. Not for publication. There were years of them. Local scandals hushed and hidden.

NO STATE CHARGES
IN TABORVILLE CORRUPTION
By Harold Carson

Taborville Mayor Lockley Rose will not face corruption charges, the state attorney general has confirmed. AG Herbert Conroy told the Times the investigation was closed after crucial witnesses retracted their statements. "Effectively, we no longer have a

complaint," he said. He refused to speculate on the reason all three witness statements were recanted simultaneously. Mayor Rose had been accused of accepting cash bribes from developers for favorable consideration by the City Council.

Mike remembered meeting old Lockley Rose, long left office by then but still influential. A tall, haggard figure with a shock of white hair. The kind of man who might live in a haunted house and scare kids. Apparently, his back wasn't the only thing that was crooked.

SHERIFF STOPS ROBBERY WITH EMPTY GUN

By Harold Carson

A robbery at Dewey's Gas Station was foiled Saturday by Sheriff Winston Hargreaves and the perpetrator taken into custody. Confronted by the Sheriff as he exited the store, the thief threw down his switchblade and surrendered when the law officer pulled his service weapon.

Many citizens witnessed the aftermath as Sheriff Hargreaves marched the man, said to be 29-year-old Cecil Ducloux, to the jailhouse. Owner Robert Dewey was fulsome in his praise of Harg-

reaves. "He drew on him without hesitation," Dewey said. "We know the Sheriff's not allowed to have ammunition, because of the drinking and all, but that didn't stop him. He just faced that fella down."

Halfway through the folders, Mike came across a file marked "Andrew Carson." Carbon copies, mostly faded now, of Tigers' football games. Uncle Harold wrote glowingly about his nephew; about his speed and grace; his calm under pressure in the pocket; his unerring aim and ability to throw the long ball when needed. Mike smiled with pride as he read the pages. His brother may have been an asshole, but he was a helluva player. He turned a page and the smile dropped.

The pages in Mike's hand were carbon copies, which meant the originals had been submitted and not rejected by the editor.

STATE AG TO CONSIDER
CHARGES IN CARSON DEATH
By Harold Carson

The death of Taborville Tigers quarterback Andrew Carson, in a single vehicle collision, may lead to criminal charges, according to sources close to the investigation. A file on the incident has been sent to Tabor County District Attorney Thomas Carson.

The DA is understood to have forwarded

the file to the state attorney general. Sources suggest there is the possibility of evidence tampering and other felonies. DA Carson has recused himself. The deceased is his son.

Andrew Carson, who took the Tigers to the State championships, died at the scene. First reports indicated he was the driver of the vehicle, a Mercedes sedan owned by local businessman, Duke McMillan. Other occupants included Zane McMillan, Rowdy Hargreaves, Jenny Patrick, Jill and Leslie Stricker. A spokesman for the state attorney general said the office was waiting for a full report from the Medical Examiner's office.

(In the interests of full disclosure, it should be noted that this reporter has familial connections to both DA Thomas Carson and the victim.)

There was nothing else in the file. Mike was certain the story was never published. Why would charges be considered against the passengers when his brother was driving the car? He remembered his father's bristling fury at the mere mention of the accident.

"Pop, why was Andy driving Mr. McMillan's car?" Mike had asked.

"How the hell would I know? Was I there?"

"Don't ask stupid questions," his mother said, and made it clear Mike was not to bring it up again.

He went through the stack of personal journals and pulled one from the pile. He flicked through the pages until he found the date. There were lots of heartsick words about Andy's loss, and then this.

Need to interview responding officers Henry Cargill and Ronnie Littlejohn. This stinks.

Mike closed the journal and wondered if either of them was still alive.

Henry Cargill had retired from Taborville PD and lived on two acres about ten miles west of town. The house and yard were neatly tended. A three-car garage and a large metal workshop were set farther back. Mrs. Cargill answered the door to Mike's ring.

"He's out back in the workshop. He's expecting you."

Cargill was medium size, maybe five feet, nine inches and looked fit. He was working on the suspension of a Fox body Mustang, raised on a two-point lift, when Mike walked into the air-conditioned space. His gray hair stuck out from an oily baseball cap, on backwards to accommodate the headlight he was using.

"Be with you in a minute. Don't want to forget to tighten this sway bar."

He double-checked the tightness with a torque wrench, wiped his hands on blue mechanic's overalls, and greeted Mike.

"Said you wanted to talk about your brother."

"Yes, sir. Andy."

"Beer?"

I'd kill for a cold one right now to take the edge off. I could start again tomorrow but... it's always tomorrow, tomorrow, tomorrow. "No thanks, you got a water?"

Cargill pulled a beer and bottled water from a small fridge on the workbench and handed the water to Mike.

"Hell of a football player, your brother, heck of a talent. God knows how far he could have gone. Such a tragedy. What can I help you with?"

"You were one of the investigating officers at the crash site."

"That's right, me and Littlejohn. We were first on scene, just ahead of fire and ambulance. It was a mess."

"I remember. I went out there on my bike the next day."

"Are you sure you want to go into all this? It's a long time ago. Sometimes it's best to let things be."

"I'm certain."

"Don't say I didn't warn you. What do you want to know?"

"I came across stuff in my Uncle Harold's journals about charges being considered, but nothing happened."

"Charges should have been brought, in my opinion."

"Why? It was an accident."

"Accident for sure, single vehicle lost control and hit a tree. No question. Two things bothered me and Littlejohn. How come a young man, firmly strapped in the driver's seat, had a broken neck? And why was windscreen glass and wood bark deeply embedded in his skull?"

"What?"

"I warned you. We concluded your brother didn't crash the car."

"But he was behind the wheel."

"Yeah, he was. We figured he was the front passenger, not

wearing a belt for some reason. Went through the windscreen, hit the tree and broke his neck."

"Oh my God."

"And then his friends, not sure you'd call them friends, picked him up, and strapped him into the driver's seat."

"Who was driving?"

"Most likely Zane McMillan. It was his father's car, after all."

"This is sick. Jesus."

"Sick is the word. Thing that always bothered us, bothers me to this day now I'm talking about it again, is how a bunch of drunk teenagers could come up with something so damn weird. I mean, that's some cold, calculated shit right there."

"You think they maybe had help?"

"We never could prove it. Zane McMillan called home, according to the car phone records. The call lasted four minutes, and it was another ten before he called 911. Draw your own conclusions."

"I can't believe this. Jesus."

"I said you should leave this alone."

"Did you write it up the way you told me?"

"We wrote up the facts, but not our full theory. We suggested the possibility that your brother might not have been driving, but we were hoping the medical examiner's report would fill in the holes."

"Did it?"

"I don't know. We never saw it."

"And that was the end of it?"

"Shouldn't have been. The chief was away on vacation at the time, fishing in the Gulf, if I remember right, so me and Littlejohn sent a prelim report to the DA. When the chief got back, we were taken off the case and told to investigate actual crimes, not be concerning ourselves with accidents."

"Why would my father not have acted on it?"

"That's a question for him, wouldn't you say?"

"I don't suppose you kept a copy of your report?"

The medical examiner's office was not a cheery place. Mike knew the woman was trying to be helpful—painstakingly diligent, but horribly slow. She struggled with the old computer in that frustrating, binary way government employees sometimes do. He wanted to press her but figured she might be on the spectrum, and it would likely backfire. If she lost her place, she'd have to start over, and that was an excruciation he didn't need.

"No," she said.

"No what?"

"No record. It's not in the system. No Andrew Carson. Sorry."

"This is the medical examiner's office. Correct?"

"Yes."

"You have records of all the autopsies carried out by medical examiners. You have to keep those records. Correct?"

"Yes."

"Then why the f—Why is there no record of my brother's autopsy?"

"I told you, sir. It's not in the system."

"Why is it not in the system? Has it been buried, deleted, hidden? What?"

"Oh, Lord no. Of course not. Gosh. The system only goes back to 1993, but they are digitizing all the time. I thought it might have been there, but unfortunately not."

"All you're saying is, it is not in the computer."

"Correct."

"It exists somewhere?"

"There'll be a hard copy in the archive."

"Great. Can you get me a copy of the hard copy please?"

"I'm afraid not."

Mike gritted his teeth.

"Why not?"

"We don't hold the archive in this building. It's across town in a warehouse. We need climate and humidity control for the physical records, you see."

"OK." Finally getting somewhere. "And you can give me the address and whatever authorization I need to access it?"

"Of course, it would be my pleasure," she wrote on a Post-it. "If you're going over there now, I'll be glad to call ahead."

It took two hours, but Mike finally had the pages in his hand. Fifty cents a page.

"Sorry, sir, can you believe the price of ink? You know if you were to buy it by the gallon it would cost—"

"Fifteen thousand dollars," Mike said.

"Oh, you know that."

It was a tough read—cold, clinical descriptions of the bone, tissue, muscle, and organs that had once been his brother. A headache started at the base of his skull and flowed across his brain like a drop of ink in water. It was all there, everything Cargill had told him. The cervical fracture, the unexplained contusions and abrasions, the tree bark, the auto glass. All of it. Injustice pounded in his head, and the unanswered questions attacked like migraine clusters. All he wanted was the dark, but what he needed was the light.

On the drive back, Mike wondered about next steps. He wanted to march into McMillan's office, face him down, drag him into the street, expose him for the sick sonofabitch he was. There would be a visceral satisfaction in letting everyone in town see the truth behind downtown's philanthropic savior.

But there was no proof McMillan told his son to move the body. No proof Zane was driving the car. Mike needed confirmations and more independent sources.

He had subconsciously driven to McMillan's office. He parked across the street and sat, dejected, still processing his outrage. His brother had become the town's James Dean: live hard, die young, forever encased in the preserving amber of taking Taborville Tigers to State. The quarterback who had never been sacked and never lost a game. Your actual, genuine, local hero—forever.

Mike noticed the door of McMillan's office open. The executive secretary walked out. Long after six o'clock. Not a stickler for time. What was her name? Patricia? No, Pamela. Pamela Patrick. Surely not. His mind back peddled to the list of girls in the Mercedes. The Stricker twins. And Jenny Patrick.

He hustled to the *Times* office.

Mike scanned the town databases. No Strickers, they must have moved. He searched the archive for Jenny Patrick.

TRAGIC DEATH

FORMER MISS TEEN TEXAS

The language danced around it, but it was suicide. Drug overdose. In the bathtub at the family home, the body discovered by her younger sister—Pamela Patrick.

Deeper research revealed the entire Stricker family had moved to Oregon in 1993, less than seven months after the accident. A small piece in the social column quoted Mrs. Stricker, a noted local patron of the arts.

"It is sad to close our business here, and leave so many good friends, but we feel a change and new opportunities will be good for our family," she'd said.

Rowdy Hargreaves was dead too—an inexplicable head-on collision with an eighteen-wheeler in broad daylight on a straight road. He had never married. Zane McMillan was the last man standing in Taborville. The sole survivor.

It was evening by the time Mike had tracked down potential numbers for the Stricker family in Oregon. He tried four different Strickers before locating the parents in Portland. Mrs. Stricker answered.

"Mrs. Stricker, my name is Mike Carson. I'm a journalist. I'm Andy Carson's younger brother."

"I remember he had a brother."

"I'm doing a story about his death."

"After all this time? Why would you do that?"

"I've come across some information that was not available at the time. Something that puts a different complexion on what happened."

"Oh, God."

"There's evidence that my brother was not driving the car, that he was put in the driving seat afterwards."

"I can't help you." She cut the call.

There was no listing for a Jill Stricker, but there were two Leslie Strickers. The first was a veterinary surgeon in Salem. Mike really hoped she was the right one. He had to get to Leslie Stricker before her mother could warn her.

"Stricker."

"Leslie Stricker?"

"Yes."

"Mike Carson, Andy Carson's brother, the journalist."

Silence.

"From Taborville."

A long sigh. "I see." Her voice was soft as lamb's wool.

"I'm doing a story about my brother's death. There's new evidence."

"What new evidence?"

"That my brother wasn't driving the car, that you guys put him in the driver's seat, and lied about it."

"Jesus, God. Nothing's ever really dead and buried, is it? I swear I never touched him. I want you to know that I loved him or thought I did. It's all so long ago. We were young. Young and stupid and naïve."

She said Zane, Rowdy, and Jenny Patrick had moved the body. Leslie's twin, Jill, had been violently ill, and Leslie had taken her deep into the trees to throw up. When they got back, it had all been done, and Zane was calling 911.

"I couldn't look at him, messed up like that. And then Zane told us what his father said—we were all guilty, accessories to a crime that would ruin the rest of our lives. You know how scary Zane was." *Was she looking for understanding?* "Why should all our lives be ruined when Andy was already gone? That's what he said. We needed to keep our mouths shut. And if we didn't, he'd shut them for us." *She was looking for forgiveness.* "What were we to do? We were only young."

Mike gulped his anger down and said, as evenly as he could manage, "I understand." But he didn't.

"None of us ever got past it, not really."

"How's your sister?"

"I won't talk about my sister."

"Off the record."

"Nothing is ever really off the record, is it? Please don't contact my sister. She's, eh, not resilient. Please."

"You have my word."

"Does Zane know?" Leslie said.

"About the evidence? No, not yet."

"You should be careful. They're dangerous people."

"I know."

"Can you keep our name out of it?"

"I'll try."

Mike felt sorry for them, in a way. These kids had been told silence was their best option. Not so much—two dead and two in dread. Life sentences.

CHAPTER THIRTY-THREE

NEXT MORNING MIKE drove to McMillan Enterprises. He didn't bother with the niceties and marched straight past the executive secretary to McMillan's office.

"Excuse me," she said, scampering after him, but he was already opening McMillan's door. He slammed it in her face.

McMillan looked up and smiled. He was one cool customer, Mike thought. You had to give him that.

"It's alright, Pamela, no cause for alarm. Mr. Carson, to what do I owe the pleasure of this intrusion?"

"This." Mike slapped the file on the desk but did not let it go. "This file of sick shit you and your son did to my brother."

"I don't know what you are talking about. Are you drunk?"

Mike ignored the jibe

"Zane was driving the night my brother was killed."

"Was he now? And what makes you come up with such an outlandish story? Of course, that is your reputation, isn't it? False stories. Fake news. Isn't that why they fired you? A death involved, wasn't there? Or was it the drinking?"

"Oh, believe me, McMillan, I've checked, double-checked and verified everything." He brandished the file like a weapon.

"I have a police report, the medical examiner's report, and interviews with corroborating witnesses."

"If what you allege actually happened, why did your father not bring charges?" McMillan was calm as a hurricane's eye. "Andrew was his son, after all."

"You know damn good and well that my father was disqualified from acting for that exact reason. It was a conflict of interest precisely because Andy *was* his son. He couldn't prosecute, but he sent the file up to the attorney general. One of the few things he did that was maybe honorable, and that's where you got it quashed, right? You had a state senator in the family, didn't you? A few words here, a promise there, and it's disappeared. *Poof.* Like it never happened. Not that it matters now because I have all I need to nail you to the cross, you sick sonofabitch. You can kiss goodbye to your good name, and so can your asshole son. How could he do that to his best friend?"

The hurricane eye was close to passing, but McMillan was still in control of his emotions. He met Mike's fiery gaze.

"I think you need to be careful, Mr. Carson. Truth is always followed by consequence."

"Do you have a quote, or statement you would like to make, about the death of Andy Carson, and the criminal role you and your son played in it?"

"Get out."

"With pleasure."

"You shouldn't cross me, Carson. You'll learn it's not a good idea."

Mike stopped in the doorway and wrote on the back of the file.

"Oh, I guess you wanted to make a statement, after all."

McMillan leaped from behind the desk. *Not so cool now.* Mike pulled the door shut and marched out of the building.

Duke left his office a couple of minutes later and drove to the Industrial Park. He parked inside the Horny Toad building but had to wait to open his door as a box truck pulled in beside him. Too fast and much too close for comfort. The driver jumped out and moved to the back of the vehicle without even glancing at him. Duke squeezed out, careful not to damage the car's paintwork.

"Hey." The man turned. "You need to be more careful." He pointed to the BMW. "This car is worth more than you make in a year."

"Sorry, *jefe. Perdone.*"

"Show some respect."

"Lo siento."

Duke took the stairs two at a time. He nodded at the staff. Zane was out of his chair and had the door open by the time Duke crossed the space.

"Dad, what's up?"

"Is that a new guy down there?"

"Yeah, Luis Arapiento, Arapuerto, something like that. He replaced Rafael."

"Rafael?"

"Houston, the accident. He's still in the hospital."

"Right. Well, that Luis needs a driving lesson and some manners, nearly sideswiped the Alpina."

"I'll have a word. Anyways, what gives?"

Duke gestured to the door. Zane closed it.

"Mike Carson just stormed into my office. He knows about the accident at Piney Creek."

"Everyone knows about the accident at Piney Creek. It's old news."

"He knows what really happened, Zane. He knows you were driving, what happened to Andrew."

Zane hammered a fist against the wall.

"Control yourself, son."

Zane swung around, fist still raised. "That bastard. How the hell? I thought you had this covered? You said you buried this."

"I thought I had. I truly did, but he's like a damn mole digging, digging, digging. Digging into everything."

"He can't do anything about it, though, can he?"

"Of course he can. He has the medical examiner's report, a police report, interviews. He's a pain in the ass, but he's not stupid and wouldn't have shown his hand if he didn't have what he needs."

"You can't let him publish." Zane's face was turning red, blood pulsing, muscles tightening, the same gearing up for battle Duke had seen so often on the football sidelines, effective there but dangerous here. This was a time for brain, not brawn.

"You need to calm down, son."

"I will not let that sonofabitch—"

"I said, calm down. I will handle this."

"That's what you said before, but you didn't handle it, did you?"

"Watch your mouth."

Zane stared back, unapologetic.

"You know, Zane, sometimes I wish you and Karter would realize I'm your father, not your damn janitor."

CHAPTER THIRTY-FOUR

MIKE SQUATTED by Uncle Harold's gravestone and watched her. She walked up the hill and turned left on a gravel path. She rearranged the blue flowers in the posy as she went. A warm breeze made the live oaks speak as she kneeled and placed the posy reverently on the yellowing grass and blessed herself.

Prayers done, she sat and caressed the grass, picked some fallen leaves from it and scrunched them. She appeared to be talking aloud, although Mike could not be sure. Even at this distance, he felt like an intruder, hidden in the closet of someone else's emotions. He tried not to move or draw attention.

At last, she had said her piece and tidied the grave to her liking. She kissed her fingers and touched the stone, lingered for a moment, and walked back along the gravel. Mike waited. As she drew level, he rose, and her head turned towards him.

"Miss Patrick."

"Mr. Carson."

"Could I talk to you for a moment?"

"No."

"It won't take long. I promise."

"Mr. Carson, I have no interest in you or anything you have to say. I came to visit my sister, and I would like to be left alone."

"That's what I want to talk to you about, your sister."

"You don't have that right. My God, after—"

"Please."

"My sister is dead because of your brother."

"I know."

"She was never the same after the crash. She was—"

"Traumatized."

She nodded, close to tears now.

"I know why," Mike said.

She'd read the pages three times now. They were in Ken's Koffee—Texas toasted, not Seattle burned. *The words will not change through some kind of magic*, Mike thought. The medical examiner's report may have remained hidden all these years, but what it said was crystal clear, and Mike's notes from his interview with Sergeant Cargill confirmed it.

"This is why you charged into our office?"

"Yes."

"It was Zane?"

"Yes."

"Not Andy."

"No."

"It's disgusting."

"Yes, yes, it is."

"And they made her help. Jenny."

Mike nodded.

She looked at the pages again.

"They didn't come up with this themselves," Mike said. "They were just teenagers."

"You think Mr. McMillan?"

"Zane called him on the car phone, according to Cargill, and I've confirmed it with another source."

"No wonder she... I mean, it's something from a horror film."

"And once they helped, they were accessories. Locked into the lie and terrified to say a word because Zane threatened them."

"Poor Jenny. Poor, poor Jenny." She stared out the window at the parking lot, lips tight, small gulps in her throat, eyes defying tears.

"It was drugs in the end, wasn't it?" Mike said.

"Yes, an overdose. Oxycontin laced with fentanyl, they said."

"About that..." He had her attention now. "I have something else to show you."

The video on Mike's laptop puzzled Pamela. They had driven to Uncle Harold's, and she was sitting at the desk. Mike perched on a kitchen chair beside her.

"I'm not sure what I'm looking at here."

"This is a place on Bluebonnet Road, at the corner of Horton Creek Drive. It used to be the Gerlich farm, if you remember, before they sold the land to the Lignite Mine Company. You can't see the old farmhouse; it's hidden behind the bushes, but this is the property's old mailbox you're looking at."

"It disappeared."

"Yes. I figure it's on a hydraulic lift and drops underground. This is how addicts in Taborville get their fix."

Pamela watched as the mailbox popped back in the frame. Mike fast-forwarded through the footage until Pete Baker reappeared. She saw him open the mailbox, turn, show the bottles to the camera, then put them in his pocket.

"Do you think this is where Jenny—"

"I don't know how long this has been in operation."

"And you think this has something to do with Mr. McMillan?"

Mike shocked her with the story of being run off the road, shot at, and hunted through the woods by Karter McMillan and Jess Scroggin.

"There's more." He clicked on another video. "This is Flores Trace, about halfway down, the back entrance to the farm."

Pamela leaned forward as the rusted gate slid into the hedge.

"My goodness."

She gasped when she recognized the courier van.

"That's one of—"

"Yes, it is."

"What would it be doing?"

"I think it is delivering raw material and collecting finished product. I trailed the van a few nights after. It went straight to the Horny Toad Courier warehouse. Later, fourteen trucks left at three in the morning."

She sat back, shoulders slumped. Her face sagged into her hands, and she sobbed. A refined and gentle leak of ancient pain. Mike put a hand on her shoulder, and she jumped, wiped her eyes.

"This is all supposition. This is your speculation." Defiant now.

"There's no supposition about the drugs in the mailbox. I have evidence. You've seen the video. I have interviews with addicts and," he opened the desk drawer, "I have the drugs." He rattled the container. "Oxycontin laced with fentanyl."

"The—"

"The same thing that killed your sister."

The defiance left her eyes like gun smoke on a western breeze. Tears glistened where her eyes had blazed.

"What do you want from me? How can I help?"

CHAPTER THIRTY-FIVE

IT WAS pure chance Holly noticed them. She'd just finished a Meal Simple from the deli department at H.E.B. supermarket, her favorite stuffed salmon with asparagus, and sat in her armchair to check out Fox News when she noticed one of the crosses on her wall was crooked. No one wants a crooked Jesus. She smiled at her own little joke as she went to adjust it. Movement outside the window caught her eye. An old farm truck, one she did not recognize, stopping on the road outside. Two tall men and a very short woman climbed out of the single cab. Bandanas covered the lower half of their faces. The driver, a tall, skinny looking guy, reached back into the truck and handed the woman a pistol, pulled a baseball bat for the other man and an assault rifle for himself. Men and women weren't really the words for it, they were more like kids.

Holly ran for her phone and dialed 911. The dispatcher said there was a big wreck on Highway 71 involving all units. It might be forty minutes before officers arrived on scene. Could she get out of the house? The dispatcher asked her to stay on the line, but Holly hung up and called her two nearest neighbors. One went straight to voicemail, the other rang and rang and rang....She glanced out the window. They were almost at the door. No more time. She ran to the bedroom. *Hide, but where? And from what? Who were they? What did they want? Doesn't matter, girl, they're not making a social call or from Jehovah's Witnesses. Hide yourself.* Moments later, she heard the front door splinter and heavy footsteps enter the living room.

"Holly," a male voice called, "we know you're here. Your truck is right outside."

"Come on now," the girl, "where are you at?"

She could hear them moving around the living area. The shatter of broken glass.

"Strike one," the second male voice shouted.

Oh Jesus, help me Jesus. Holly turned her phone to silent and tried her neighbor again. Still ringing out. She heard another door opening. Bathroom—from the squeak. More glass breaking, and porcelain too, a deeper, more ominous sound.

"Strike two."

Another door clunked slightly as the hinges sagged. Second bedroom.

"Holly. We know you're in here. Come on out now. Don't make us come to get you," the first male voice, more menacing now.

"You got something don't belong to you, girl. We need to get it back," the female said.

"We're not going to hurt you," the first male again.

"Sure as shit gonna hurt you, if you don't come out," the girl, "cos we are gonna find you, that's for damn certain."

"Strike..."

Crash.

"...three."

Holly heard a wall cave in. The entire trailer echoed and shook.

"Goddammit, you are in for it now. We are gonna rip this place apart."

Holly held her breath, closed her eyes, and prayed to Jesus.

The bedroom door opened.

Holly texted Mike in the dark.

```
come quik arm men
at house help
```

The text flew silently away. She could only hope now. The footsteps pounded into the bedroom. Holly dared not breathe. She heard them pause outside the closet door.

"You asked for it."

The hollow echo of metal hitting wood and then, one by one, the bullets kept coming.

Mike raced down the narrow road, cutting corners, straight lining through curves. Just a few more minutes. He hoped he was not too late. He slid to a halt and had the car's door open but waited a moment. Observe, assess, act. Holly's truck was still outside. No other vehicles. Were they still here? He crept up the steps and listened through the open door. No sound of movement. He went inside. The place was trashed. There were five bullet holes in the living room wall, exit holes by the look of them. He eased through the rooms, wreckage everywhere. He got to the main bedroom. Someone had shot through the closet door. He reached out and levered it open with his fingertip, stomach churning. Empty but for clothes. Did she get away, or had they taken her? He ran outside to her truck, looked inside the cab. Nothing. He turned back to the house.

"Holly," he yelled. "Holly. Holly, it's Mike."

A small voice answered.

"I'm here," from underneath the trailer home.

"Where?"

"Here." Mike located her voice and pulled the neat white latticework from the bottom of the outside wall. She crawled out on hands and knees, covered in dirt and cobwebs.

"Are you alright?"

"Thanks be to Jesus, and Adam."

"Adam?"

"He built a little concrete crawl space under our bedroom, in case a tornado hit in the middle of the night. There's nowhere safe in these manufactured homes. He put a trapdoor in the floor so we could get down there quickly. Whoever was here didn't notice."

"Who was it?"

"They were wearing bandanas, kids though, from the look of them, two tall guys and a real short girl."

"McMillan and the Scroggins, I'll bet."

"They wanted to kill me, Mike. When I heard the shots, I..." She seemed close to breakdown.

"I know."

"They said I had something that didn't belong to me and wanted it back, and then I could hear them destroying the house when they couldn't find me or whatever they were looking for."

"Whatever they were looking for, they must want it bad. What the hell would make them so desperate?" Mike said.

"Maybe..." Holly turned to crawl back under the house.

"Hang on," Mike said, "I'll go."

She shook herself and was all business again. "That would be stupid. I'm already dirty. And I'm smaller."

And before he could argue, she disappeared under the trailer. She re-emerged a couple of minutes later, dragging a gray metal lockbox. Mike helped her to her feet. She crouched and worked the combination lock.

"Adam kept all our important papers in here, under the house, where they'd be safe." She opened the box. "Woah." She pulled files out, one by one, handing them to Mike, each marked with a letter and a number.

"Those are land documents," Holly said. "They shouldn't be here. What did you do, Adam? It's an offense to remove documents from the courthouse. He told me that."

Mike opened a folder. R317463. "Sale of land to Martha Gates."

"That's the chief's ex-wife," Holly said. "Nice woman. Episcopalian."

And on it went. VanDorn's daughter, McMillan's wife, Pryor's niece, Isaac Brook's brother.

"This must have been what Adam was trying to figure out, you know, on the notepad. Little tracts of land, too small to build a house," Holly said, "You take them. I don't want them here."

There was a yellow Post-it note stuck to one file. R317354 with a question mark beside it.

Back at Uncle Harold's, Mike fired up the Tabor Central Appraisal District website. He'd helped Holly straighten up the double-wide and waited until a neighbor arrived. He'd advised her to leave, go to her sister's, but she wouldn't hear of it. "They will not run me out of my own house," she said. Mike decided it would be best for him to leave before the police arrived.

He punched in the reference R317354. Up came Christian Taylor. The county judge. Roughly the same size as the land in each of the files. He checked all the others, then went back and did it again, this time putting a small highlighter mark on the county map screen as each property came up. The highlighter marks formed a narrow line from Taborville to San Antonio. He dialed the courthouse.

———

The county judge was a formal man, one who stuck rigidly to the rigors of a mannered society.

"Coffee? Tea, Mr. Carson?"

"No, thanks. You don't drive?"

"Sorry?"

"I saw your space outside, empty."

"I can't imagine my vehicle is relevant to your readers."

"I'm a car guy, just curious is all."

"You had some questions?"

"Yes, I'm doing a piece on the murder of Adam Polley."

"Mr. Polley, tragic, shocking, truly shocking."

"Indeed. I believe he worked for the county."

"He did. A valued employee."

"And—"

"I should make something clear. He was not working for the county at the time of the, eh, unfortunate incident."

"I'm aware. He was actually working for us, delivering papers."

"Something that is specifically prohibited by our HR policy."

"Delivering newspapers?"

"Any secondary employment without prior written approval."

"What exactly did Mr. Polley do here?"

"He was part of our land registry team."

"Which...?"

"Records and authenticates sale of real property in the county."

"Was he good at his job?"

"I would say excellent. Well, I would have said excellent. We had no knowledge of his drug habit."

"He wasn't a drug user."

"The police chief said the murder was drug-related, your own paper reported it."

"We reported the chief's statement but Mr. Polley was clean. Medical examiner confirmed it. And no drugs were found in the car or at the scene."

"That's a relief. The poor man, machine gunned to death like that."

"Machine gunned?"

"Someone told me the car was, literally, riddled with bullets."

"Who told you that? There's been no mention of a machine gun."

"I'm not sure now, possibly someone at the police department. Please don't quote me on that. I may have been misinformed."

"What do you think happened?"

"I have no idea. Perhaps he was in the wrong place at the wrong time. Perhaps he came across a drug deal. Maybe he had enemies. I really don't know. How could I?"

"What about his work here? Any possibility someone was upset with him?"

"I can't imagine. Recording transactions is not exactly the stuff of passion."

"Can you tell me what this is?" Mike slid an index card across the desk. R317354.

"Let me see." Taylor squinted. "Certainly, it's a property ID number."

"Any idea why he'd have this ID written on a Post-it note at home?"

"No."

"Can you tell me anything about that property?"

"Not without looking it up."

"Surprising."

"Excuse me?"

"I thought you'd be familiar."

"Why?"

"Because you own it."

"I own a lot of property in the county. I don't memorize the IDs of all of them."

"I thought you might remember the last one you bought. Just a couple of months ago."

"I think you are mistaken. I have not bought property in over a year. Anyway, I thought you were here to talk about Mr. Polley."

"You're right. I am. Just trying to cover the angles. The possibility the shooting was about something else."

"You're not suggesting..."

"No, no, of course not."

The judge looked straight in Mike's eyes as he slowly rose from his seat.

"Mr. Polley was a valued member of our team at the county. His tragic death shocked and saddened everyone on our staff. Our thoughts and prayers are with his family at this awful time. I think that does it, don't you?"

As soon as Carson left the office, the judge picked up his

private line and called the deputy chief of administration at the Tabor Central Appraisal District.

"Brent...Judge Taylor. Look, I'm terribly sorry to bother you with this, but we've had an unfortunate administrative error over here. Yes, rare indeed, fortunately, but it needs correcting since it has made its way to your office and website. R317354. No such parcel exists. Incorrect transaction reporting. Needless to say, there will be repercussions in Land Registry. I'm grateful. Say hello to Melissa for me, and that tiger of a softball player, eh? Why, you're so welcome. It is always a pleasure to help. Children play better when they have sharp uniforms, I always think."

When Mike got back to Uncle Harold's, he opened the appraisal district website again. Judge Taylor was lying his ass off. He punched in R317354 and leaned forward. The spinning wheel of death. Then finally...

No result

The Keller Aquifer Authority met on the fourth Tuesday of the month when there were issues to consider. They were in a weird mood tonight more Spanish Inquisition than local government body. Duke McMillan waited for his turn like a stand-up comedian peeking from the wings of "The Comedy Store" as the act on stage got savaged.

The authority's new rigor stemmed, in part, from two lawsuits filed by Texans for Transparency and an NPR investigation into partisan rulings and mismanagement. There had been several conflict-of-interest allegations leveled. Now they were in the spotlight, members were meticulously following the letter of the regulations. Things understood in the shadows no longer applied.

The secretary called Reflow Logistics, and Duke walked to the public podium.

"Duke McMillan for Reflow." He looked at the men and women he had been cultivating for two years, and saw a row of deliberate, unsmiling faces. They flatly rejected his application for an extension.

"I think we have made it clear, Mr. McMillan, not once but on several occasions, Reflow Logistics must show it has an end user before we will issue a certificate," said the chairman. "It is the view of the Permits and Enforcement Committee that you have had ample time to secure customers. We will vote on the application at our next meeting."

Duke turned away and left. He would make phone calls later, remind members of favors done and contributions made. He knew it would make no difference. They were in a bind, and he was collateral damage. This would have to be solved another way. Taborville City Council would have to be made to agree to the water deal at the next city council meeting. Everything depended on it. His partners had stuck with him through the Magnolia Trails disaster, but their patience was razor thin now. They wanted to be made whole, fast and with interest, lots of interest. He could not contemplate failing them again. There would be no forgiveness...and retribution would not be calculated in dollars alone. Of that, he was certain.

CHAPTER THIRTY-SIX

ZANE MCMILLAN SEETHED. The anger coursed, demanding an outlet. He'd prowled the Horny Toad office, then the warehouse floor, checked the vans and trucks, looking for something, someone to unload on. He returned to his desk, unsatisfied. There was no question about it. His father was getting soft. There had been a time when stuff got dealt with promptly, no dicking around. Warnings given, actions taken, problems solved. Not these days, though. It was all talk and patience and the long game. But there was no long game to play with people like Mike Carson. Players like him needed to be tackled hard and sent to the locker room, preferably on an injury cart. He picked up the phone.

"Yes?" His father sounded tired.

"That thing we talked about. Is it handled?"

"It will be. I've been dealing with something else, something more immediate."

"That thing with Karter?"

"Yes."

"So, when—"

"I told you, this is in hand. Go tend to your business."

Zane slammed the phone down onto the receiver. *This is my business, father dear, very much my business.* He stalked out and stopped by the key rack at the bottom of the stairs. His Porsche was in the shop, so he reached for a set of keys to one of the company trucks. *Wait up.* He spotted Karter's key chain hanging at the end of the rack and sniggered. *Much better.* He'd love to see the look on the arrogant little shit's face when he got back from the Houston run and saw his pride and joy was gone. Zane was still grinning when he climbed up into the blue Dodge Ram and went in search of Mike Carson.

Enjoyment was not a word Mike would use about being sober. Sure, there were benefits. No ibuprofen in the mornings, no throw-ups in the middle of the night, no wondering about missing minutes, no puzzling why there were two uncooked pieces of bacon on a plate beside the bed. But his body betrayed his brain by shaking in the morning, and there was a constant sense of unscratched itch inside. His evenings were a struggle—a constant screaming match inside his head made worse by the unwelcoming embrace of empty sheets, the soul-destroying solitude, the graceless taste of guilt. The impending sense of doom he'd endured for years had lessened a little, and sometimes there was even a tiny glimmer of clear-headed hope. Clear-headed and clear-eyed was what he needed now. So easy to say, but he had his teeth firmly in the story and would not, could not, *must* not screw this up. It was an iceberg, no telling how deep it went, maybe deep enough to go national.

Daily meetings were getting him through and, thankfully, there were enough within driving distance. Mike had not spoken at any of them. He politely declined each invitation to share, since an acceptance would involve saying the words he was not yet prepared to own fully: *My name is Mike, and I am an alcoholic.*

The blue truck slotted in behind his Elantra, about two miles from the Taborville City limits. Mike sensed the danger before he saw it. The truck was so close behind he could only see the grill and hood in his rearview mirror. *Damn truck hog, pass if you want to.* But the truck stayed glued to his bumper. As the truck filled his mirrors, he began to get a real bad feeling. He was running the speed limit, fifty-five, but he put his foot down, conscious of the hollow in his heart and the prickle on his scalp. The truck hit him in the rear quarter panel when he was just past sixty-five. *What the?* The car slewed wildly, but he accelerated and dragged it back in line.

He could not outrun the powerful pickup on this straight stretch of street. The Hyundai would be more agile where there were corners. Tabor Lake Road was just half a mile away. He needed to stay ahead till then. The bull bars smashed into the back of the Elantra and the truck kept pushing, trying to force him to spin. Mike coaxed the motor faster. Eighty-five now.

Glued to his mirrors, Mike saw the truck close the gap again. *Who the hell was that?* Tinted windows hid the driver. Mike could see the turnoff just ahead. At the last possible second, he sliced to the right, onto the shoulder, braked hard, and threw it into the turn. *Please hold.*

He heard the tortured scream of rubber on asphalt and saw the cloud of smoke in his mirrors as the truck attempted to follow. It looked as though he'd pulled it off, but his little jolt of joy faded when he saw the big pickup had somehow negotiated the turn.

He had to focus forward now, head up, eyes well ahead, just as he'd been taught—when it was an exercise. Mouth dry from adrenaline panting, he tried to stay calm. He had not driven this road in a long time but remembered it and started to visualize what was coming. It was Taborville's unofficial Lovers' Lane, a regular haunt for teens seeking romance with an overview of the lake and stars twinkling in the dark Texas sky.

What Mike gained in the corners, he quickly lost on the straights. The truck kept pace. *Goddammit.* There was a tight right hander coming up. Maybe he could fool them. His hands were strangling the steering wheel. He needed loose hands. As they approached the acute bend, Mike slowed way down. Sensing an opportunity, the truck closed in and when it filled his mirrors, Mike accelerated hard into the turn. The rear tires immediately lost grip, and the car was sideways, pointing at the trees. *Feel it, hold it.* Mike fed in opposite lock on the steering wheel and kept his foot on the gas. The slide seemed way past the point of saving, but the front wheel drive hauled it through. *Made it.*

The truck shrank in the mirrors and Mike pressed on and remembered to breathe again. He'd hoped to be clear by now, but the Dodge was still there. The Elantra sped through a left hander at well over sixty when a woman in an SUV picked that precise moment to reverse out of her driveway. *Jesus.* He swung right and flashed through the closing gap. The pickup rounded the corner and had to screech to a halt.

Clear.

Success–but now he remembered. This road had no outlet. His hollow heart was heavy now, sinking. He blinked salty sweat away and saw the yellow corrugated steel where the asphalt finished. Mike slowed and turned onto a small track through the trees. He followed the path, hoping he might find a place to turn into the pines, but, all too soon, he crept out onto open rocky ground. A parking place for awkward midnight fumbles, deserted in the day. The lake shimmered in the sun, deep blue and inviting, over ninety feet below. Ahead lay the cliff edge. Mike braked. This was not just a place for lovers. It was a place for losers. Those who had lost hope. For some, in desperate despair, this was the end of the road. Their exit was the rocks and water below. As it might be for Mike, who had no more cards to play.

The huge blue Dodge crawled out of the woods, taking its time. It straightened up, revved a predator growl, then came hard, smashing into the back of the car. The Elantra, with its 1.6-liter engine, was no match for the raw grunt of the Ram's 6.7-liter power plant, pushing it towards the cliff three hundred feet away. Mike had both feet on the brake pedal, but his tires just slid along the dirt. He selected reverse and gunned the engine, releasing the brake. For a moment, the movement towards the edge slowed, but the Ram engine roared louder, and the car inched towards the precipice again, faster now as the trunk crumpled. Desperate, Mike contemplated jumping from the car but knew he would be more vulnerable on foot. Whoever was in the truck had deadly intent and would probably be armed. He was running out of time and space. Space. There might be enough space. Barely. He slammed his left foot on the brake, selected drive. The car slid faster towards the edge.

He waited. Just a little longer. He released the brake and pressed his right foot to the floor. The Elantra shot forward, hurtling towards the cliff, rapidly being caught by the charging truck. Six car lengths, five, four. Mike took his foot off the gas, selected neutral, pulled the handbrake and spun the wheel. The car slid neatly through 180. He shoved it into drive, hit the gas, and shot back the way he came.

The truck braked, but even the ABS could not stop its forward momentum. The pickup slid to the edge. In the rearview, Mike saw it teeter for a moment, then topple over. He braked, threw the door open, and sprinted toward the cliff. The truck was in the water, sinking, rear wheels still spinning, sending waterspouts high into the air. He could just make out the driver slumped over the wheel. Must not have had the seatbelt fastened. *Serves the bastard right. The water will wake him up.* But it didn't, and the lake continued to swallow the pickup.

Mike ran to his left, where the cliff was not so sheer, and scrambled down. *Are you really going to do this?* He tossed his jacket, kicked off his shoes, and dived in. Almost all the cab was under water. He had never been a good swimmer, not since he shattered his shoulder when he was ten. This was a race against gravity and physics, one Mike could not win.

The tailgate slid under when he was still thirty feet away. He thought about diving, knew the lake was deep here, but decided to try. He made it maybe ten feet down before running out of air. The truck was still descending. He surfaced to grab another breath and saw three sets of ripples on the water. *No, no, no, no.*

Mike was twelve when it had happened. The fishing competition had been suspended, cut short by the boy's horrendous screams. Mike, Uncle Harold, and the other participants were confused until the boy's legs were dragged from the water, and they saw the deadly turmoil in his jeans. Someone spotted a thrashing tail, hauled it out and threw it, scattering the onlookers. Water moccasin. It slid through the tall grass with surprising speed back to the river. The boy's voice was almost inhuman, but it was drowned by the wail of approaching sirens. When the EMTs cut the boy's jeans away, three more water moccasins slid away. The boy stopped breathing.

Water moccasins. Aggressive, deadly, terrifying. Mike sucked in a large lungful of air, thinking he had time for one more attempt. But the ripples moved steadily in his direction, excited by the disturbance in the lake-water. Mike's courage fled, and he swam back to shore as gently as he could. The snakes passed ten feet to his right. He hauled himself across the rocks on hands and knees, panting, then retrieved his jacket. He dried his hands on the sleeve, pulled his phone from the pocket, dialed 911, and waited.

Mike sat handcuffed on a rock, drying uncomfortably in the sun. Police, fire department, EMS, all milling around, not sure what to do. It had been an hour now. Could someone survive that long in the cab? Acting Police Chief Harden Pletch pulled up in a cloud of dust and stone chips. He'd been bumped up after Wally Gates was put on administrative leave.

"What in hell's name is going on? Ain't nobody gone in after him yet?" he yelled.

Excuses and explanations answered him.

"Goddammit. Don't none of y'all ever read a damn manual. There's a protocol for this."

He grabbed his phone and walked around kicking rocks, waiting for an answer.

"SMART, yeah, this is Chief Pletch over in Tabor County. We got a situation here. A truck's gone into Tabor Lake. Uh-huh. One individual, so far as we can tell. Gotcha. We sure would be grateful. Two hours, huh? Well, I guess by that time we're talking recovery, not rescue. I understand."

He walked back to the awkward group, none of whom wanted to meet his gaze.

"San Marcos Area Recovery Team is mobilizing. Hope to be here in a couple of hours. Gotta get their team assembled and pick up the boat." He pointed across the lake. "One of you go over there, secure the launch ramp, and keep it ready."

He issued clear, concise orders, and cruisers took off to do his bidding. Mike was impressed. The acting chief marched his way.

"You're Carson, right? You want to tell me what happened here?"

"A truck tried to push me off the cliff. I got out of the way. He went over instead. I tried to get to him, but the truck was too deep."

Pletch looked dubious. "And why in the hell would someone want to do that?"

"Beats me."

"So... what? You're just sitting here admiring the view, and a truck tries to push you off the cliff?"

"No. The truck tried to run me off the road. It chased me here, then it tried to push me over the cliff."

"A road rage thing?"

"He had no cause to be angry with me."

"Recognize him?"

"No. Couldn't see in the rearview. It was a big blue Dodge Ram with a lift kit."

"Blue with a lift kit? Like metallic blue?"

"Metallic, yeah."

"Goddammit. Karter McMillan's truck most like. Goddammit to hell." He stomped away and dialed again, but Mike could not hear the conversation. Pletch returned.

"Just how in the hell did you Houdini your way out of being pushed over the cliff anyhow?"

"I did an anti-terrorist evasive driving course for one of my articles. I remembered what to do. Have you seen the back of my car?"

"Yessir, I have. It's consistent with your story. I'll take off these handcuffs if you give me your word that you'll stay put."

Duke McMillan looked distraught. He huddled with a group of officers, demanding action. There was nothing anyone could do. The recovery team was on the way. They had ordered up a long arm crane, which was due within the hour, although there was some debate about whether it could negotiate the narrow tree-lined road.

The conversation must have switched, Mike thought, because Duke looked at him every couple of seconds. He figured they were telling him what had happened. McMillan broke away from the officers and ran at Mike. *Here we go.*

"You bastard. What have you done?"

Mike avoided the roundhouse punch easily. McMillan had telegraphed it. Mike backed up as officers ran to get between them.

"I'll kill you, you lowlife drunk. If anything has happened to my boy..."

Oh, something's happened to your boy, alright.

The officers pulled Duke away.

"Don't go saying stuff like that, Mr. McMillan, threats and such."

"Get your hands off me." He turned back to Mike. "You're done, you hear me? Done."

They put McMillan in a cruiser immediately after the diver surfaced and gave a thumbs up to the SMART boat. They had found the truck. The black-and-white peeled away towards the launch ramp. McMillan didn't see the diver bob up again, thumbs down. He didn't see the lifeless form dragged from the water and hauled, ignominiously, into the Boston whaler.

A buoy marked the truck's location. The giant crane had successfully negotiated the narrow road, but pieces of broken branch and foliage littered the top of the vehicle. It maneuvered into position as the whaler, with its sad cargo, headed respectfully back towards the launch ramp. Mike heard the primeval howl clear across the lake a few minutes later. An animal sound, then—

"Zane!"–-screamed loud and long, echoing off the cliff face.

Not Karter.

Sam Washington arrived from Austin, as water cascaded from the Ram, suspended ten feet above the wavelets.

"What's your status, Mike?"

"Not sure. They had me in cuffs earlier. I've given my word I'll stay put till they tell me otherwise."

"Nice outfit. You should consider wrinkle free." He walked towards the crane.

It took another full half hour before the Dodge was on solid ground. Mike watched as they unhooked it from the crane. Sam conferred with two of the officers, pulled on a pair of nitrile gloves, and opened the driver's door. He jumped back as brown sludge threatened his Oxfords.

He opened all four doors of the crew cab in turn, examined everything inside, careful not to get any crap on his suit. He nodded, and the officers closed the doors. Willy's Breakdown winched the pickup onto a slanted low loader. Sam peeled off the blue gloves as he walked to Mike.

"You will not believe what's in that truck," he said.

CHAPTER THIRTY-SEVEN

SAM WASHINGTON PUT the used gloves into his jacket pocket.

"Don't leave me hanging. What's in the truck?" Mike said.

"Can't tell you," Sam grinned, "not officially, not at all actually, not even a little bit."

"Come on, man. Stop screwing with me."

"You can't print this, or even hint at it."

"OK. OK."

"There's a MAC 11 machine pistol, full auto, which is illegal, unless owned by a certified gun dealer, and I'm prepared to bet actual, real money neither of the McMillan brothers are certified dealers."

"I knew it."

"That there was a machine pistol in the truck?"

"No, no. I figured Adam Polley was shot with a MAC 11. It was the only thing that made any sense."

"And how would you know about a MAC 11?"

"Did some research out at the gun range."

"We'll know for sure real soon. Only problem is which brother owned the weapon? Could be either."

"At least you'll be able to establish it was the murder weapon, if it was."

"One of the weapons. There's still what we are assuming was a .357. Anyways, I gotta go. I'm heading back with the truck. Make sure there's no funny business at the station."

"What about me?"

"What about you?" Another grin. "I think Chief Pletch is playing with you a bit. He'll get bored with it soon enough. Just hang tight and be patient." He walked away, thought about something, and retraced his steps. "Did you get a sponsor yet?"

"Sponsor? Oh, for AA. No."

"How about me?"

"Aaah, I don't know."

"Think about it. Who else will call you on your crap?"

It took another hour before an apologetic Acting Chief Pletch handed him his phone and confirmed he could go. Mike got the usual warnings about not leaving the jurisdiction and was told to come to the station later to make a formal statement.

"What can I report about this?"

"From our point of view, the Taborville Police Department is investigating the circumstances of the drowning of a local man whose truck went into Tabor Lake."

"I can quote you on that?"

"Police department spokesperson."

"What about the rest?"

"Up to you. You were here. I'd be careful, though. This is a continuing investigation."

"Understood."

The Elantra was still drivable. Mike took it easy on the way back to town because the rear fender assembly looked like it could fall off any minute. He doubted Alamo would thank him if it dropped on the highway and caused another accident. He wasn't looking forward to explaining his second wrecked rental.

The phone dinged. A *Taborville Times* Facebook update.

TRAGIC ACCIDENT AT TABOR LAKE

Local businessman and philanthropist Zane McMillan has died tragically in an accident at Tabor Lake. The former football star was CEO of Horny Toad Couriers and drowned when the pickup truck he was driving went into the lake this afternoon.

Dozens of emergency personnel responded to a 911 call, including a dive rescue team from San Marcos.

"We have not yet established a full picture of how the truck ended up in the lake," said a Taborville PD spokesperson. "We are keeping an open mind, and appeal for witnesses to come forward if they have any information."

Police have not named the victim, but the man's father, Duke McMillan, confirmed his identity.

Tragic accident, my ass. Mike slammed the phone into the cupholder and headed to the *Times* office.

Cathy Ross jumped when the door flew open. Mike stuck the phone in her face.

"Are you responsible for this? Who fed you this crap?"

"Steady there, tiger."

"I asked you a question."

"I don't do angry." She pulled on her jacket. "If you'll excuse me." She moved towards the door.

Mike blocked her.

"Here we go. Big macho man, eh?"

"It's a simple question."

"Maybe I'll answer it when you stick your ego back in your pants." She stepped around him.

"I made the 911 call," Mike said.

"You were there?"

"Yes. I was there. And this story is pure crap. Zane McMillan just tried to kill me."

The Road King Bar and Grill had a back entrance and overflow parking lot where vehicles could not be seen from the street. The owners had reserved the front parking space for bikes. A cluster of Harleys looked disdainfully at their cheaper Honda cousins. A few Japanese sports bikes loitered a little farther off, respectful of the American iron. Rice rockets were tolerated here, but only barely. Anyone who entered in race leathers with their distinct, hunched crab walk could expect derisive snorts of laughter from the tattoos and doo rags at the counter.

The only access to the private dining room was via the rear entrance or through the kitchens. Xander VanDorn looked up as suspended Police Chief Wally Gates walked in. It was already five past the appointed time and Duke McMillan had not arrived. Xander's phone rang.

"Put me on speaker," County Judge Christian Taylor said. "You'll have to excuse Mr. McMillan. He won't be attending. He's had some terrible news, a death in the family. His son, Zane, just drowned in Tabor Lake." Shock registered on the faces around the table.

"There was a lot of chatter on the scanner this afternoon," Wally Gates said, "but I didn't know it was Zane."

"It is public now," Taylor said. "I've just seen it on the *Times* website. It appears Mr. McMillan is trying to direct the narrative. Tragic accident of local hero, etc." They all reached for their phones. "I have spoken to Mr. McMillan, and he is doubly upset, as it appears Mike Carson is involved in this somehow."

"Bastard," spat Wally Gates.

"Unnecessary and unhelpful, Mr. Gates. Gentlemen, we have a bigger issue at hand. I have ascertained, from Mr. McMillan, that the Aquifer Authority has refused an extension to the required permits." Dismay on the faces now. "It is therefore imperative the city votes in favor of our supply proposal at the next meeting. Is that clear?"

VanDorn, Brook, and the mayor exchanged glances.

"I'm not sure that's possible," VanDorn said. "It's one meeting too soon."

"There will be a first reading at the next meeting," Mayor Pryor said. "It can't pass until the second reading."

There was a moment's pause. Everyone focused on the phone in the middle of the table like it was some sainted relic with mystical powers, or perhaps something darker.

"There are sections in your charter which allow the mayor to combine first and second readings—is that not so?"

"Well, eh, yes. I believe so. I'd need to check," said the mayor.

"I just have."

"Doesn't it have to be an emergency circumstance?" said VanDorn.

"Please do not tell me that you, Mr. Brook and Mayor Pryor, cannot argue the critical nature of the proposal while Texas is in drought, and the very survival of our area is in imminent jeopardy."

"Navarro won't go for it," said the Mayor.

"No, she won't," VanDorn agreed, "and she'll pack the audience with her wild bunch of radicals to oppose it."

Another pause on the phone.

"Perhaps she won't be there."

"She hasn't missed a council meeting or workshop ever, even when she had surgery," the mayor said. "Not one."

"Even if she wasn't there, Mike Carson has been sniffing around enough to make a big deal of it," VanDorn said.

"Perhaps neither of them will be there. Yes. Neither of them there. Mr. Gates, you should pay a visit to Mr. McMillan tomorrow afternoon, convey your condolences, etc. He will have something for you, and I shall be in contact later with some thoughts on how to proceed. Take heart, gentlemen, the game is not lost."

The line went dead.

Mike woke at 4 a.m. desperate for a pee. For a second, he couldn't work out where he was. His head was beginning to throb, and someone had dumped cotton in his mouth. He closed his eyes, took a deep breath, and could smell the sex. Then he remembered. He looked over at the other pillow where Cathy Ross was sleeping quietly, the sheet tucked over her nakedness.

He sat on her toilet, remembering snippets. Mediocre food and great whiskey at The Copper Kettle and stories, lots of stories, which she loved. Lots of drinks and stories and admiring eyes and comforting hands and the nightcap invite back to her place and the delicious sweatiness on the bed and the welcome sleep that followed it.

You're a piece of work, Mike Carson, you know that? A real piece of work. Someone tried to kill me today. *But he didn't.* But he could have. *People tried to kill you before. You didn't lose your shit then.* This was different. *Yeah, this time you said you wouldn't drink.* I know, but...give me a break...asshole. *Prick.*

Mike didn't want to wake her. He got back into the bed and closed his eyes. He was grateful for the darkness.

He woke again to the sound of keys. Cathy standing beside the door in running gear.

"What time is it?"

"It's only 6:30 a.m. go back to sleep. I'm just getting my run in. I'll make you breakfast when I get back."

Mike didn't realize the phone in her hand was his. He closed his eyes and tried to drift off.

Duke McMillan thought she was a welcome distraction from the horror he was going through, bouncing down the road like that in her form fitting Lycra.

"Morning, Katie. You have something for me?" She handed him the phone. "What's the password?"

"785489."

"Look at you, secret agent. How did you get it?"

"Simple really...PULITZ as in Pulitzer. I saw him do it last night. What are—"

"You can have it back in forty-five minutes. I'll be right here," Duke said.

She looked a little distressed.

"Don't worry. Nothing bad is going to happen, Miss Magruder. Not to you. You've done the right thing."

Duke put the BMW in drive and pulled away.

CHAPTER THIRTY-EIGHT

MIKE WAS FRYING eggs when Cathy knocked. She wasn't smiling when he opened the door.

"Don't trust me in the kitchen, huh?" she said.

"Nah, it's not that. I just couldn't get back to sleep. Thought I'd walk downtown, pick up the car, come home, and get some fresh clothes."

"Right," she said, unconvinced. "Anyway, you left this at mine." She pulled his phone from her bag.

"I was wondering where that was. I thought I had it in my jacket pocket."

"Must have fallen out. I found it under the chair. See you later?"

"Yeah, maybe. Got a lot of calls to make. Now that I have my phone." But he was talking to an empty doorway.

Acting Chief Harden Pletch insisted on personally handling Mike's statement about what was being referred to as "the Tabor Lake incident." Mike recounted the sequence of events with as little emotion as he could muster. Officers had tracked down the SUV lady on Tabor Lake Road, who confirmed the story. As Mike signed the statement, Pletch shifted uncomfortably.

"I have to hold your vehicle," he said. "By rights I should not have let you leave with it yesterday, but I think we can keep that detail to ourselves, yes?"

"Sure. How will I explain it to Alamo, though?"

"I'll run you over there myself and have a little chat with them."

Reassured by the chief that the incident had not been Mike's fault, the Alamo agent produced another vehicle.

"I'll bet you're glad you took full insurance," she said. "You don't have much luck with cars, do you?"

As Mike climbed into an identical Elantra, he noticed a black Toyota parked on the roadway. He was almost positive he'd seen it outside the police station when he got into Chief Pletch's cruiser. One guy in the driver's seat. Watching. Mike eased out of the parking lot and headed back to the house. The Toyota followed. Mike turned left at the Cornerstore and back tracked towards the *Times* office. The black sedan stuck on his tail. Mike took a few more unexpected turns, and when there was no doubt he was being followed, he headed back to the house. He stopped at the four-way intersection, then sped through and slammed on his brakes just as the Toyota cleared the junction. Mike ran back, house keys jutting out between the fingers of his right fist, and hammered on the driver's window.

"Why are you following me?"

The furtive, little white-haired man seemed not much of a threat. He slid the window down.

"I'm sorry. You're Mike Carson, right?"

"Why are you following me?"

"I have some information for you."

"Who are you?"

"Joe Kass, Texas Water Conservancy League." He pulled a business card from the top pocket of his shirt. "Can you get in for a second? It's important. I'll drop you back to your car in a few minutes."

Mike weighed the risk, shrugged, and climbed in. Unless the guy had a gun, he should be OK.

Kass checked his mirrors constantly as he drove.

"You could have called me," Mike said.

"Didn't have your private number and coming to the *Times* was too dangerous."

"Forgive me for saying it, but all this is paranoid."

"When you've had as many death threats as I have, you can talk to me about being paranoid. These are powerful people. Dangerous people."

"Right. So, what do you have to tell me?"

"McMillan's consortium is planning to drain the aquifer."

"What?"

"The amount they are talking about harvesting every year is so far beyond the needs of the city. They've got to have a plan to sell it."

"Fact or speculation?"

"Fact about how much they plan to pump, but the rest is my guess. What I know is they need a contract with the City of Taborville to get their permits."

"OK."

"No end user, no permit. Their time is running out. The Aquifer Authority won't give them an extension."

"That's why they are pushing so hard."

"They are going deep, real deep. Could make shallower

wells dry up," he turned towards Mike. "These are corrupt people. You should ask yourself where's all the money coming from?"

"Eyes on the road, please. Why have you come to me?"

"I don't trust anyone at the city anymore. That place leaks like a sieve. It would come back on me. McMillan's lot need to be exposed. I've researched you and you could be the man to do it."

"How do you know you can trust me?"

"I don't. But I can always deny I spoke to you. You've made things up in the past. I checked."

"Ouch."

Mike gave Kass his cell number before being dropped back to his car. He shook his head as the little man drove away. *There goes a guy who might believe in a conspiracy or two.* But almost every conspiracy contains a grain of truth.

In the house, he dialed Nadia Navarro.

"I was wondering if we could meet," he said. "I've got some information that might be useful, and a few things I'd like to discuss."

"You can't tell me on the phone?"

"Not really, no."

"I'm out of town. Texas Municipal League meeting. I won't be back until late tomorrow afternoon."

"How about dinner, then? My treat."

"Dinner would be nice. I could do without cooking after the drive, but I don't accept gifts from constituents. I'll pay for myself."

"Fair enough. How about Walkers at seven?"

"Done."

At the end of the AA meeting, Mike followed Sam to the line for coffee. He took a pass on the stale cookies.

"Do we really have to do the coffee and chat thing?" he said.

"It's about the fellowship," Sam said.

"But the coffee is vile, and anyway, I need to talk to you about other stuff. Let's get out of here. Please?"

When they were settled in Romano's Little Italy, with good coffee and antipasti, Mike said. "You've got to admit this is better."

"Better food and coffee, but not necessarily better for your recovery. The program is as much about the people as the steps. Alcoholics understand you because they are you. They have made all your mistakes and more, besides."

"Look, I'm doing the meetings."

"Are you getting it?"

"I'm not drinking, am I?"

"Not this second," said Sam.

"Meaning?"

"Do you want to tell me you've been sober since the last meeting?" He waited. "I didn't think so."

"I had a few last night."

"More than a few, judging by the look of you today."

"Yesterday was rough, you have to admit. Not every day someone tries to push you off a cliff. And what is it I hear everyone say? I haven't had a drink today."

"Good. Try to keep it that way."

"I'm not dodging, but I need to talk about something else."

"What?"

"Adam Polley."

"Not sure what I can tell you."

"Any news on the MAC 11?"

"Are we on the record?" Sam said.

"Let's talk, and you can tell me what's on the record at the end. You know I'll respect it."

"The MAC is one of the murder weapons. Ballistics confirm it. Chief Deckrow can be very persuasive when he needs to be. NIBIN made it top priority. Problem is we don't know who fired it. The weapon was in Zane's possession but was in Karter's truck. Whose is it? We don't know."

"Why don't you ask Karter? Might be revealing?"

"Might be, but he says 'no' and what have we got? I prefer to talk to suspects when I have more in my pocket than they realize. Takes a little time, but it's more productive, and I love the look on their faces when they go *oh shit, he knows*." Sam laughed.

"What can I write?"

"Let's see...Investigators have established that a weapon recovered from the truck in Tabor Lake is connected to the murder of Adam Polley. No details on the weapon, understood?"

Mike nodded as he made notes. Sam was staring over Mike's shoulder at the wall, wrestling with something. Mike turned to look. Some print of an old bridge in Venice.

"What's going on?"

"The Bluebonnet thing," Sam said.

"Yeah?"

"It's going down soon."

Tantrums were not part of Duke McMillan's nature, but circumstances alter people. *That bastard Carson.* He looked at the screen again in disbelief and fired the phone at his office door so hard it cracked the glass. Pamela Patrick jumped in shock. The others had left on the dot of six, as usual, but she always kept Duke's hours in case he needed anything. Pamela moved towards his office.

"I'm sorry, Pamela, nothing to worry about. Slipped out of my hand."

Liar.

She spotted the cracked door glass. "I'll get someone in tomorrow to replace that."

"Thank you."

"Are you alright?"

"Yes, just some frustrating news I could have done without. Bad timing."

"If you need to go, I would be more than happy to put everything away and lock up."

"Would you? That would be a great, actually. A big help."

"My pleasure. I have a few things I need to finish up, anyway. It's no trouble. I'll just need the keys."

"Of course, and you know the codes?"

"Yes."

"Thank you." He pulled on his jacket and hat, marched out to his BMW, revved hard, and pulled away.

Pamela knew all about his frustration. The same alert from the *Taborville Times* online news had popped up her smart phone.

Weapon found in McMillan truck tied to Polley murder

Pamela had waited for this opportunity. She closed and locked the front door, drew the blind, collected the financial files, and headed to the copier. Her heart was pulsing faster and her temples throbbed with the beginning of a headache. She had never, ever, stepped outside her position of trust. She'd been loyal to a fault—her fault, her failure to understand the character of the man she had served faithfully for years. The boss who deceived her every day. She felt tiny slices of retribution with each scan of the copier. Pamela looked at the stack of documents she'd collected and hoped they were enough to nail McMillan.

The town of Winchester, Texas, was one of the earliest communities in Fayette County. Contrary to some of the tall tales told to visitors, the town was not named after the famed rifle, which played such a key role in winning the West. The first Winchester firearm didn't appear until almost forty years after the town had been established in 1827. Oliver Winchester, the future repeating rifle tycoon, was just a lad of seventeen in Boston, Massachusetts, at the time. The little settlement was one of over twenty-five in the United States, named after a cathedral town in Hampshire, England. At the dawn of the twentieth century, the community hosted eighteen businesses and thrived during the railway era of the locomotive. Highways and road haulers killed off Winchester's heyday, and it now had a population of just fifty. It was off the beaten track, far away from prying eyes—which was why Mike had picked it for the meeting.

He sat in the last surviving commercial building from those good old days. A store, built by German immigrant C.H. Schmidt in 1913, name and date immortalized in brick above the corrugated metal awning protecting the sidewalk. The faded pink building, with its red windows and doors, now housed Murphy's Steakhouse, an establishment known for great T-bones. Mike had taken a table opposite the old post office paraphernalia, remnants of the building's once vital function. When Pamela Patrick entered, he raised a hand to catch her eye. She was still dressed in her business suit and carried an elegant brown leather briefcase, which she placed discretely beneath the table as she sat.

"I'm glad you came," Mike said.

"I'm not sure how I feel about this. It's like being in some Cold War movie or something."

"Yeah. I'll bet it feels pretty weird."

"Can I trust you? Really?"

"You have my word. I understand what an enormous risk you've run, but I can't do this without you and if—"

"Oh, I want that man to get his comeuppance, believe me. It's just...he's already paying in terrible ways. With Zane, I mean. And now, suspicion on Karter. Was it you who wrote that?"

"Yes, it was. One or other of the sons is likely a murderer. There's no way of knowing which one yet. At the very least, the boys know who killed Adam Polley. The murder weapon was in Karter's truck. Seven bullets from that gun were in Adam's body."

"I'm embarrassed, I guess, and a little ashamed. I didn't know who these people really were. I guess that makes me naïve, a small-town girl."

"Nothing of the sort. They're very good at what they do. They've been fooling folks for decades. Seriously. Look, let's get some food into you. The steaks are excellent."

When they cleared the plates and brought the coffee, she lifted the briefcase onto her lap and pulled out stacks of copies. She handed them to Mike in sequence, explaining the relevance of each as he skimmed the pages. A low whistle escaped. It was a clearly curated roadmap to a dark and hidden secret. He looked up.

She forced a smile. "I guess this is what you needed."

CHAPTER THIRTY-NINE

JOSHUA SCROGGIN WAS AN EARLY RISER, always had been. The orchestra of nature started early outside town, each species with its solo. The roosters and the donkeys sang the verse, the horses and birds chimed in with the chorus. He walked onto his second-floor balcony, steaming cup of coffee in hand, and settled in his easy chair. He looked across Bluebonnet Road at the land that mocked him every morning. Beyond the abandoned Gerlich farmhouse, a low ground mist hung over on the fields, becoming clearer as the sky lightened.

There had been a handshake deal between old Gerlich and Joshua's father—the Scroggin family would have the right of first refusal to buy the land when the time came. But the Gerlich kids didn't honor the deal and sold to The Lignite Mining Company. Every morning the land shot him the middle finger. Fields that should be Scroggin land. But soon....

This was his favorite time of day, a time to reflect, a time to plan and ponder, no phones, no interruptions, the clock moving in lockstep with the natural order. Lesser humans laid abed and rose later to accept what was in store for them, blithely unaware that plans had been made for them while they snored.

We are so close now, he thought, *so very close to securing our future, so close to legitimacy.*

Generations of Scroggins had battled the land and tamed it, defied the Comanche and the Tonkawa, stood strong against drought and flood, brutal heat and merciless cold, had spit in the eye of road agents and Mexicans, the Union and its carpet-baggers.

Every generation had built and expanded. Until this one. Until it was under Joshua's stewardship. Duke McMillan, Christian Taylor, and the disastrous Magnolia Trails development had dragged them to the point of ruin. Joshua had endured the shame of selling some of the hard-won land to avoid bankruptcy and losing everything the Scroggins had built in Tabor County. But soon he would restore it and no one would know what a close-run thing it had been. There were still some obstacles, but the end was beckoning, and all would be fine. He smiled.

Joshua was savoring a second pour of fresh coffee when the soundscape changed, nature's song interrupted by the hammering of man. He stood and searched the skyline, ears guiding his eyes, until he saw them. Two dots in formation, just above the tree line. Helicopters moving fast. Coming straight at him.

In the lead chopper, Sam Washington activated his radio.

"All units, all units. Air One is two mikes out. Two mikes out. Execute. Execute."

In those two minutes, state troopers blocked three intersections—Bluebonnet and Weimar roads, Bluebonnet and Flores

Trace and finally, Weimar and Flores Trace. The old Gerlich farm was now totally locked by road.

A black, armored SWAT BearCat sped hard up Flores Trace, the 6.7-liter twin turbo engine hustling its bulk along. Approaching the disguised electronic gate, the run-flat tires arced left at speed. The gate was no match for 9,000 pounds of accumulating momentum and was ripped clean out of the earth, hauling twelve feet of hedge and concrete posts with it. The armored personnel carrier dragged the fencing to one side. Vehicles raced through the gap like Crusaders after a castle breach and headed for the farmhouse, shredding the ground mist as they hit the field. Drivers and crews involuntarily ducked as the helicopters skimmed over them. The choppers skidded towards the house, side doors open, teams ready.

Sam jumped from the lead chopper before it came to a halt and ran forward. Teams of DEA, FBI, and Texas Rangers had the building surrounded in under thirty seconds. Sam paused at the back door.

"DEA, FBI, open up."

Nothing.

"We have a warrant. DEA. FBI. Open the door or we breach it."

Nada. He nodded to the breacher. The rotten wooden door splintered, but the battering ram bounced backwards and put the breacher on his ass.

"Steel door," Sam radioed. "Bring up the BearCat."

The armored truck extended its twelve-foot battering ram. It maneuvered into position, set the circular end plate on the door, and revved hard. The door and the brickwork securing it disappeared in dust. FBI SWAT officers tossed two flash-bangs inside and followed quickly after the explosions.

"Clear."

One by one, the team cleared the rooms and the adrenaline

ramped down. The house was empty and looked as it might have when the last Gerlich had quit.

"What about the garage?" Sam asked nobody in particular.

"Clear," called a sergeant, "but signs of recent occupation."

Sam stepped down from the kitchen, took in the old sagging shelves with dried out bottles of half empty fertilizers. A few old license plates nailed to the wall. A single naked lightbulb hanging from the flyspecked ceiling. But the floor....

The floor was immaculate. Clean. Painted. He stamped his foot. And metal. Beside the door to the kitchen were two switches. He pressed one, and the corrugated garage door cranked up, climbing on well-oiled chains. More officers moved in once the door was fully open.

Sam pressed the other switch.

The entire room started to descend.

Sam's arm shot up in reaction, but the switch was already out of reach. They were on their way down to whatever awaited. The SWAT team reacted with practiced precision and kneeled, covering all four corners. The leader gestured Sam to do the same. They scanned continuously, weapons ready, hyper-alert as the floor crept down through dirt and rock and concrete reinforcing. They emerged in a cavern, dimly lit by fluorescents on the walls. Narrow-gauge railway tracks led into a tunnel at one side of the space. It had the feel of a large chapel—if they built chapels in the shape of igloos. The faint sound of generators whispered from the tunnel, and Sam noted the rails were shiny, recently used.

They were in the old lignite mine, had to be, but he'd never heard about caverns. A quick glance around told the story—what had been here was gone. Gone in a hurry. Sam got his bearings in the cavern, based on the farmhouse above. Below the front yard, stretching toward the road, was a large temporary platform, a bunch of eight by fours assembled on prefab legs, like stages in a convention center. Sam counted fifteen across the narrow end and four long. Almost 2,000 square feet of workspace. Littered around were empty cardboard boxes, some with Chinese symbols, discarded plastic wrappers, and other detritus.

"Touch nothing," he said. "Crime Scene will want to go over all this."

They settled onto another platform, about ten feet above the cavern floor, with a metal staircase. The SWAT team filed down the steps and spread out. Sam realized what they had been standing on was a large metal plate welded to the top of a giant scissor lift. He glanced up and estimated they were fifty feet below the surface. How the old farmhouse had not collapsed into this hole was a mystery. The SWAT team cleared the cavern, and on a signal from the leader, moved into the tunnel in two lines, hugging the walls. Sam clicked the radio.

"I'm heading topside for reinforcements. Got anything?"

"Nothing so far. We're moving slow. Making sure we miss nothing. It's a rabbit warren. High threat probability."

"Understood."

"We're gonna need some big ass lights down here."

Sam punched a large red electrical button on a plinth beside the scissor lift, and the platform rose. He was staggered by the scale of the place. Whatever had been down here must have generated huge profits.

The Crime Scene folk were organized and methodical. They identified and taped off the areas most likely to be evidence-rich. Next, they prioritized the scissor lift, and having recovered all they could, released it for use. Then they combed and cleared a staging area with space for a command post. The scissor lift went into constant motion, ferrying personnel and equipment.

Sam and the incident commanders from DEA, FBI, Texas Rangers, and Texas State Troopers became concerned when all radio contact with the SWAT team got patchy and then ceased.

"We need relay stations. They're out of range, most likely," the Ranger captain said. The team ordered up two ATV four-wheelers and some radio boosters. A couple of additional SWAT members straddled them and roared down the tunnel. It took a long time for one to return.

"The lead team must be three miles out now. We're going to need more people. Team leader says they can be regular officers. Doesn't appear to be anyone down here but us." He turned and headed back to rejoin the search.

The SWAT team emerged into daylight, five miles away, at the site of the original mine works entrance. They found a tiny locomotive and a chain of empty carriages. There were motor vehicle tracks everywhere.

"That's how they got everything out," Sam said, "and how they got people in unseen." The abandoned mine, and the land above it, was locked in litigation. The entrance was remote. He had to admit, it was damn smart.

CID Chief Wiley Deckrow arrived soon after the scene had been fully secured. He quickly got over his awe at the scale of what he saw and marched over to the command table.

"Which one of your agencies is harboring the traitorous bastard who tipped these assholes off?" he demanded. "Huh?"

Nobody had an answer.

"Best get to finding them."

"It's hard to keep something this big quiet, Chief Deckrow," said the Ranger captain.

"Are you serious right now, George? Really? That's what you're going to say to me?"

"Just saying there were a lot of moving parts, multiple agencies, multiple asset movements—"

"And one corrupt loudmouth who undid all our hard work. I want him found. Him slash her or they slash them, to be politically correct about it." He pulled Sam aside. "What do we know?"

"Not much, Chief."

"What do we think we know?"

"There's a good possibility the local drug store owner's kids are involved. They have the training, ability to get supplies, and there's a connection. They attacked Mike Carson when he was out here investigating."

"The journalist fella you unwisely brought to my office?"

"The journalist fella who tipped us off to this whole thing, Chief. From the scale of what you see here, this could account for almost all the opioid traffic in the state."

"Except we got nothing. Anything else?"

"Involvement by the McMillan family through the sons, and their courier company—Horny Toad."

"Anything tracking back yet?"

"Not so far. That big scissor lift is a $120,000 item, manufactured in Germany, sold to a corporation registered in Panama that has since gone out of business."

"God, I hate it when they're smart."

"We're trying to track how they got it down here."

"Keep at it." Deckrow looked around the cavern. "This is so damn disappointing."

Sam was uncertain for a second but spoke. "I'm not sure DEA is keeping us fully in the loop."

"What now?"

"It's just a feeling, but their guy has too much of a shit-eating grin for an operation coming up this empty. Like I say, just a feeling, but I think they might have something they're not sharing."

"We'll soon see about that."

"Go easy, Chief. You catch more—"

"Flies with honey. Yeah, yeah, yeah." He wheeled and stalked over to the command table. "Hey, DEA, front and center, we need to take a walk." When the offended supervising special agent joined him, Deckrow placed his huge arm around the guy's shoulders, and squeezed hard. "Are you holding out on me, son? You are, aren't you? Got something up your sleeve, you don't want to share with the class?"

"I've been instructed—"

"Instructed, my ass. You'd best fess up, son. Before this all goes the shape of a pear, because I can guaran-damn-tee you'll be digging through fish guts in Alaska looking for non-existent cocaine pretty damn soon. Do you know the attorney general, son? Or the DNI? Or the president? I didn't think so."

"We may have something."

"What may you have?"

"We're tracking vehicles from the courier company."

"And you didn't think to mention it?"

"It could be nothing."

"Or it could be the whole damn ball game."

CHAPTER FORTY

MIKE ALMOST LOST his footing when Sam pressed the button, and the garage floor descended. Sam's laughter exploded and Mike smiled in spite of himself.

"You could have warned me."

"Where's the fun in that?"

They dropped into the cavern.

"Sweet Mother of God," Mike said.

"Impressive, isn't it? Based on the preliminary evidence we've gathered, we reckon it's the largest opioid manufacturing facility we've seen in the state. There's evidence of fentanyl, some Chinese, some Mexican, which probably came in through McMillan's courier operation."

"But there's nothing here."

"Lots of trace evidence, enough to give us a pretty clear picture."

He gave Mike the quick tour. "Oh, you'll like this," he said, when they stood on the abandoned work platform. He punched a button. With a whirr of oiled chains, the drunken mailbox descended.

"Same basic technology as garage door openers."

"Where's everything gone?" Mike asked.

"Loaded onto narrow rail carts and hauled out to the mine entrance, transferred to a fleet of trucks and down the road."

"How did—"

"Tip off from someone, possibly a state trooper, although we're not sure. Could have been something as simple as our choppers and vehicles being spotted assembling at the airport a couple of days ago. Someone might have put two and two together."

"So, they are going to get away with it? Goddammit. Goddammit to hell and back."

Sam clamped a hand on his shoulder. "Oh, ye of little faith, do you really think we'd let that happen?" He looked around the empty space. "No one's here because the command post has relocated. These smart asses think they've got smooth away with it and now they're on the move, but, as my boss likes to say, we're on them like ticks on a hunting dog."

The blue-and-white Cessna 206 was anonymous. Cruising at 7,000 feet, its tail number and callsign could not be traced to the agency that owned and operated it. It had been equally anonymous when it was seized after landing on the Chihuahua Desert floor in Big Bend Ranch State Park, an area so remote and rugged it was called *El Despoblado*—The Uninhabited. The man who'd flown it was now in a seven by twelve cell at the Supermax in Florence, Texas, and the heroin and cocaine it carried were long since destroyed. The plane, having gone through the proper legal procedures, became one of the fifteen different types of fixed-wing aircraft and helicopters operated by the Drug Enforcement Agency. DEA Aviation Division had over a hundred aircraft, commanded and controlled from the Aviation Operations Center at Alliance Airport in Fort Worth.

The Special Agent Pilot and observer flew slow, intersecting right-hand circuits over Interstate 10 as they kept a visual on the convoy of courier vehicles heading east. Trackers on the vehicles were displayed on a screen in the cockpit. As operations went, this was smooth and routine, except for a slight diversion around Houston's international airport.

On the ground, nine unmarked agency vehicles had the small convoy contained. Innocuous SUVs and pickup trucks, for the most part. There were a few high pursuit vehicles—two BMW M4s and a hot AMG Mercedes, seized from drug dealers. State troopers were stationed near every off-ramp and leapfrogged each other on the service road to stay ahead of the courier trucks.

Karter McMillan hated being alone, and he was really on his own now. Zane was gone and Father wouldn't look at Karter, morphing like some freaking alien between mourning and murder. The Duke had completely lost his shit when they found the MAC in Karter's truck.

"You told me you got rid of it. Was I not specific? Was I not clear?!"

For a second, Karter thought Father might come after him, beat the crap out of him, and he'd have to take it. He wasn't Zane, didn't have his build or his temper. Or his balls. Zane would stand there and face Father down, make him back off. Father didn't know how to read Zane, how to judge when the volcano would erupt. Karter could decipher every little nuance of his half-brother's face and body language. He knew exactly where the boiling point was. He could poke and provoke Zane until he lashed out that moment before his temper completely took over. Karter would run then, yelling for help, and Zane would be in trouble. Karter loved the game—even that time he miscalculated and got his jaw broke—because he was the one in charge, pulling his brother's strings.

The only good thing about being alone was the music. He had Dixie Witch cranked to the max on the crappy van speakers, and he was banging along with them, on the dash, the steering wheel, the window. Jess ridiculed them, said they were a bunch of pathetic old men pretending to be rockers, but he really liked Trinidad's hard vocals and heavy drums. She was all about Cardi B. It was too much for him, not that he would admit it. All the flapping ass cheeks and tit waggling took the mystery away: it was full, Jess though. She agreed with Cardi—broke boys didn't deserve pussy. You had to have the Benjamins if you wanted to hang with Jess, and he did. He kinda wished she was with him, but she'd gone ahead with her brother Peter to get the new location ready. Maybe it was better she wasn't here. She'd be giving him earfuls of grief, too. What could he say? He really liked the gun. Gone now, along with his truck, and the Morel sound system and all the upgrades. He knew Zane took it to spite him. *That didn't work out for ya, brother, did it?* Karter looked at the speedometer and then his watch and wondered how much longer he'd have to be in this piece of shit van, driving the limit, at the back of the convoy.

In the command post, Chief Deckrow made a few calls while the DEA supervising special agent paced. Deckrow didn't appear to like what he was hearing. Sam worried a little about what might happen next.

"How is that even possible?" Deckrow asked. "I see. It

always comes down to that, doesn't it?" He ended the call. "Mr. Supervising Special Agent, sir. What exactly is your name?"

"Myles Carney, sir."

"Irish. Well, Myles, I've just been told this here task force is mainly funded by the DEA, which makes you, technically, in charge, whether or not I like it, which I don't. Sam and I sure would appreciate knowing a few things."

"I'll be happy to answer what questions I can."

"How are you tracking these vehicles and on what legal authority?"

"They are being monitored by air and ground, in a joint operation by DEA, Texas State Troopers, and the Texas Highway Patrol. As to the second question, that's a bit more delicate."

"In what way?"

"The authority comes from a warrant issued on foot of information from a confidential source. I'm not at liberty to say more."

"Confidential source," Sam said, "not confidential informant." He understood it right away. The DEA interest in McMillan went back a long way.

"They have an agent on the inside," Sam told Deckrow, "probably one of the drivers."

Carney said nothing. Bingo.

"Where are they headed?"

"East on Interstate 10,"

"How many?"

"Seven box trucks and a small cargo van."

"East," said Deckrow. "How far east?"

Carney walked back to his computer. "Coming up on Vidor."

"Jesus, that means they'll be at the state line in—"

"Twenty-five minutes," Sam said.

"Yes, that's our assessment."

"You're not stopping them?" Deckrow asked.

"Our strategy is to follow and find their new location."

"Oh, hell no," said Deckrow. "These guys don't get to leave the state. This is a Texas case."

"As you have acknowledged, Chief Deckrow, I have operational control here. DEA is grateful for the cooperation of our Texas partners. We're bringing Louisiana resources on board once they cross the state line."

Sam thought the special agent was about to lose some teeth, but Deckrow's meaty fist came up with a phone. Deckrow called the Governor of Texas. The gears of government grind slowly, but the pressure of politics can cut through obstacles as swiftly as a water cannon through a protest. It took seven minutes for Carney's phone to buzz. Within seconds, he was nodding.

"Yes, sir, I understand sir, yes, sir. Immediately, sir." He turned to his team. "Stop them now."

Karter McMillan noticed the trucks begin to slow. The convoy had been clipping along at a conservative sixty-five, not to draw attention. Maybe there was a wreck. When they slowed to forty, he got concerned. There was a sign for an off-ramp and the service road looked clear. He got off the highway. Maybe he could get far enough forward to see what was happening. He passed the box trucks as the highway traffic came to a walking pace. It must be a major accident, maybe a tractor trailer blocking the highway. He didn't notice the black Highway Patrol Dodge Charger on the service road behind him.

Karter climbed a hill, stopped at a traffic light and crested when the light turned green. About a mile ahead, blue and red flashing lights blocked all lanes. It was a massive roadblock. Now alert, Karter noticed the Charger behind him, maintained the speed limit, and looked for an exit off the service road. The patrol car maintained his pace, twenty car lengths behind. It might mean nothing. Coincidence. The contents of the trucks were legit. Machines and supplies being delivered to a registered pharmaceutical facility just outside Baton Rouge. Innocent, appropriate stuff. He glanced through the metal cage at the stack of brown cardboard boxes he was ferrying. Nothing innocent back there. Karter needed to melt quietly away from law enforcement with the contraband and rejoin the convoy later.

He saw a sign for Farm to Market 1442. The road would be narrow. Hopefully, the police cruiser would stick to the service road and pass by. He slowed, signaled, and turned onto the two-lane blacktop, passed a gas station on the right and a Dollar General on the left. He glued his eyes to his rearview mirror. No sign of the Charger. According to the signage, he was in Orange County, where they had built a convention center next to their stinky landfill. Weird. He went past both facilities into fields and scrub trees. Karter maintained a steady pace, constantly checking his mirrors.

The road took a big right-hand curve at the county veteran's office, and he became more confident. He wondered if he should make a call, but Father had been adamant. No live cell phones until everything was safely delivered and the vehicles were at least fifty miles from the Baton Rouge location.

More trees and fields meandered past, broken occasionally by dirt roads leading to houses. There were little clusters of them as the road moved left. He checked the rearview again. The Charger was there, closing fast. No lights or sirens but hammer down. Karter increased his speed. It could still be a coincidence. He went through an intersection, bumped hard across railway tracks, and passed a church. The Charger was gaining.

Another road appeared on his right. He took it at speed. The light-bars flashed on the Charger as it followed. Karter spotted a dirt road to his left and turned onto it, grinning. He loved driving on dirt and was good at it. He had Sprint Car Dirt Series trophies to prove it. The Charger got all serious and flipped on the siren. *As if I didn't know you were there.* Karter planted his right foot to the floor, flashed across a drainage ditch and was airborne for a second. He raced between two corn fields and decided to hang a turn as soon as he could. He saw it seconds later, two fields separated by another drainage ditch. First or second field? He picked the second, turned in and floored it. The Charger was struggling. Karter juggled the steering wheel and throttle, and the van slid hard left, perfectly controlled. But this was not a nice clay dirt racetrack like the three-eighth mile he ran in Houston.

Karter noticed the deep tractor ruts a fraction too late. Both his left wheels dropped into the ruts. The slide stopped immediately, but the momentum continued, and the van flipped on its side, slamming onto the barbed wire fence surrounding the field. A five-foot metal post pierced the thin skin of the cargo compartment and cut into three cardboard boxes. Karter was smashed against the driver's door. Suddenly it was Christmas. Everything was white. Once, he couldn't get enough, and now there was too much. He knew he shouldn't breathe and kept his mouth firmly shut as he tried to unbuckle his seatbelt. The seat was twisted and he scrambled for the red release button. The powder was everywhere. He almost gasped when the seatbelt released but resisted. He reached for the passenger seat and tried to pull himself upright.

Karter's lungs were burning, head pounding. His right foot was caught between the brake and accelerator. He reached down to free it, to pull his foot from the cowboy boot. It was too much effort for his remaining oxygen. In fatal desperation, he took a breath of Christmas. His heart rate slowed, his blood pressure dropped, the powder stuck to his clammy skin. He began to vomit. He noticed his fingernails turning blue before his eyesight dimmed. Then he stopped breathing. He had two words in his head before he slipped into the coma that would kill him within minutes.

Fucking fentanyl.

CHAPTER FORTY-ONE

WALKERS WAS A DISCRETE LITTLE PLACE, sandwiched between an attorney's office and a title company. High-end engraving on the brass plaque bolted to the ancient redbrick tried to give the veneer of a private dining club. Inside, the small, tasteful bar area was well stocked and served customers with gentility and respect.

The impeccably dressed maitre d' escorted Mike to his reserved booth in the cozy dining area. Fine starched linen, heavy cutlery, and wine glasses you could swim in. Mike wondered if the place could survive. From what he'd heard, locals did not frequent it because the owners were Californians and just a little too liberal.

Nadia arrived on the dot of seven. Mike rose to greet her, bounced his crotch off the table's edge, and plopped back onto the soft brown leather, which let out a suspicious puff of air.

A small guffaw escaped her.

"Oh, I'm sorry. I hope you didn't do yourself an injury."

Mike grinned and glanced down.

"I think all the vitals are intact."

She slid into the booth.

"Thank you for coming, Ms. Navarro. How was the drive?"

"It's Nadia—the usual I-35 mess, roadworks all the way. Anyway, I'm back in one piece." She picked up the menu. "Have you tried the surf 'n turf? It really is divine."

Mike closed his menu. "That's me decided then."

She ordered a glass of pinot grigio when the server came to take their order.

"And for you, sir?"

"I'll just go with the water, thanks."

"You don't drink?" Nadia said.

"Let's say it's a matter of debate at the moment."

"I'm intrigued. Who's winning?"

"If it was a political debate, I'd say it's too close to call."

"Fascinating. You must let me know how it turns out. I love a political thriller." Her smile was broad and extended to her eyes.

"Anyway," she said, "you wanted to discuss some things. I assume we are off the record."

"Of course. It's about the water."

She leaned forward, full of attention mode.

"I got a tipoff from a source, and I've been doing some checking. Reflow Logistics—that's the McMillan consortium—has an application with the Keller Aquifer Authority to pump 500,000-acre feet a year—"

"That's way more than—"

"Exactly, way more than the city needs. They obviously intend to sell it elsewhere." He watched the penny drop.

"San Antonio—has to be," she whispered.

"One of the fastest-growing cities in the nation. That would be my guess too. The thing is, they don't have a permit—yet. Can't get one unless they have a signed contract with an end user."

"The 'bargain' contract they offered to us."

"There's a time crunch. The authority won't give them an extension on their permit application."

"And there's the urgency. McMillan said they'd drill deep," she said.

"I remember."

"They'll suck our water out from under us, pump it off, make our own wells go dry, and then they'll be our only option. And you can bet your last dollar that's when they'll renegotiate the price. What a bunch of scum-sucking assholes. Sorry, that wasn't very parliamentary."

"Well, you're with friends."

She studied his face, took her time.

"I am, aren't I?"

"Yes," he said.

The lobster and filet steak arrived, accompanied by elegant slim fries sitting proudly in their own stainless containers, perfectly steamed broccoli, and five different sauces.

She approached her food with mannered determination. Savored every mouthful, but made quick work of it.

"How did you get into politics?" Mike asked.

"When my husband passed, I found myself with a lot of time on my hands."

"I'm sorry."

"Yes, prostate cancer years ago now. God rest him. Anyway, he made sure I was taken care of, didn't need to work. So, I had time to fill."

"If you don't mind me saying, you're a little fiercer, more of a crusader than filling time suggests."

She laughed.

"How rude. Me? Fierce?" she laughed again. "True, I guess. That comes from my grandfather. He was a real crusader back when fighting the establishment could get you killed. Brave man. What about you? The journalism?"

"My Uncle Harold, all my Uncle Harold's influence. I took after him, much to the annoyance of my father."

The conversation flowed through the crème brûlée, into coffees, and finally waned when the waiters hovered with more polite intensity. Mike realized they wanted to close.

Nadia insisted on separate checks. Outside, a gentle breeze embraced the street.

"I enjoyed that," Mike said.

"Me too. It's nice to have an ally in the press."

"Oh, I'm a neutral observer."

"Of course you are."

They both chuckled.

"I hope the information was useful," Mike said. "I'll keep you posted if I come across anything else. Good night."

"Ditto."

CHAPTER FORTY-TWO

ALL THE NEWS outlets in the Gregory Group ran with Mike's *Taborville Times* story. The biggest opioid drug bust in Texas history. A huge seizure of production items, pill-making machines, pharmaceutical raw materials, and fentanyl. The details in the story were breath-taking. Mike's words painted vivid pictures of the production lines in the secret cavern, the hurried escape down tunnels to a fleet of Horny Toad Courier box trucks, the aerial surveillance of the illicit convoy heading for the Louisiana border, the drivers unaware they were trapped in a complex, rolling roadblock. Eleven Mexican nationals had been arrested—men who, according to some sources, had likely connections to the Esperanza Cartel.

All of this had been happening within three miles of Main Street. Shockingly, for the town, the younger son of a prominent entrepreneur and philanthropist, Duke McMillan, had died in a police chase. Karter McMillan and Zane McMillan were both dead within days of each other, both in suspicious circumstances.

The Associated Press picked it up and within the hour, TV news crews from the local affiliates of ABC, CBS, and NBC had been dispatched from San Antonio. The CNN Dallas Bureau sent a crew and a national correspondent. They would arrive four hours behind the locals, but they were confident in their superior reporting. Fox News scrambled a crew from Dallas, too, while MSNBC relied on their local affiliate and the expertise of their anchors in New York.

Mike fielded calls from major papers and radio stations all over the country, including one from *The Philadelphia Inquirer*.

"Congratulations, Skippy," said Frank Wolfe, "that's a heck of a story."

"Thanks, man. Want a quote?"

"Nah. I already know it would be unprintable." He chuckled. "The boy is back," and hung up.

The next call shocked him.

"I always said you could throw a sentence together."

"Ron?"

"Good story, kid. Sounds like you got some mojo back. Imagine all that happening in your own backyard. I mean, what are the chances?" Ron Knowles paused, then, "How are you?"

"Better now. Sober."

"Very glad to hear it."

"Ron, I—"

"I'm sure you're up to your eyes. We'll talk." The editor of the *Los Angeles Times* ended the call.

Mike had first met Ron fifteen years earlier, shortly after joining *The Dallas Morning News*. Mike was a junior reporter on the team covering the trial of George Rivas, mastermind of the Texas 7 prison break, and subsequent murder of Officer Aubrey Hawkins. Knowles was sent by *The New York Times* to write features. He was known for detailed research. He read every report available before he wrote a single word. On the third day of the trial, he sat beside Mike in the press box.

"Mike Carson, *Morning News*, right?"

"Yes."

"Ron Knowles, *New York Times*."

"I know who you are."

"You have flair, keep it up. You can throw a sentence together."

Five days later, he gave Mike his card before returning to New York.

"If you ever need advice, call me." Ron slapped himself on his balding forehead. "Jesus, what have I let myself in for?" He laughed as he walked away. "See you down the road." He turned. "Keep learning."

Mike got in touch about once a year to maintain contact. It took seven years before one call changed his life.

"How are you doing, Mike?" Ron said. "I've been keeping tabs. You kept learning."

"Thank you."

"Reason for the call. I'm at the *Chronicle* now, and some idiot thinks I should run the news desk. Long story short, one of my guys deserted to the *Post* in Washington, and I'm wondering how you'd feel about coming to New York? Salary is not great to start but there are benefits and opportunities, and I'm sure it's more than you're making at the *Morning News*. Oh, and we pay moving expenses. No pressure."

Mike accepted in a heartbeat, gave notice to his pissed off editor, and prepared for his move to the big time. New York. The city of dreams. And nightmares.

Holly chose Longhorns for their catch-up meeting. Mike would have preferred somewhere more discrete, but she was insistent. She would not hide from anyone. Mike sipped his coffee.

"So what are you saying?" she asked.

"One of the brothers shot Adam, but they don't know which. Might never know for sure. Not that it matters. Both of the bastards are dead."

"All deaths matter. You know that. They were still the Lord's children."

"I'm not sure the Lord would claim them. I can't believe how calm you are about all this. One of those two evil fu—people shot your husband. Those two are devil spawn."

"Don't you say such a thing, Mike Carson. Jesus loves the sinner, even if he hates the sin. We must find forgiveness in our hearts."

"Both of those lowlife vermin tried to kill me. Zane killed my brother. I have no forgiveness for that. I hope they rot in hell, if there is such a place. I'm glad they're gone, and I'm delighted that McMillan is suffering."

"Your soul is in mortal danger if you continue down this path." She skewered him with an intense stare. "What you are saying now is an invitation to Satan. You might as well say, 'Come and take my soul.'"

"He's welcome to try. Bring it on. Do your worst."

"Don't."

"Don't what?"

"Do not tempt the Devil. He will find you."

CHAPTER FORTY-THREE

MAYOR PRYOR SCHEDULED a press conference for 3 p.m. The city's PR company assured him it would give the TV affiliates time to package their pieces for the early evening news. His phone buzzed a minute after the announcement was posted across the city's social media pages.

"Have you completely lost your mind?" hissed Xander VanDorn. "I'm the mayor pro-tem, and you didn't think to call me? My God, you are dumber than a San Juan brown trout and that—"

"How dare—"

"Look Bill, you're mayor because we put you there. Stop trying to do things you aren't equipped for. Now is not the time to think for yourself."

"Why are you so upset? We have to hold a conference."

"Of course we do, but we don't have to wait till CNN and Fox News get here to do it. We don't have influence there. They won't be asking softball questions and, from now till then, we'll have local news crews all over town, turning this into a bigger thing than it needs to be. Duke tells me there's a crew outside his office right now."

"He only has himself to blame for that."

"Excuse me? What did you just say?"

"Nothing. Nothing."

"This concerns us all. All. Understand? The future of the town is at stake. Make no more decisions without me."

Duke McMillan didn't know why he had come to work, but he had to get out of the house. The pain fit him like Lycra and the leaden lethargy was worse, but he couldn't bear to look at his wife's impassive face. She was mother to neither of his boys—his poor, lost sons—and she was about to divorce him, anyway. He hadn't slept. The police had questioned him for hours, but he'd held his nerve and been careful with his answers. He could tell they didn't buy it. Surely, he had to know what his sons were up to? But they couldn't prove a thing. Not yet.

He looked around his desk, picked up random pieces of paper, stared at them for minutes at a time, and put them down again, unsure. How long had he been here? Hours and nothing to show for it, not a single thing accomplished. He picked up an invoice, pulled the check book from his desk drawer, reached for a pen. *Pay to the order of*—he copied the name from the invoice, filled in the amount. *For*—for what? He looked at the invoice again. *Services.* What services? He pushed the invoice away and returned the check book to the drawer. Damn woman could have tried to pretend she cared about them—the boys, him.

The TV crews outside were getting bolder. They fired up their lights and were trying to shoot through the windows. The office staff was freaking. He'd seen the shock on their faces when they arrived and realized he was there. They kept sneaking looks towards the window in his office, expecting something, an explanation maybe. He couldn't make sense of it himself. Best to give them the day off and close the office. He needed to get out of the building—without going through the media scrum. There was nothing he could say to the cameras. They'd see him broken if he spoke, and he had no intention of giving them that guilty "avoiding the media" footage they loved to show. He called Pamela.

"Can you move my car into the back alley? I need to get out of here."

"Of course, Mr. McMillan, no problem."

"And could you close the office for me?"

"Sure. I'm so sorry Mr. McMillan, it's awful."

"I know, thank you."

"I'll need the keys."

He handed over the keys to the BMW and the office.

Pamela stopped outside and waited till the reporters quieted down.

"I'm going to get some coffee for the team," she said. "Would you like some? I should tell you—you're wasting your time here. There will be no statement."

None of the journalists took her up on the offer of coffee, nor believed they were wasting their time. She walked calmly across the road to McMillan's BMW. After circling the block, she slipped down the side of the old bank building and parked behind the office where Duke was waiting, peering through the cracked doorway. She left the engine running.

"Thank you, Pamela. I'm grateful. No need to let anyone know..."

She nodded and he drove away. Pamela completed the charade by returning down Main Street, holding four coffees in a cardboard tray, smiling at the cameras as she entered the office. She dismissed the staff, warned them not to utter a single word to the press, and closed and locked the door behind them.

"Where's Duke McMillan?" yelled one reporter.

"Not here."

She turned off the lights in the main area, drew the blind on the front door, and retreated to Duke's office. She hefted the keys and wondered what other evidence she could find for Mike.

The news teams roamed the town like jackals in search of prey. Each of them turned up at Bluebonnet Road, where crime tape, police cruisers, and taciturn officers barred the way to any decent pictures. All requests for access to the now-infamous cavern were denied. "Active crime scene" was the excuse from all agencies. They rolled footage of the deserted Horny Toad Courier building and the state troopers guarding it. Requests for interviews with local, state, and federal officials were denied, and reporters were directed to the press conference where, they were assured, all agencies would be represented. The TV teams filled their time by stopping random people on the streets.

"I had no idea."

"It's such a shock."

"A terrible thing for the town."

"You people are disgusting."

Even a few "fake news."

Mike was holed up at Uncle Harold's fielding phone calls. He was forced to get very specific about what he would, and would not, talk about on the radio. The longer interviews wanted to talk about him, rather than the story, and that led to questions about him being fired from the *Chronicle*—and related questions he was not prepared to answer. He picked up the next call. Quintin Smith, from the *Times.*

"I've been asked to ask you to stay away from the press conference."

"Who's asking?"

"The city, my boss, me."

"Why?"

"People are concerned you'll get questions about what else you're investigating here."

"How is that a bad thing for you?"

"You've had a lot of leeway."

"Meaning?"

"For God's sake, just don't turn up."

"I'll think about it." Furious, Mike realized he desperately needed coffee. He opened the cupboard. Empty can. *You have got to be kidding.*

Mike put on a pair of loafers and walked to the Cornerstore, noticing the huge headlines on the paper racks as he walked in. He nodded at the surly cashier and went in search of coffee. When he came back to the counter, red can of Folger's in hand, and reached for his wallet, a gravelly voice interrupted.

"You're the Carson boy, aren't you? The one who went east." The flimsy stool holding this gargantuan was straining. Larry Lomax, longtime city council member, termed out but still desperate to be mayor someday. Even his good friends referred to him as Jabba—behind his back. The retired bus driver divided his time between the Cornerstore and Scroggin Drug Store, Taborville's primary gossip centers.

"Yeah, Mike Carson, pleased to meet you." He extended his hand. Lomax folded his arms across his man breasts.

"Shoulda stayed out east. We don't need your kind here."

"And what kind might that be?"

"Goddam, interfering troublemakers." He pointed at the newspaper rack. "We don't need this kind of shit associated with our town."

"Then maybe you shouldn't have this kind of shit going on."

"Why don't you take yourself back to where you came from?"

"Why don't you go screw yourself?"

He paid and left but heard Lomax's parting comment.

"That boy never had no manners. Not like his brother."

CHAPTER FORTY-FOUR

THE PACKED press conference at Taborville City Hall went wrong almost as soon as it began. Mayor Pryor had just introduced Chief Harden Pletch when a question interrupted the prepared flow.

"Isn't Pletch the acting chief? Where's Chief Gates?"

"We'll be taking questions at the end of the press conference. Thank you," the mayor said.

"Is he still on administrative leave?"

"Yes, Chief Gates is on administrative leave, but that is regarding a different matter."

"I thought it had to do with the Polley murder," the reporter continued.

"Correct, now—"

"Which was drug-related, according to the Taborville Police Department statement."

"As I say, we'll be happy to take questions at the end."

"Is the Polley murder related, or not?"

A CNN producer shut the reporter down. She pulled him aside, reminded him they were live and to quit grandstanding.

He didn't want his name added to a "never call for comment" list.

Acting Chief Pletch was blunt and very brief. Sam Washington stood to one side of the council chamber, well out of camera view. His boss, Wiley Deckrow, told the assembled press those bits of the story he was happy to make public. He handed over to the FBI and DEA for the juicy details. The FBI senior agent in charge's description of the events was dry as desert air. He concluded by saying all further updates would come from Dallas.

The reporters' questions were endlessly repetitive and ultimately unproductive. No more details were forthcoming. The mayor stepped up again, thanked the journalists, then the line of spokespeople filed out. The nation's press was unlikely to be back in this room again.

Sensing her opportunity and noticing there were still red transmission and record lights on some cameras, Nadia Navarro walked past the podium and addressed a seemingly private remark to the mayor, loud enough to be picked up by the microphone array.

"I guess we only have the water scandal to deal with now."

When she emerged from city hall twenty minutes later, some reporters and crews were waiting.

"Council Member Navarro, what did you mean by the water scandal?"

"Oh, I'm sorry. I didn't intend for anyone to hear that. I may have misspoken. 'Water situation' would be a better way of putting it. It's just the city is being put under a lot of pressure to strike a deal with a specific water supplier without being given an opportunity for due diligence. It concerns me."

County Judge Christian Taylor watched the broadcast from his office. He had declined an invitation to attend. It was a matter for the city, he said. Taylor was not an emotional man. It served no purpose. Setbacks were part of every ambitious enterprise, and there were no straight paths to any worthwhile goal, but he was getting concerned now. He unlocked a desk drawer and picked out one of three phones in a zipped plastic bag. He inserted the battery and SIM card and dialed.

"We're running out of time," he said. "We need to get this mess cleaned up."

Disinvited from the press conference, Mike sat in his rental car looking out at Tabor Lake. The biggest story to hit Taborville in decades and he couldn't even be there to follow up. The emergency bottle of Bulleit twelve-year-old sat on the passenger seat. Mike picked it up, studied it. It was a solid, smoothed rectangle. A no-nonsense bottle but refined, nonetheless. None of the ostentation of Willet Pot Still or Blanton's. A man's bottle. He couldn't wait to taste it.

He carried it to the cliff edge and sat. Tabor Lake was troubled, waves unsure where to go in the shifting winds. *Just like me,* Mike thought. *They don't want me here, doing my thing, digging into their underwear and finding the soiled places.* The town was full of Larry Lomaxes, who relished the simple comfort of a blind eye. *And here I am peddling truth which is definitely not as tasty as the snake oil.* He was angry at Quintin. *I've given him the story of a lifetime, for free, and I don't get to be there.* Intellectually, he understood the pressures on the young editor, but a better man would have fought. A Ron Knowles would have fought. Back before....

Quintin didn't really appreciate him, but Mike supposed it

was hard to put a value on a service when it's free. Truth be told, Taborville wasn't a place he'd ever felt appreciated. This was Andy Carson's town—Mike was the insignificant little brother. Who Mike was or wanted to be meant little here.

The wind was getting up, whipping the confused waves into white caps as the gloom descended. "Storms a-comin'," Uncle Harold used to say. And he was always right.

Fisher Creek Mall was a fraud. Fifty-thousand square feet of retail and office space built to serve the Fisher Creek subdivision but never opened. The mall was maintained in pristine condition—the grounds mowed and manicured, parking spaces repainted every year, windows washed. Move-in ready, according to the glossy advertisements, but rental space was cheaper in Manhattan. The mall was a gigantic tax loss designed to offset obscene profits from the development of the subdivision itself.

A small, unnamed creek flowed through the land, which had been part of Merit Cottle's family ranch for generations. The soil was too poor for grazing and had been colonized by Texas sage, mountain laurel, and prickly pear. All it did was push up their property taxes and provide the Cottles with a little distance from the noisy highway. Merit applied, unsuccessfully, for commercial zoning nine times in fourteen years. It shocked him when Duke McMillan and Christian Taylor made an offer on the acres and accepted their modest check before either of them changed their mind.

Three months later, the entire tract was rezoned for single-family housing and associated commercial. The injustice of it literally killed Merit Cottle, brought about the stroke, and then the aneurism. He raged until the end, stuck in his wheelchair, a tough but kindly man consumed by anger.

Nadia Navarro only knew this from stories. She'd met Cottle once, at a fundraiser for the Food Bank, where he always gave generously, but Merit was bitter by then.

She shouldn't have come here, didn't know what the hell she was thinking. She knew better and wouldn't have considered it for a single second if the message had been from someone else. It was not her habit to trust strangers, although he was hardly a stranger now. They'd had dinner. The wind whistled in her part-opened window and some leaves flew past, horizontal. She didn't like this, not one bit, parked in back of the mall, hidden from the highway. Alone. Vulnerable. But the town was in jeopardy. She owed it to the people she represented, needed to be fully informed so she could fight. Instinctively, she knew this would be the biggest battle of her political career, one she could not afford to lose, one the town could not afford to lose. She looked at the message again.

```
Essential we meet.
Info on the water plan.
Documents.
10.15 back of Fisher
Creek Mall.
```

She understood the need for discretion, but this cloak-and-dagger stuff made her uneasy. She had come a little early, despite her misgivings. Tardiness was just plain rude. She lowered her window farther for a moment and listened to the traffic whizzing by on the highway. Minutes stressed past. The dark claustrophobia of night worried at her with scratchy little fingers. She switched on her high beams, picking out the clean industrial dumpsters that had never been used.

Where the hell was he? Anxiety crawled around her back like a cluster of spiders. Something flashed across her lights. Coyote? Fox? She closed the window. She would stay five more minutes. Maybe four. *What the hell was she doing?* She fired up the engine and turned the car to face the entrance from the highway. Two more minutes.

Finally.

Another set of headlights came around the side of the mall. *Thank God.* Nadia killed her high beams, but the other car didn't. She lifted her arm to shield her eyes. The white glare persisted as the car drew beside her, driver to driver. The window lowered. She hit her down button. Nadia couldn't quite make out the face in the shadows and squinted. A hand extended, offering her something. She reached for it and hesitated. It wasn't a document; it was something snub and black.

CHAPTER FORTY-FIVE

SERGEANT GREEN REACHED for the ignition in the unmarked car as they saw the suspect trotting down the steps.

"Let him go," Acting Chief Pletch said. "It will be easier to search if he isn't there."

He picked up the radio. "You got ears, Brown?"

"Yes, Chief."

"Follow and stick with him. Let me know where he's going."

"Chief."

Brown's cruiser went past, following the suspect down the street. Five minutes later, Brown reported.

"He's at Longhorns. Having breakfast, looks like."

"Stay on him," said Pletch. He turned to Sergeant Green. "Let's go."

They made a big show of announcing themselves with a loud hailer before they broke the door down. Neighbors spilled onto front yards to watch. Pletch walked from room to room. Nothing. Three officers combed through the outbuilding. Zilch. Pletch was pacing the yard to work off his frustration when he saw it—an access hatch beneath the porch. He looked around and spotted a young, fresh-faced officer.

"Hanson, get yourself under there, son. Be thorough, now. Get the big Maglite."

Minutes later, Hanson called out.

"Got something, Chief."

"Don't touch it till the crime scene boys get down there."

Diners heard the approaching sirens get louder. Must be a big wreck somewhere. Or a fire. Louder and louder. The sirens stopped mid-tone, but the walls and ceiling of Longhorns pulsed in strobes of blue and red. Moments later, police crashed in through the front entrance, weapons drawn, and banged through the kitchen service door in back. Some diners threw their hands up in automatic response.

"Everyone, stay seated," Sergeant Green called in a strong, authoritative voice. "Nobody move."

The officers behind him echoed his instructions. Green scanned the room and fixed his eyes on a booth in the corner. He nodded left and right. The officers threaded through the tables to the booth.

"Hands on your head. Now."

The man dropped his fork into the eggy hash browns and complied. Two officers covered him with a Mossberg and a Glock while Green pushed him forward, snatched his hands behind, and snapped the cuffs.

"Michael Carson, you are under arrest on suspicion of murder."

It had been two hours. Mike was sick of this familiar interview room where they had him sat on the same chair, handcuffed to the same desk. They should charge him rent. He had not spoken a word, nor had anyone else. They were letting him stew. Standard police tactic and a good one. His mind was racing. Were they trying to pin Adam Polley's murder on him? Possible, but unlikely. Sam had taken over that case and they couldn't make arrests without him. Someone else. But who? Holly? Jesus, please no. Had they got to her again? Unlikely, since she was on her guard now, as were her friends and neighbors. Plus, she had reported the first attack, given descriptions. But maybe they came back to shut her up, or one of them did. Except he couldn't be mistaken for any of her previous attackers, could he? Hopefully not Holly. Cathy Ross? Possible, but why? Shit—

Duke McMillan.

He had motive and history and witnesses to swear to their animosity. Who would want Duke dead? Jeez, who wouldn't?

When did it happen? Did he have an alibi? Not for last night. Or the night before. Crap. Calm down. Useless to speculate. But murder. It was a death penalty in Texas. And the governor had no hesitation about it. They freakin' loved it here. The more the merrier. Judicial killing by the hundreds, five times more than any other state in the Union. Five hundred and sixty lost souls in forty years, mailed back to their maker. Some of those souls were atrophied by anger, shrunk by sin, but not all. At least nine had been innocent. Getting strapped down and dispatched for a crime you didn't commit was more than possible in the Lone Star State.

The door banged open. Two guys in suits. One stocky dude with military hair. The other an overweight wheezer, asthma most likely, maybe COPD, too. Stocky stood and Wheezer flopped onto the chair.

"I'm Detective Sergeant Stevens," Wheezer said, "and this is Detective Delaroza. We have a few questions."

Taborville could afford detectives now, apparently.

"Lawyer," said Mike.

"Pardon?"

"You heard me. Lawyer. John McKinney."

"You don't want to go that way, Mr. Carson. We just need to clear a few things up."

Mike turned and looked at the wall.

"OK," Wheezer said, "it's your funeral."

McKinney arrived an hour later. The door clanged behind him and locked.

"Have you said anything?"

"Of course not. What's going on?"

McKinney paused, not sure how to put it.

"Nadia Navarro was murdered last night."

The words hit like a blue norther and froze him to the marrow. Breathing became a willful thing, a conscious effort to survive. Gradually, understanding thawed the words and melted them through his eyes

"Jesus Christ."

"Shot twice in the face. They are probably going to charge you."

"Me?"

"Listen—"

But he wasn't. He could hear words that made no sense, familiar phrases he often reported but had not absorbed, sentences whose magnitude he had never understood.

"—evidence. Got a warrant and searched your house this

morning. Say they found a gun, same caliber, recently fired. They're convinced it's the murder weapon."

"A gun? I don't own a gun."

"Good to know. Nothing registered in your name?"

"No."

"Helpful, but they seem convinced you're their guy."

"Why? Why would I do that? Why would someone... She's...she's, you know... an extraordinary person, brave...oh my God."

"She was."

Mike looked up at Honest John's blurred face. The man was embarrassed.

"Sorry, it's hard to grasp." Mike swallowed hard. "What now?"

"Where were you last night? She was killed around ten."

"I was out at the lake."

"Why?"

"Thinking about stuff."

"Anyone see you?"

"I don't think so."

"They're going to hold you till they get ballistics back. You'll probably be here for seventy-two hours, the max."

"Three days?"

"Looks like." Honest John scratched his stubble. "I don't like this."

Mike was listening now, and these were not the words he hoped to hear. He needed to hear everything was going to work out fine. Nothing to worry about, just a big mistake. Honest John lifted himself out of the chair, walked to the door, and knocked. While waiting for the lock to turn, he adjusted his Stetson.

"I really wish you had a solid alibi."

CHAPTER FORTY-SIX

THEY HOPED the case would be assigned to Judge Cartwright. Honest John had described him as an affable and considered man, much loved by the community. Instead, they got Judge Neiman, who was notoriously irascible, and who was reputed to have sentenced his own son to five years for petty theft—the judge being white, the son being Black and the relationship never having been acknowledged.

Mike wriggled nervously at the defense table and glanced over his shoulder. Word had spread like a California wildfire. The small courtroom was packed. There were even people standing along the walls. The mayor sat next to the county judge. Sofia Navarro, Nadia's sister, was in the first row, much too close for comfort. Her laser anger targeted him with precision, although it was Honest John who caught the spittle and had to wipe his jacket when he sat at the table.

Holly sat two rows farther back and gave him a wan smile. Mike spotted Levi Forrest by the wall. Juan and Rosa Alvarez sat on the left of the courtroom and appeared to be praying. Mike's eyes were drawn to the middle of the room, more by sense than movement, where Duke McMillan sat and stared with unabashed hatred. Quintin Smith and Cathy Ross perched at a small press table. They had added a larger one for the six out-of-town reporters. Quintin was impassive, professional. Cathy had her head down, tweeting. Sam Washington stood at the back.

The court was gaveled into session.

"Michael Carson's counsel has asked for an examining trial," Judge Neiman began. "This is his right under Article 16.01 of the Texas Code of Criminal Procedure. We are here to examine the truth of the accusation brought against Mr. Carson, prior to an arraignment or grand jury inquiry. Evidence given shall be recorded and offered at any subsequent trial."

District Attorney Bryan Paxton got to his feet. "Your honor, this is an extremely serious case. The heinous murder of a public official, a member of our city council, a woman who was lured to her death while performing her civic duties by the accused, Michael Carson. The facts are these." He looked around for emphasis. "Council Member Nadia Navarro went to Fisher Creek Mall in the mistaken belief the accused would give her information about matters of critical importance to the city. She was, instead, brutally murdered, shot twice in the head. She died instantly at the scene. Evidence obtained from the council member's phone resulted in a search warrant for a house owned by Mr. Carson. During the subsequent search of those premises, a weapon—a Glock 19—was recovered. Forensic analysis has confirmed this weapon was used to murder Ms. Navarro. Police took the accused into custody immediately following the discovery of the weapon."

"Murderer." Sofia Navarro's voice was broken anguish.

"Quiet," Judge Neiman ordered. "I will not have outbursts in the court."

Sergeant Oliver Green, the first officer on the scene, took

the stand. He responded to a 911 call of shots fired at Fisher Creek Mall, where he found a deceased female in her early fifties in an SUV behind the mall. He recognized the individual as Council Member Nadia Navarro. When Green completed his testimony, Honest John rose.

"Sergeant Green. Was there anything unusual about the 911 call?"

"I didn't get the call. That would be dispatch. I just responded to it."

"Who made the call?"

"I was told it was a male caller who refused to give a name."

"Would you describe the Fisher Creek Mall as isolated?"

"I suppose so, yes."

Honest John thought for a moment. "What is the nearest building to the mall, in your estimation?"

"Probably the Texaco station."

"On the other side of the busy highway."

"Yes."

"It didn't strike you as odd that gunshots were heard from a very isolated location, beside a busy highway, with a lot of traffic noise?"

"No, it did not."

"Fisher Creek Mall has never been open for business, isn't that correct?"

"So I believe."

"Has it ever been vandalized, to your knowledge, in the ten years it has been vacant?"

"Not to my knowledge, no."

"Why do you think that is?"

"Calls for speculation," said Bryan Paxton.

"Apologies, Your Honor, quite right," said Honest John. "Let me rephrase. Sergeant Green, I don't know about you but I'm a bit of a looky-loo, and I have to admit I have driven around Fisher Creek Mall," he turned towards the audience, "wondering, like most people in town, I suspect, why it never opened for business." There was a little ripple of agreement. "In fact, I went out there yesterday. I couldn't help noticing all the surveillance cameras. I counted fifteen. Are you aware of those cameras, Sergeant Green?"

"I am."

"Did you attempt to retrieve surveillance footage from those cameras for the night when the unfortunate Ms. Navarro was murdered?"

"We did."

"Can you produce that footage?"

"No. The surveillance system malfunctioned that night."

Little intakes of breath from the audience.

"Was it working the night prior?"

"Apparently."

"And the night after."

"I can't speak to that, but I believe the fault was rectified."

"Interesting," said Honest John, looking directly at the judge, then at the court before sitting down.

Wheezer—Detective Sergeant Stevens—lumbered into the witness box. He had found the council member's phone and the message on it directing her to Fisher Creek Mall for the fatal rendezvous. The text had come from Mike Carson's phone. Mike's head dropped. He was responsible. She was dead because of him. He wished he'd never met her, had never come back, hadn't started digging. Honest John rose.

"Pretty damning evidence, don't you think?" he said.

What the hell, aren't you supposed to defend me?

"That's for a court to decide," the sergeant wheezed.

"Quite true. The police department has Mr. Carson's phone, correct?"

"Yes."

"And you have found a corresponding text from Mr. Carson's phone to Ms. Navarro?"

"No."

"How do you explain that?"

"He probably deleted the text."

"Or possibly never sent one." Honest John moved closer to the witness box. "Have you sought information from the cell phone providers?"

"Yes."

"What does it tell you?"

"We have not received the information at this point."

"I see." Honest John towered over the witness box, and his tone hardened. "Have you considered the possibility my client's phone may have been cloned?"

"Not really. It's highly unlikely unless someone could physically get hold of his phone, take out his SIM card, and copy it."

Mike jerked around to look at the press table. Cathy Ross's head shot up, shocked. Their eyes met for a split second before she grabbed her laptop and fled. *Oh Cathy,* Mike thought, *what did you do?*

"Detective Sergeant, this text message is the only connection between my client and Ms. Navarro. Correct?"

"Apart from the murder weapon at his house."

Honest John hesitated.

"No further questions." He resumed his seat.

"Are you trying to get me fried?" Mike hissed. "You and Cathy and the whole damn town."

Acting Chief Pletch nailed the coffin shut with his graphic account of the search and discovery of the Glock 19 pistol beneath Mike Carson's porch. Ballistics tests confirmed, conclusively, it was the murder weapon. One hundred percent. Mike could almost sense the straps gripping his wrists and ankles in the execution room. He looked back at Sam, but his friend's face showed nothing.

"Did you find any fingerprints on the weapon?" Honest John asked the chief.

"We did not. Probably wiped clean, or maybe he wore gloves."

"Did your forensics team examine my client, his clothes, and all the clothes at his home?"

"Yes."

"Was there any trace of gunshot residue on my client or the clothes?"

"No. He most likely showered and disposed of the clothes."

"Did you discover the clothes he supposedly disposed of?"

"No, we did not."

"Chief Pletch, is the porch at Mr. Carson's house accessible from outside the building?"

"I believe so."

"Thank you."

DA Bryan Paxton concluded his presentation. "Your honor, I respectfully submit to the court there is ample probable cause, and propose we move to arraignment, where we would ask for bail to be denied, due to the severity of the crime."

There was a grumble of agreement from the room, which cut off abruptly when Judge Neiman tapped his gavel twice. The judge turned. He caught Mike's eye and suddenly Mike felt cold. Neiman looked inquiringly at Honest John, who stood again.

"Your Honor, the district attorney's office has presented a compelling case, I must admit. A really compelling case. I would like to introduce evidence which will cast a very different light upon the events."

"What kind of evidence?" asked Bryan Paxton.

"Location data from Mr. Carson's vehicle." Honest John handed the judge and DA some documents. "Your Honor, my client does not own a vehicle. He rents one from Alamo here in town, and, as you may know, rental companies install tracking devices in their vehicles in case of theft or non-return, or the need for breakdown recovery. This is a printout of the vehicle's location at the time of the murder. There are affidavits of authenticity at the back of the pack. On the second page you will see the coordinates place the vehicle at Tabor Lake at the time of the murder."

Mike dared to hope.

"Proves nothing," Bryan Paxton interjected. "The car may have been there, but that doesn't mean the accused was there."

Honest John ignored him. He reached into his large briefcase and his huge hand emerged holding a rock.

"The next piece of evidence, Your Honor, comes from a hidden surveillance camera I installed in my client's yard. It was my belief he might be targeted because of his journalistic investigation into the recent death of Adam Polley. Not only has he been harassed by the police department, but there have also been attempts on his life."

That got a loud murmur from the audience. The judge frowned and smacked his gavel none too gently. Honest John extracted an SD card from the flat bottom of the rock and held it aloft for all to see. He placed it on the table, lifted a thumb drive, walked to the side of the court TV monitor, and inserted it.

"This is an extract of that surveillance footage, Your Honor. You can see it is time-stamped to the dates in question. I can make the full, unedited and authenticated video available to the DA's office."

"Objection. How do we know this is genuine, Your Honor, and has not been interfered with?" Bryan Paxton asked.

"I am an officer of the court," said Honest John. "I personally collected the SD card and delivered it to the state attorney general investigator in charge of the Polley case. An examination of the video by experts will prove its veracity. It is not the primary evidence I wish to offer, merely a building block."

"Since this is an examining trial, I'm prepared to allow some leeway," said the judge.

The image was remarkably clear. A side view of Mike Carson's house with a full view of the front porch and driveway. Dawn was breaking. The time stamp said 5:33 a.m. The figure of a man walked across the yard from the rear of the home, squatted by the porch, pulled open an access hatch and placed something inside. He stood, turned and could be seen full face. Honest John paused the video. "For the benefit of the court, I've had this image enlarged." He hit play.

There were audible gasps in the courtroom.

"Good God," said Judge Neiman.

"Your Honor's reaction is understandable," said Honest John, "I think we can all agree, from our own personal experience, this is the face of Police Chief Walter E. Gates, currently placed on administrative leave by the City of Taborville, pending the outcome of the state attorney general's investigation into the Adam Polley murder."

When the court settled, Honest John continued. "I now call the chief investigator of the attorney general's Criminal Investigation Division, Sam Washington."

When Sam was sworn in, he told the court he had reviewed the footage given to him by the attorney and then sought a warrant to obtain cellular and location data from Chief Gates' cell phone provider.

"Using that data, we could track the chief's movements in the days prior to Council Member Navarro's murder. The day prior to the killing, we placed the chief in the vicinity of a small strip mall on the outskirts of San Antonio," Sam said. "We obtained security camera footage from several stores in that location and were able to determine Chief Gates visited a business called Bell Cleaners. He was seen entering that business carrying a package and leaving without it."

The courtroom was silent as a nun on retreat. People leaned forward, not to miss a word. Mike listened with an odd detachment, as if the life discussed was not his own.

"We got a search warrant for Bell Cleaners and detained Samuel 'Sonny' Bell. We also recovered a weapon, which we have linked to five killings in the state."

"Thank you," said Honest John.

"This weapon you found, Investigator Washington, was it used to murder Council Member Navarro?" said Bryan Paxton.

"No."

"In that case, Your Honor, this testimony is irrelevant."

"Noted," said the judge.

Mike lost his grip on the sliver of hope. Honest John had his back to the defense table. *This guy is going to kill me.*

"I now call Samuel 'Sonny' Bell to the stand," said Honest John.

A door opened at the side of the courtroom, and two Texas Rangers escorted Sonny to the witness box.

"Mr. Bell," said Honest John, "did Michael Carson, the accused, shoot and kill Council Member Nadia Navarro?"

CHAPTER FORTY-SEVEN

SONNY BELL KNEW he should have shut down Bell Cleaners the moment County Judge Taylor mentioned Wally Gates, but he figured he was protected and, anyway, he'd worked hard to build the cover and the contacts. Too late now. Too late the second they busted into the store to arrest him. Much too late. They'd hauled him to Taborville, stuck him in an interview room, and left him.

The room had tones of gray, not a hint of color anywhere. Sonny thought it was probably deliberate. No color, no hope. He'd been there for two hours and twenty-seven minutes, handcuffed to a desk, on a metal chair with a numb butt. His head was full of questions. Nobody had said a word to him. No answers in the back of the cruiser or when they put him in this room. He'd had time to think. His best bet was to keep his mouth shut, let them do the talking, let them reveal their hand. Then he could figure out his defense. Definitely the best strategy. He sat back and relaxed as best he could and wiggled his butt to ease the numbness. He was used to his own company.

The big, Black dude in the shiny suit came in thirty minutes later, two minutes to the top of the hour. Looked like he'd been shot in the face. Sonny hadn't noticed that before, when they arrested him. Dude must have been careless. Or unlucky. There was another dude with him, stocky white guy, mean looking, Western shirt, bolo tie, snakeskin boots. Ranger, maybe.

"Mr. Bell, my name is Sam Washington. I'm an investigator with the state attorney general's office. I see from your face you are not familiar. No reason why you should be. Let me put it this way, I have jurisdiction across the whole state, and I investigate all kinds of cases—cold cases, ones that local cops give up on, public corruption, and issues inside police departments themselves. This is Randall Gilbert from the Texas Rangers. We may be joined by other officers from different agencies later."

They sat down, put notebooks on the table, and a recorder. *Other agencies? Could be ICE for his workers, but ICE usually comes alone. Anyway, don't speculate. See what they've got.*

"Now, Sonny," the Black dude said, "I'm going to call you Sonny, because we will be spending some time with you, and Mr. Bell is a bit formal. I'm going to be real honest with you. Your life was over the minute I laid eyes on you this morning. You need to accept that. The life you have known, at least. Over." He paused, like he was thinking, then smiled, "You'll have woken up today, completely unaware it was the last time you would ever enjoy freedom, the last time you could make decisions for yourself, indulge your passions, choose your food, step into the sunshine whenever you want. None of that is possible now."

Sonny stared, expressionless.

"You might have done some things differently had you known. Maybe got a different breakfast, took a walk, I don't know, but what I do know is your life as you know it is done."

They got nothing yet, Sonny thought. *This is meaningless bullshit. Scare tactics.* He looked at them both and smiled. The Ranger reacted.

"You won't be smiling soon, shithead."

"Now, now. Please excuse my colleague, Sonny. He's a bit upset. But that's no excuse for name calling. Is it Randall?"

"No. I apologize."

Sonny grinned. *Round One to the Bell. Ding dong.*

"Sonny, it's possible you might come to understand and appreciate the reason he's upset, but we'll see."

He looked Sonny directly in the eye. His eyes were still kind of smiling.

"James Hensley."

Sonny kept his face straight. Two in the head, Parking Lot B, IAH Houston after landing from Paris.

"Oliver Jones."

Dallas, three years ago.

"Robert Guthrie,"

Austin, an alley, in back of Fourth Street.

The names continued, each one perfectly pronounced, given weight like accusations, which they were. Sonny squeezed his cheeks together. He needed the toilet. The Black dude stopped talking. They looked at Sonny like they were sizing him up for a coffin.

"Like I said, Sonny, your life is over. But how long your life will be depends on one thing—what you tell me about the name I did not mention. The last one on the list. What you tell me about that name will determine if you get strapped down to a table, and get a needle in your arm, and wait for the three chemicals to push into your veins, and rid us of you, or...."

Sonny wasn't fully convinced and stayed silent. They had a list of names was all, a list of unsolved murders, murders with the same pattern maybe, but it didn't mean they could pin it on him.

"You know what gets real careful criminals caught, Sonny? No matter how cautious they are, they get a little overconfident after they get away with it for a while, and then, at some point, they change their routine."

Sonny shifted in the chair. His butt was getting really painful. This did not sound good.

"Contract guys like .22s for close work, because they are effective, small, light, no recoil, pretty quiet as firearms go. And cheap. Cheap is important because at the beginning, they toss the gun. Onetime use."

Sonny shifted again. A .22...damn.

"In the beginning, it's any cheap .22 they can buy on the down low, untraceable, right? But then sometimes a guy stumbles onto something that he really likes, feels good in his hand, like a carpenter's favorite chisel. Maybe he tosses the first one but then he gets to thinking, that's four, five hundred bucks a time I'm tossing in the river. Five hundred bucks that could be in my pocket, and every time I have to buy a piece, I'm exposed. And the cops don't suspect a thing, all these hits are a mystery. So, maybe I'll just keep this one, and I can always toss it later, if things get hot."

Things were hot for Sonny right now. His butt was sweating.

"Hey, man," he said, "I need a bathroom break."

The Black dude turned to the Ranger.

"He speaks. What do you think? Should we take him?"

"Well, I guess, if he has to go, he has to go. Don't want him pissing his pants in here."

The Ranger stood and watched him the whole time he was on the shitter, shackled his left hand to a rail in the stall, so he could use his right for wiping. Sonny felt humiliated and angry. And very small.

He once got in a wrestling match at school with this

popular dude called Travis Woods. When Travis had him on the floor, somebody shouted, "Pile on!" And they did. Eight of them, and he felt the crush and the breath leaving him and how hard it was to move his chest to suck in more air and the vision shrinking—that's where he was now. Heading for a blackout.

There was a package on the desk when the Ranger brought him back. The Black dude was all smiles and fake manners.

"Feeling better? I'll bet that's a load off. It does that, you know—there are all kinds of studies—bad news, it has an effect on the bowels." He laughed a big laugh that filled the room. "I guess the term 'scare the shit out of you' has to come from somewhere, right?"

Then all the funny stopped.

"Sonny, I'm running out of time and Randall here is running out of patience. I understand what's in your head. You're thinking they know a lot, but they don't have me. And you're wrong. You couldn't be more wrong."

Randall leaned in.

"You think we're amateurs, Sonny. You think we don't know how to do our jobs? It's insulting, real insulting. We're professionals."

"Now, Randall, let's be fair. Sonny, here, is a professional too. Well, more of a semi-professional. But let's give him that."

He smiled again.

"He's just a semi-professional who made a big mistake. A guy who thought we wouldn't dismantle every filthy vacuum cleaner in his shop till we found this."

The Black dude unveiled the package—Sonny's matte black Sig Sauer Mosquito and his 22X suppressor.

CHAPTER FORTY-EIGHT

THERE WAS a deathly silence in the court when Honest John McKinney turned and walked towards the witness stand. Ears strained; necks craned.

"I'll repeat the question, Mr. Bell. Did Mike Carson shoot and kill Council Member Navarro?"

Sonny paused and looked around the courtroom, like they'd shown him in witness prep the day before.

"No. He didn't."

"How can you say that with such certainty?"

"Because Wally Gates paid me $5,000 to do her, with a Glock 19."

Honest John allowed the collective shocked gasp to run its course before continuing.

"And what happened to that weapon?"

"I gave it back to him, right after he paid me the balance for clipping her."

The courtroom erupted. Sofia Navarro made a run for the witness box, shrieking an incomprehensible mix of languages, but the bailiff tackled her before her clawed hands could grab Sonny Bell's throat. Judge Neiman hammered his gavel and ordered the courtroom to be cleared, which was easy to say but impossible to accomplish. The Texas Rangers moved swiftly to stand guard over Sonny Bell. Sofia Navarro was escorted into the corridor, and a couple of local women went to console her. Holly got up to help but realized she wasn't needed and sat back down.

"I will have order," Judge Neiman insisted. Silence dropped like a guillotine.

"Please continue."

Honest John stepped forward. "Your Honor, based on the evidence presented, I would ask that my client be discharged forthwith."

DA Paxton stood. "The district attorney's office will not pursue charges against Mr. Carson."

"Michael Carson, please stand. You are hereby discharged."

"Thank you, Your Honor," Mike said, then his knees betrayed him, and he slumped back down onto the chair. Honest John shook his hand, gathered his papers and was putting them in a large black pilot's case when the judge inquired.

"Investigator Washington, if I may. What is happening regarding Chief Gates?"

"We have issued a warrant for his arrest," Sam said, "but he has fled the jurisdiction. He boarded a flight in Austin two hours after Mr. Bell was taken into custody. He transferred in New York and flew to Paris. We have alerted Interpol."

Sam followed the mayor and county judge out onto the courthouse steps. He waited while they shook hands briefly and parted. Sam nodded to two Texas Rangers who had followed him out. They closed the gap quickly.

"Christian Taylor," Sam said, "I need you to come with me."

"Why, may I ask?"

"I have some questions for you about the Polley inquiry."

"I'm happy to cooperate. If you'll call my assistant, I'm sure—"

"No, sir. Needs to be now."

"It's not convenient at the present time."

"It will get a lot less convenient if I ask the Rangers to take you into custody."

Taylor turned, bewildered for a moment, and saw the unsmiling Rangers, one of whom reached for the handcuffs on his belt.

"Of course," Taylor said, "there's no need for that."

He walked alongside Sam as if they were two pals going for a stroll and smiled broadly at each constituent they passed on the way to Sam's Escalade.

Christian Taylor did not speak other than to ask for his lawyer, former DA Landry Stout, who arrived thirty minutes later. Stout was belligerent and confrontational and accusatory. The rhetoric bounced off the investigation team like the weak pickle balls Landry served at weekends in his senior community. When he had read the warrant from top to bottom for the third time, he started to listen.

Sam took the lead. Texas Ranger Randall Gilbert glowered. He was very good at it.

"I know this feels outrageous to you, Mr. Taylor," Sam said, "an affront to your position, and believe me, we thought long and hard before acting. It's not a good look for the county, for the city, for the community."

Taylor nodded at that.

"But the thing is, no one is above the law. Not me. And certainly not you."

Taylor sat, unmoved.

"The problem is, Christian, may I call you Christian?"

"I would prefer Judge Taylor, if you don't mind."

"Of course not, Judge Taylor, happy to do that. Although it won't be a title you can hold on to for long. You are going to be incarcerated, of that there is no doubt, none whatever. We have overwhelming evidence."

Landry Stout ran a hand across his thinning, white strands of hair.

"I sincerely doubt it," he said.

Sam turned to Randall.

"What do you think, Randall? A little preview maybe?"

"Why not?" Randall pulled a thumb drive from his pocket and stuck it in his laptop, turning it sideways so everyone could see.

"Judge Taylor, Mr. Stout, this is footage of the pursuit of Adam Polley immediately prior to his murder." Sam said, and Randall pressed play. Adam Polley's car sped into view and turned off the road at speed. When the two following cars stopped on the road, Randall paused after the first figure emerged.

"That is Chief Walter Gates getting out of the Charger."

Randall pressed play again. A man emerged from the Ford Mustang. "And this is you, Judge Taylor."

As the two figures turned and walked to the edge of the road, Sam leaned over and hit pause. Detectives and investigators are trained to lie, and Sam was very good at it. He ignored

Taylor and addressed all his remarks to Landry Stout. All of it was speculation, but they didn't know that.

"Let me explain what you are seeing here, and what you cannot see." Sam hit rewind until Adam Polley's car appeared just before it left the road. "Adam Polley is fleeing from something, driving very fast. He suddenly pulls off the road into the trees. Why? Because a large Dodge truck has blocked the road, blue in color, driven by one Karter McMillan, now deceased. Karter McMillan got out of that vehicle, armed with a MAC 11 machine pistol, with a thirty-shot magazine, and discharged the full magazine at Mr. Polley's car. It took just over a second. Are you clear so far?"

Stout nodded.

"Seven of those .380 ACP bullets entered Mr. Polley's body. Astoundingly, none of them hit vital organs. He might have bled out eventually, but at this stage, according to the medical examiner, Mr. Polley would have been alive." Sam pressed "play," allowed the footage to run, and paused again when both men walked off the road. "One of those two men is in possession of a large caliber handgun, most probably a .357 Magnum." The footage ran again until the men reappeared on the roadway. "Mr. Polley is now dead. Shot point blank in the head with a single bullet, which ripped half his skull away, and finished what Karter McMillan could not accomplish."

Sam stared at both men, switching from one to the other several times.

"The position here is simple. You and your client know it doesn't matter which man pulled the trigger. They are both guilty of murder. You understand how cooperation can affect your client's treatment by the court." He smiled. "I'll give you a little time to consider your position on the murder charge before we talk about the public corruption, which I'm really looking forward to, by the way." He nodded to Randall. They gathered their materials, knowing little of what they had revealed would stand up in court for a myriad of reasons, and left the room.

Twenty minutes later, Landry Stout informed the detectives his client would be happy to make a comprehensive statement once he had a guarantee of immunity from prosecution for any of the crimes they were investigating.

"I don't think you understand your position, Judge Taylor. This is not a negotiation. There is no immunity on the table. You killed Adam Polley or Gates did. Say nothing and you'll both be charged with murder. Make a full confession and we'll see what we can do about reducing the murder charge. One way or another, the investigation into public corruption will continue until we have a clear picture of what has been going on here."

Color drained from Judge Taylor's face.

"Could you give us a moment?" Landry Stout asked.

"Certainly," Sam paused at the door. "Just FYI, we've now been asked to take over the Navarro murder case. We'll be digging around in Taborville for quite some time."

CHAPTER FORTY-NINE

MIKE SAT in the courtroom until it emptied, unsure whether his jelly legs would support him. He caught glimpses of people in his periphery but didn't turn. They seemed unwilling, or unable, to move past the bar. That little swing gate separated the spectator from the suspected, the audience from the accused. They didn't risk stepping into the business end of the courtroom and eventually eased themselves away.

The DA offered a half-hearted apology when he slid Mike's phone onto the table, still stained with fingerprint powder, inside a plastic baggie. Mike did not acknowledge the words or the gesture. He jerked when the bailiff tapped him on the shoulder.

"We have to close up now, Mr. Carson, everybody's gone."

The bailiff let him out through the staff door at the back of the building, and he trudged the lesser streets until the light lay down and he could slip back to his house, unseen. Sleep scorned his efforts to embrace it, and sometime in the night he had driven to the lake, where the dark enveloped and protected him.

He reached across for the bottle of Bulleit 95 Rye Frontier.

The emergency bottle of twelve-year-old. Keeping it unopened had been his challenge. He stroked the bottle, played with the cap, then stepped out of the car and walked to the cliff edge. He drew his arm back and fired. The bottle flew high and long, end over end, until the water caught it—a throw even Andy would have been proud of.

As dawn broke, a jon boat left the ramp, and put-putted across the limp water, a father and son going fishing. They didn't speak as they cast, their lures piercing the surface in search of the gullible and unwary. The boy was maybe twelve and easy in his father's company. Mike envied him.

The bottled water in his car was no longer cold, but he needed to wet the dry. He had no speaking words and could not trust the cords in his throat. The earthquake he'd endured had fissured all roads to verbal expression. The grinding plates had ruptured the last of his tectonic vanities, and the cloak of journalism offered no protection. He was not an investigative reporter, he was just a man—a fortunate but sad and lonely man envying the life of a boy he didn't know.

After the phone charged, it shimmied around on the passenger seat, vibrating away from all the media inquiries. Frank Wolfe had called and so had Holly. They'd left messages and texts, which he hadn't listened to or read. The phone fell into the footwell and, as he retrieved it, he saw Ron Knowles calling and hoped he had a voice to answer.

"Been reading about you," Ron said, "a piece by someone called Quintin Smith. Who's he?"

"The *Times* editor."

"Doesn't have your flair, kid. I thought you said Taborville was a sleepy little backwater."

"Used to be."

"Until you showed up."

"I guess."

"Seriously, how are you doing? That had to be pretty scary."

"I don't know how I am, boss. I truly do not know."

"You've been through the wringer, kid."

"Ron."

"Yeah."

"I'm an alcoholic."

"Not exactly news."

"I'm sober."

"Good for you."

Mike knew he should offer more, but he didn't have it. Eventually, Ron grew impatient.

"What happens now?"

"Dunno. I'm tired, Ron, so, so tired. But there are elections here in a few days and I guess people should know who they're voting for. I'll talk to Quintin. She deserves that, don't you think? Nadia, I mean... she was...she worked so hard...." Mike felt a sudden blush of anger redden his brain and linger. "You know what? No. I'm going to write it myself. I'm going to blow the freakin' lid off."

"You should send it to me."

"Yeah?"

"Yeah."

Two days later, the streets around the high school were a sea of political yard signs, getting ever more dense the closer they got. Every foot of permitted space on the edges of the sidewalks bristled with competing promises. The eco-friendly cardboard signs soaked by rain and sun-bleached beyond their color tolerance curled their edges in anticipation of the recycle bin.

Seasoned campaigners had parked spare vehicles at

strategic street corners days before. These were now replaced by pickups sporting wooden A-frames in their truck beds, with eight-foot by four-foot signs of smiling, earnest faces asking for support. Pop-up canopy tents, portable tables, and lawn chairs were pre-set for the morning by campaign volunteers.

Although there had been five days of early voting, few had exercised the privilege. The hours were carefully calculated, minimizing commuters' opportunities while appearing to offer generous access. Citizens working in San Antonio or Austin were on the road before the polls opened and still in their vehicles returning home when the stations closed. Taborville City Council's representation was determined by the few hundreds of voters in downtown and the historic district. It had always been so. These were the folks who turned up on election day.

None of the canny political observers could predict with any certainty how the vote would go this year. It was impossible to forecast how the town would react to the stories and tragedies. Tomorrow would tell the tale.

CHAPTER FIFTY

VANS, cars, and kids on bikes tossed newspapers onto drives from Los Angeles, California, to Lubbock, Texas, and all points in between. The newspapers had different banner titles, but the headlines were all the same:

TEXAS SCANDAL
Murder, corruption, drugs and water

By Mike Carson, *Taborville Times*

As Taborville, TX goes to the polls today, voters are reeling from a series of Texas-sized scandals that rocked the city to its core in recent weeks. One candidate was murdered; two more are being investigated for corruption.

Police Chief Walter Gates is a fugitive being sought by Interpol on murder charges. Texas's biggest opioid ring

has been busted three miles from downtown, and state and federal authorities are investigating a scheme by local businessmen, politicians and criminal elements to dupe the city into a fraudulent water contract.

The conspirators planned to extract vast quantities of water from the aquifer beneath the town and sell it to nearby San Antonio, one of the fastest-growing cities in the nation.

Anti-corruption investigators from the state attorney general's office are leading the inquiries.

"This is a complex case," said chief Wiley Deckrow, head of the criminal investigation division. "We are investigating two murders, illegal drug manufacturing and distribution, major fraud, money laundering and public corruption in both the city and the county. These may all be connected."

Local cleaning contractor Samuel "Sonny'" Bell has been indicted for the contract killing of Council Member Nadia Navarro. At a recent court hearing, Bell testified that Gates ordered and paid for the assassination.

County Judge Christian Taylor has been indicted as an accessory to the murder of Adam Polley, a county employee in the Land Registry Office. Gates is the primary suspect in the case. Polley is believed to have made a connection between a series of apparently random land purchases and a proposed water pipeline from Taborville to San Antonio.

Mayor William Pryor and Council Member Xander VanDorn, both running for re-election, were involved in the land purchases.

Businesses founded or owned by local entrepreneur Duke McMillan have been shuttered by the investigation, including Horny Toad Courier. McMillan's son Karter died in a police chase near the Texas-Louisiana border.

The courier company vehicle he was driving carried commercial quantities of the synthetic opioid fentanyl. The DEA has seized seven other Horny Toad vehicles.

Duke McMillan heads Reflow Logistics, the recently incorporated company behind the water scheme. The company's

primary source of funding is Tabor Trust Bank, also headed by McMillan.

VanDorn, a water broker, and Isaac Brook, a local real estate agent, are on the board of the bank and also have majority stakes in corporations that have invested in Reflow Logistics.

The damning facts continued relentlessly onto a second page where there was a secondary feature on Nadia Navarro. All of Taborville's dirty laundry was laid out for the voters as they headed for the high school to cast their ballots.

CHAPTER FIFTY-ONE

HOLLY SCANNED her wall of crosses, then fixed an accusatory stare on Mike, sitting in the armchair opposite her.

"You failed me, Mike. You got answers for everyone, but none for me. I still don't know how Adam died or why."

"I'm sorry, Holly, truly sorry. I did what I could. I think you need to be patient. The only people who know for sure what happened that morning were those who were there."

"I've been patient. Lord knows I've been patient."

"You have, but you have to wait a little longer. You can't quote me on this, but I heard that Judge Taylor has made a full confession. It will all come out when he goes to trial."

"If he goes to trial." She looked at the crosses again. "Tell me a story, Mike. It doesn't have to be true. Tell me what happened to my husband."

Mike swallowed. "The best I can figure it, they were having a secret meeting real early at the Scroggin house. All of them, probably, McMillan, Gates, the judge, VanDorn, Brook, and Scroggin, when Adam showed up in the Crown Vic. Maybe Adam saw them and took off, or they thought he was a fed and went after him. Either way, they chased him down the road. My guess is that the McMillan boys were running security for the meeting, screwed it up and then panicked. And they shot at Adam."

Holly winced as if the words were bullets.

"In the end, though, I think Adam died because of what he knew. He'd figured it out, and they knew it."

She looked up. A single tear glistened on her cheek. "Poor Adam. His patterns lost us our home and our money, and a pattern cost him his life." She wiped the tear away. "I hope there are no patterns in heaven."

Nobody in town could say with any certainty the year it started, but it became a tradition for a large board to be hung outside *The Taborville Times* after the polls closed on election night. As the county courthouse counted the ballots, observers phoned results to the editor, who wrote them on the board—these days with dry erase markers. Anyone with a keen interest in politics stood in the street and cheered or moaned as the numbers came in. Some brought folding chairs, flasks, and bottles.

In recent years, the good ol' boy candidates gathered at Gold Spurs, where Duke McMillan declared a free bar that would stay open until the last results were in. He wrote it off as a combination of political contribution and advertising. This was not a night for tradition.

The others normally hung at Longhorns, a smaller, fiercer group of dedicated election soldiers, outraised, outspent, sometimes outraged but never, ever outworked. This year even Longhorns sat empty. Nadia Navarro's supporters endured their grief alone or shared it in small groups in private houses. None of them wanted their desolation to be seen by the other side, and few could stomach laying eyes on any of those who might have been involved in her death.

The crowd outside the *Times* was smaller than usual. Mayor Bill Pryor didn't have a challenger and had refused to stand down, despite the scandal. There was already talk in the town of mounting a recall. Quintin Smith, the editor, stepped up with his marker.

WILLIAM PRYOR—572

Less than half of the votes he got when he ran in a contested election two years earlier. Commentary crabbed through the crowd. Next was Xander VanDorn in a contest against law enforcement officer Mac Johnstone.

MAC JOHNSTONE—673
XANDER VANDORN—678

Cheers from some, curses from others. The man was made of Teflon. Nothing seemed to stick.

Holly Kingston shivered at the back of the crowd. Her soul was colder than the surrounding air. She watched Quintin answer his cell phone. From his body language, he appeared not to believe what he was being told. He stepped back in the building, iPhone glued to his ear and emerged a few minutes later. He ascended his small step ladder, eraser and marker in hand, and adjusted the figures.

The shock was audible and visceral. A smattering of tentative applause grew slowly to a drum roll and finally to a cheer that filled the street.

NADIA NAVARRO—1208
ANTONIO GONZALEZ—43

In that moment, Holly made a decision—her hsband Adam's death would not be in vain.

CHAPTER FIFTY-TWO

MIKE STOOD in front of the Cornerstore, surrounded by the entire Alvarez clan, admiring the three-quarter view of Uncle Harold's house—once again pristine, glistening in the morning sun, rehabilitated and restored. The realtor's "For Sale" sign stood invitingly in the front yard, close to the road.

"She is whole again," Juan said. "She is beautiful. She will make a fine home for someone."

"I hope so."

The family lined up to embrace Mike, then piled into their vehicles, and left him alone to appreciate their work. Mike could almost see Uncle Harold on the porch on the old swing and, in an instant, knew he could never part with the property. He marched across and pulled the "For Sale" sign out of the ground. The house was decency and legacy, heredity and history. It was Carson, honest. It was everything he was and wanted to be.

But he could not live here. Not now.

The level of backlash to his stories had stunned him. Social media burned with vitriolic chatter. There were people who believed, fervently, he had assassinated Nadia Navarro in some twisted act of vengeance, despite all the evidence. Why he would want revenge was never explained. His detractors claimed the stories he'd written were proof he wanted to destroy the city's reputation.

Nadia Navarro's team of tough ladies were on the streets, rapidly collecting signatures for the recall of the mayor, Xander VanDorn, and Isaac Brook. The town was dividing into factions—downtown versus subdivisions—but the women were confident they would prevail.

Levi had launched a legal suit with Honest John McKinney against Duke McMillan and Judge Christian Taylor, Tabor Trust Bank, and a host of their companies to recover the losses he incurred when the Magnolia Trails subdivision collapsed. Other investors now wanted to join the class action.

Mike and Sam embraced again, under the watchful eyes of Willie and the Highwaymen inside Texas Roadhouse, with promises not to leave it so long again.

"I ordered an audit of the evidence room in Taborville, and there was a missing .357 Magnum Coonan Compact, connected to another drug case. Never used, unfortunately, which made it virtually untraceable. Gates would have had access to it."

"Did he sign it out?"

"Nah, he wasn't that stupid. It's probably in Tabor Lake somewhere. Doubt we'll ever find it."

The editor of *The Taborville Times* beamed as Mike pushed through his half-open door.

"I don't suppose there's any point—"

"Not a chance. I've done my pro bono work for now," Mike said.

"But I'm down to just me now. This is it."

"No word of Cathy?"

"Not since the trial. Gone girl, you might say."

"You'll find someone good. Do me a favor and do a background check next time."

"I will. Those stories really boosted our circulation, and having our name out there across the nation, well, let's say, the owners are well pleased."

"The paper's in excellent hands, Quintin. I won't say, 'If there's anything I can do' because I know you'll take me up on it. So I'll just shake your hand and wish you luck."

Quintin pumped the offered hand with both of his.

"I'm keeping this," Mike brandished the *Times* press card. "You can always say I'm your secret correspondent if you ever get a call."

None of the goodbyes were easy, but the cemetery was hardest. He kneeled beside the mounded clay at Nadia Navarro's grave, still without a headstone, and put his hand into the dirt, reaching through the sadness and the guilt. If she'd never met him, maybe she would still be alive.

He sat with Andy for a while and made peace with a spirit he'd resented for almost all his life. Andy's end may have been born of recklessness but was not of his own making. That was something.

Mike lingered longer with Uncle Harold and told him everything—the intrigues and the plots, the building of the story, and the reaction to it after publication. He didn't know if it was possible wherever Uncle Harold was, but could he please make sure McMillan, and Scroggin, VanDorn, and Gates got what they deserved?

A dove landed nearby and watched him until he walked back to the road.

Justice had not been done. Not for Nadia, not for Holly. Pryor, VanDorn, and Brook were still on the city council. McMillan, the Scroggins, and Christian Taylor were not in jail.

Wally Gates was safely domiciled in a villa overlooking the Adriatic Sea in Montenegro, a tiny nation with a pleasant climate and no extradition treaty with the United States. Gates had been funneling money to Montenegro for years.

Sam Washington was sure he'd get them all one day, but Mike was less hopeful.

CHAPTER FIFTY-THREE

THE OFFICIAL WORKING hours of Taborville City offices began at 7:30 a.m. The city secretary was responsible for opening the building and always arrived thirty minutes early. She liked to have herself settled before dealing with the public. It surprised her to see a lone figure waiting at the door when she pulled the heavy set of keys from her purse.

"Ms. Kingston," she said, "you're here early. Let me open up." She unlocked the door and killed the alarm. "What can I help you with?"

"The special election," Holly said, "I've been praying on it. I think I'm going to run for Nadia Navarro's seat. I heard the candidate application pack is available this morning."

"It certainly is, Ms. Kingston, and it will be my pleasure to get one for you. Yes, indeed." She made her way to the office, paused, and called out over her shoulder. "You go, girl, you show 'em."

Xander VanDorn always walked to breakfast. It was an efficient use of time. He prioritized his goals for the day as he marched along and sorted through the conversations he would have when he took his seat at the table.

Duke McMillan's continued funk might be understandable, given the police investigation, both sons lost, and now his wife, but leaving Tabor Trust Bank rudderless was unacceptable, no matter what the circumstances. The bank needed strong executive leadership. The Texas Department of Banking had started an investigation and Xander had been tipped off the previous night by a friend at Treasury that FinCON, the Financial Crimes Enforcement Network, might not be far behind. Mike Carson's article and the subsequent furor had inflicted serious damage. It was probably survivable so long as everyone did their part. McMillan would have to be taken out of the equation.

Xander opened the door of Longhorns and stepped inside. What the hell? All the seats at the table had been taken—by Nadia Navarro's witches. The damn nerve. One of the guys waved from a table farther back. Xander nodded but headed for the register. A waitress looked up from the till, but he pointed past her into the office.

"It's him I want."

The owner stepped up to the counter.

"You wanted to see me, Xander?"

"Just what in the hell do you think you're playing at?"

"Not sure what you mean."

"That," Xander said, gesturing at the table full of women. "That's our table."

"Sign says 'OPEN SEATING' right inside the door."

"So?" said Xander.

"People may sit where they want, always been that way. People left that table clear 'cos it was kinda understood. Guess it ain't no more."

Joshua Scroggin looked up from the counter as the doorbell dinged. Old Mrs. Schuler made her way towards him.

"Hello, Mrs. Schuler. What can we do for you today?"

"Mr. Scroggin, I have a new script from that young doctor. She says it will help with the arthritis. Some new drug they have. I think I saw it advertised on the TV. Maybe I'll be break-dancing, like they do in the commercial." She broke out into a wheezy laugh. "Damn fools."

Joshua looked at the prescription. "I think you might find it helpful, actually. I've read the trial reviews, and I've gotten excellent reports from folks who've used it. Take a seat and I'll get it filled."

Mrs. Schuler climbed up on the high stool. "How's the family?" she asked. "I haven't seen your youngest around the place lately."

"We're empty nesters at the moment. Amber is still in Colorado at college and the other two are out of state, working."

"Oh, I didn't know. What are they up to? Something fun, I hope."

"They're both working in pharmaceuticals. The youngest, Jess, she's specializing in sales and distribution, and Peter is concentrating on the manufacturing process—you know, making the pills."

"Still in the family business, then?"

"Oh yes, and when the time is right, they will come back with all that extra knowledge and expertise." He handed over the medication.

"Wasn't that an awful business about the McMillan boys?" Mrs. Schuler said.

"Terrible."

"You know, a friend of mine had to go out there, to that

courier place, one time. Some mix-up over a parcel, and do you know what she told me? Mexicans, the lot of them. All Mexicans, except for the McMillans. From over the border. What do you call that thing... the drug thing...cartel, isn't it?"

"I heard that story, too. Thank goodness we've seen the back of it. Well, Mrs. Schuler, that's all covered by your Medicare. Hopefully, you'll soon be doing the Macarena." They both laughed.

Joshua's phone rang.

"Excuse me, Mrs. Schuler."

He answered. "Scroggin."

"Dad."

"Jess, I was just speaking about you to Mrs. Schuler."

"Dad, the DEA just grabbed Peter."

CHAPTER FIFTY-FOUR

INTERSTATE 10 CONNECTS a continent from Jacksonville, Florida, to Santa Monica, California. One-third of its entire length crosses the Lone Star State. Texas Highway 71 meets the interstate ninety miles southeast of Austin and cuts a straighter route than the Colorado River, which meanders along a similar path towards Matagorda Bay to the Gulf of Mexico. Bastrop, Smithville, and La Grange all nestle on the banks of the Colorado's unappealing brown waters. Mike crossed the river in Columbus, "The City of Live Oaks and Live Folks." He pulled off 71 onto the hard shoulder. Ahead lay a decision, just past the interstate signs. Taborville was miles back. But was the past ever truly left behind? He moved his watch and the small question mark tattoo appeared. What now?

To his right, the road led west to Los Angeles. Ron Knowles had been vague when Mike asked if he was being offered a job.

"Come out to LA and let's talk about it," Ron said.

"It's a long way to go for nothing."

"Who said it's nothing?"

"Well, it's not something, is it?"

"Mike, I don't want to be disappointed again, can't take the chance. I'll be honest, I'm not a great believer in the reality or permanence of resurrection. Call me a doubting Thomas, but I need to stick my hand in the wound."

To his left lay Florida, father, family. He'd always accepted what he'd been told about Andy's death. Never questioned it. Never questioned the sketchy story about his runaway sister either—Sarah who, supposedly, had died although there was no grave to visit. The stories about his father, his mother, Uncle Harold—just stories. Stories he had never fact checked. Maybe it was time to fact check the whole Carson saga.

Mike laid his head back on the neck rest and closed his eyes. Ron's position was reasonable. He had betrayed the man.

Betrayed. There it was. A simple, powerful, awful word. An act of deliberate disloyalty. Not consciously deliberate, to be fair. The truth was closer to the Middle English root *bitrayen*—lying, deceiving. Still ugly. Hard to forgive.

He remembered his mother, in one of her few candid moments, turning to him, eyes hardened by hurt, saying, "You think the truth is some shiny thing but it's not. It doesn't set you free. It shines light in the dark places you want to forget. Truth is cruel and harsh and uncontrollable and unforgiving. And it's never the full story." But lying to yourself was a liquifying solvent of the soul, a lengthy fade to the gray that she had become. And he'd been heading down that same road.

The pieces he had written about Taborville were true, but not the full story. It was still being written in the minds, mouths, and hearts of the people who lived there. He opened his eyes, looked at the tattoo, and smiled. He'd given them the who, the what, the where, the when and the how, but not the why. The why was up to them to figure out. He'd given them the facts. He hoped whatever opinions they formed, as a result, would amount to more than dog spit.

The tension in his jaw relaxed. He felt a lightness he'd not experienced in forever. Decision made, Mike selected sport mode, put the car in drive, and accelerated hard onto the tarmac, speeding toward the interstate.

ACKNOWLEDGMENTS

A huge thank you to Loren Steffy, Leslie Barrett, Kathryn Jones, Danielle Acee, and all at Stoney Creek Publishing for their hard work, dedication, and faith. I am deeply indebted.

My writing tribe has supported me through the all the lows and highs. Thank you zoomwriters Emile Cassen, Lily Devalle, Catherine Johnstone, Sandy Foster, Billy Green, Niamh McAnally, Nina Smith, Ben Tufnell, and the late Wendy Williamson.

My friend and automotive mentor Bo Rivers kept the wheels between the ditches. Major Brian Jones stood me to attention on military matters. Judge Chris Duggan hopefully has kept me out of the dock on courtroom procedure, and Police Chief Jeff Yarborough helped me on police matters. Any mistakes are mine and mine alone.

Thanks to Erin Hallagan Clare for reigniting creative sparks and my dad, Ray McAnally, for always getting to the truth.

But most of all, thanks to my family—to Kay, my love, the best decision I have ever made; to Áine, Nuala, Aisling, Bébhínn, Cian and John who are inspirations all; to Aonghus, Máire and Niamh who always have my back.

And to you, the reader. *Míle buíochas.* A thousand thanks.

ABOUT THE AUTHOR

Conor McAnally is an award-winning writer, performer, producer and TV director. A native of Ireland, he is a former investigative print, radio and television journalist.

Conor has produced thousands of factual and entertainment television shows for networks worldwide including BBC, ITV, Channel 4, DirecTV, AMC, Nickelodeon, RTE, SBS, Fuse. His TV shows have garnered 22 major awards including five British Academies and five from the Royal Television Society.

His story Love Spines was the 2024 winner of the Plaza

Prize for Microfiction. His short stories Shattered Silence and The Bell Tolls were published in the anthology Stories of Place by Black Rose Writing in April 2025. The Psychiatrist's Window was a prize winner in the South West Writers short story competition and published.

McAnally created, wrote, produced and directed the hybrid youth drama series Over The Wall for BBC

In theatre he has written and performed three one-man shows — The Irish in America, Texas Independence and The Mexican-American War.

Conor's passions have included skydiving and gardening, motor racing and cooking, motor cycling and golfing, poetry and performing — although not all at the same time.

He has homes in Austin, Texas, and Galway, Ireland.

www.ingramcontent.com/pod-product-compliance
Lightning Source LLC
LaVergne TN
LVHW042112141025
823231LV00002B/2

* 9 7 8 1 9 6 5 7 6 6 3 2 3 *